ENCOMPASSING DARkNESS

CHILD OF LIGHT

Terah Marie

◆ FriesenPress

Suite 300 - 990 Fort St
Victoria, BC, V8V 3K2
Canada

www.friesenpress.com

This book is a work of Fiction. Names, characters, places
and incidents are products of the author's imagination or
are used fictitiously. Any resemblance to actual events or
locales or persons, living or dead, is entirely coincidental.

ISBN
978-1-5255-3119-4 (Hardcover)
978-1-5255-3120-0 (Paperback)
978-1-5255-3121-7 (eBook)

1. FICTION

Distributed to the trade by The Ingram Book Company

I dedicate this book to my daughter Railyn.
(You can read past this page when you are a teenager.) Love mom.
To my loving and supportive husband thanks for all that you do and for
being my support system for this book.

ACKNOWLEDGEMENTS

It takes a village to raise a child. Well this book is my baby and that sentiment definitely applies here. Thank you to everyone at FriesenPress for standing by me. If it wasn't for my Account Manager, Editor, design and formatting personnel, this book would not be what it is today. Also to my husband who encouraged me to write and get my book published, he is my greatest support system through out this process, I love you. To my test readers and my new friends, who did all the reading and went through my entire manuscript with me, you have been my life savers and I would not have done this without you. To my sister who gave tid-bits of information to run with in my story, you are the best sister ever! To the believers and non believers out there, thank you for reading my story. To everyone that supported me thank you!

ENCOMPASSING
DARkNESS

CHAPTER 1
Bouncy Clown Go Away

FOUR. I WAS FOUR—THAT'S WHAT I REMEMBERED FROM THE DREAM. SHIT, I wished sleep wasn't something that eluded me on a nightly basis. Don't normal people sleep, get up, go to work and do fun things with friends on weekends? Ugh, my life felt like a shit show. Stupid job I hate, and weekends—what were those? Ha! Friends—who were they? Maybe I was just being hard on myself. When you only get ten hours of sleep over three nights with weird nightmares or prophetic dreams, life can look more dismal than it really is.

Dragging my ass out of bed, I hit the alarm, which was deliberately trying to make me insane by reminding me it was 6:00 a.m. I went to the kitchen, put the coffee on and drained a half-liter of water with my vitamins. I didn't allow myself to have coffee until I had at least a couple glasses of water. They say the best way to start your day is with room-temperature water. I don't know if I believe whoever "they" are, but I was willing to try anything to get my ass in gear and have the energy to get through the day. As the smell of the coffee hit me, I decided it was going to be a good day. I loved that smell. I went and took a shower and did my makeup simply; I put on just enough to look like I at least tried, and I highlighted my blue eyes.

Why other women put makeup on to look like they didn't have makeup on I did not know, but I did it out of habit. Next, I pulled my wavy, chestnut-brown hair into a ponytail to keep it out of my face for work in record time so I could have some of that lovely brew. I grabbed my book off the shelf for the lunch break and picked up the box of filing I brought home from work to do on my free time. Doing the extra filing lets me have the job at the box store that treated everyone like they owned us little guys at the bottom of the work chain. But at the moment, it was what I had, so that's what I did—put in the free hours and kept a job until I could find something better.

It's not like I didn't go to school; I actually went to college a couple times. Staying in my menial job while the top brass who think they are the end-all, be-all to the world whilst they also sit in their mundane position just wasn't appealing to me. So I moved around in temp jobs till I could find something I liked.

As I grabbed a coat and headed out the door, I realized I was forgetting the only morning comfort I longed for—the giant cup of coffee. I went back in and took a moment to pour. I leaned against the counter and allowed myself the moment of the first delicious sip. Then it was back to reality and out the door I went. Forgetting to warm up my tiny red hybrid car kind of sucked this morning because it was minus-four degrees Celsius. It didn't get too cold here in Vancouver, but being Canada, cold is more of a state of mind.

When I finally got to Tony's Furniture Giant, I went around to the customer services area, which was hidden behind the front-end staff who handled the purchases.

This was my lovely job— I was the customer service rep who handled all the questions, complaints and warranty work. Tony's Furniture was a franchise that went straight across Canada, with fifty-two stores total. Thank goodness I only had to worry about this one. People really hated customer service representatives; they thought we were out to make the consumer's life hell because we work for "the man" (The big corporations that pay you to stiff the little guy.)

This was why I was so good at my job, because within the first thirty seconds I had the customer realizing I worked for them and would do what-ever I could for them within the confines of my job. I would push and bend any rule necessary, within reason, to help them—I was the perfect middle man. Which was why I would be getting a raise today; it was the first good thing that had happened at this job. So far, it had been horrible because the superior front-end management treat the staff like we owed them the world. And my direct boss—well, he was just a dick. He acted like a bitchy eighty-year-old and I was pretty sure he hated me.

No one else in the department really talked to me. But the raise made the filing and working on free time with the not-so-great co-workers more feasible. It felt good when someone finally appreciated you. Although the raise came from my boss's supervisor, Mr. Gunderson; he was the head of this store. My boss, Mr. Sean Stock, had to give me the raise suggested by Mr. Gunderson. I don't think Mr. Stock was too happy about it. I think he saw me as a piece of gum on his shoe, the little annoyance he couldn't get rid of.

Boom, just like that the phone lines started ringing; all three lines on my phone as well as on the other three desks. The phones automatically turned on at 8:00 a.m. The other three reps ran to their desks from the break room so they didn't get scolded for letting the phone ring more than four times. They were always late from having coffee in the break room. I hadn't been included in that social group yet, but I was relatively new here and I was a temporary worker. People in the workplace tended to treat me like I had the plague, because they were not sure a temp worker would stick around. I was sure it wouldn't last long. I'd only been there for over a month just about two.

I picked up my phone and put two lines on hold to deal with the first call. "Tony's Furniture. How may I help you?"

"Hello, dear, it's Mrs. Janssen. I'm looking to speak with Cali, is this Cali?"

"Hello, Mrs. Janssen. You have good luck, yes, it's Cali. I've gotten somewhere with the process of your claim. Yours is a difficult one, as your warranty was up four months ago."

"But I need that chair, dearie. I sleep in that chair! I can't sleep in a bed, as you know, because of my conditions. How am I going to sleep? I can't just go buy a new chair every two years … I don't have the money!"

"Mrs. Janssen, I am well aware of your situation from our previous conversations. As you know, we have sent someone to your home already who said the chair was not worth repair and the warranty is up. But I have talked to my manager and I actually have some good news.

I have persuaded them to have a second look, as the damage sounds structural and could be a manufacturer's problem. It might be a little difficult for you, but if you could have someone bring your chair to the Tony's warehouse, my store manager is going to have the manufacturer's representative take a look and see if my suspicions are right. I will make sure your concerns are being vocalized. This is a bit of a happy coincidence because the manufacturer usually isn't here. I will do my best to get your chair fixed or replaced. But you have to be ready for any outcome, okay? There is no guarantee."

"Oh, thank you, Cali! Thank you! I know you will help me if you can."

"I will do my very best for you." With that, I signed off from the conversation.

"You're going to need a Hail Mary to pull that off," said Tracy, the worker whose desk was directly beside mine. Tracy was a classic beauty, about my height with straight blonde hair and green eyes.

"I know," I said, "but she's really old and she's having a hard time and no one is listening to her point of view. It's an open-and-shut case for everyone that talks to her, but she said something the other day and there was something in the worker's report that leads me to believe it's a manufacturer's problem. It's just pure luck that the manufacturer is coming this week, so I am going to take that Hail Mary and run with it."

"Let's take some more calls and then go for break at 10:00," said Tracy.

"Yeah, sounds good."

As I answered another call, I was excited, thinking, *wow, I get a raise sometime today and I've been asked to have coffee with an actual person in the break room! No book for me this morning; things are looking up!*

After the break I got called into the customer service manager's office. "Hi, Mr. Stock, you wanted to see me?" I said in a slightly questioning voice even though I knew what this was about.

"Yes, have a seat. I suppose you know what this paperwork is? And this envelope?" He slapped both on his desk.

"Well, Mr. Gunderson did mention a raise … is there paperwork as well?" There were more than a few pages sitting in front of me.

"There is, apparently. This morning Mr. Gunderson talked with me and he thinks you're worthy of a full-time permanent spot if you want it. It automatically comes with a twelve-percent raise, versus the original nine-percent raise as a temporary worker." He continued in his most sulky, grumpy voice. "Though I don't particularly see why you need permanency here. If you want the permanent spot, you need to fill the paperwork out."

I pondered this—he was such a dick. For the life of me, I could not figure out if he hated just me or everyone. I think it was just me that got this delightful attitude. I contemplated being a permanent employee at Tony's Furniture Giant.

Did I want to be? I mean, a couple extra bucks never hurt anyone, but it just sounded so final. I stared at the stack of papers as I considered the positives and negatives.

Apparently I stared too long, as Sean exclaimed, "Well! You gonna sit there forever like it's Saturday and not Monday? Or are you going to sign the papers?" He shook me from my reverie and I automatically grabbed the papers. I read them over, signed the release form from the temp agency and the paperwork to be an employee and the six-month probation period disclaimer. Okay, so not so final after all—good. With that, I thanked the turd sitting in front of me who just scoffed as I left the office.

Being part of Tony's didn't have to be so final. If I didn't like the team, the work, or for that matter, the place, I could try to get back on with the temp agency. Dealing with Sean day in and day out for the unforeseeable future sounded dreary and made me panic.

"One of us! One of us! One of us!" was being chanted in monotone voices when I came out of Sean's office. I giggled at the other three reps. Sean came out of his office with a grin on his face at the sight of this. But he promptly told us to get back to work as he shook his head with a snicker. Okay, so it *was* just me he hated. I accepted quick congratulations and got back to the daily grind. I didn't know what I had done to this guy to piss him off; it was like he was mad that we were breathing the same air. I just couldn't figure him out!

He had degrees on his walls from the University of Victoria, so he had to have some intellect. He was at least 6'1" with dark, almost black, collar-length hair that was haphazardly done, like he just put his hands through it and it fell to the side. He was well built, so he was handsome to most, to me it was only if he kept his dumbass mouth shut that he could be handsome. Not that it mattered. I was not a kiss ass, so there was no need to try and figure him out. I was there to do a job, so that's what I would do. If he didn't like me, too bad for him. He had acted like a smug ass in his office, and I felt like ranting back at him. I had left a little more than just irritated. As far as he was concerned, I just signed the papers and I'd be there forever to make sure I was breathing the same air as he was! That would drive him crazy. Now that I was done the rant in my head, I calmed down and got a coffee. Maybe it wouldn't be so bad to be permanent here. A couple of extra bucks would help with the crazy cost of living. Working with good people, if they were starting to accept me, couldn't hurt either. This might be a good thing.

I finished the day and drove home. I lived just thirty minutes from work—a little longer during rush hour, but living close to the main arteries meant cheaper housing, and I lived in an older (I mean really old) home with golf courses on either side and a park to the south. This gave me a little more peace and quiet and a little less city in my face, with the comforts of having everything. Affording more would be hard on a single person's salary. Honestly, it was tough as it was, but I really wanted my own space, not an apartment. It was just a small, three-bedroom home with a single parking space, which I pulled into.

As I jiggled the keys in my door to unlock it I could hear an ornery low growl from the other side of the door. "Well, hello, Dallas," I greeted my cat while opening the door. She was my miserable little girl who had a temper like a crotchety old lady. She was not much for people, and she pretended she didn't like to cuddle. She was not a good pretender, though. She loved me and she knew it, and I couldn't be without her. She was the cranky roommate I hardly ever saw, but every so often I heard her grumpy little growl from somewhere in the house and when she decided to be fit company she crawled in beside me. I got her a tin of her favorite cat food and decided I should cook for myself as well—supper was a good idea. While I cooked, the cat finished her meal and then took off to wherever she deemed a good hiding spot.

I put some chicken in the oven and shut the door, and that's when I heard a clang and a bang and lights flickered in the kitchen. Then I heard the pissed-off cat growl. I ran out of the kitchen to see what happened towards the back of the house to cause such a cacophony. I got headed down the hall and looked into the room on the right and found the disturbance. "What in the hell!" The cat came tearing from the back corner of the room running right towards me and then through my legs. At the front of the room the mirror was cracked in pieces all over the floor, and the lamp stand was knocked over. What the hell was that cat trying to do? I picked up the lamp, and as I was straightening up I saw a dark figure in the cracked mirror pieces.

I jumped toward the doorway and then turned to face the intruder. Nothing but an empty space and a small single bed greeted me. I looked back to the mirror to see what could have caused the shadow and saw nothing.

I left the room and closed the door—I would have to deal with the cracked mirror tomorrow. Living alone for a while could play tricks on your mind. I was always seeing things. Mind you, I had been that way for as long as I could remember. I thought I would have grown out of it after childhood, but that seemed to be my cross to bear— seeing things, hearing things and knowing things that just were not apparent to everyone else. Sometimes the things I heard and saw just weren't there. Or, conversely, I was a loon, and had lost my mind. I rolled my eyes at that thought and went back into the kitchen to finish cooking my dinner. After I ate, I decided a brisk walk to the grocery store, which also housed a café, was in order. Once there, I grabbed my favorite vanilla bean latte and few groceries and walked back. The cool air was burning my lungs, but the coffee was a good way to defrost in the cool air.

Vancouver winters were not usually too cold, but tonight seemed to have a chill in the air—icy, even. The sky was clear and there was no wind, which made for a very nice night out. I decided when I got home I would put my groceries away and then double check the house to make sure I hadn't missed anything, and that there really wasn't anyone there but me and a grumpy cat.

I did a walkthrough, tidying along the way so I didn't feel like an idiot for rechecking my house when no one was there but me and a grumpy cat. Everything was fine, as I thought—just a good imagination, not an intruder. I headed off to bed early after taking a sleep aid. Time to catch up on some much-needed sleep, which came easily. So did the dreams.

Lying in bed, I am back to when I was a four-year-old girl. From my room I can see down the hall and to the stairway, but I cannot see my parents' room in the small, low-income condo we live in. I look toward the window to see how light it is outside. I am trying to gauge if it is okay for me to get up at this time of day. Then I look down the hall for confirmation; no darkness means it should be okay to be awake. At the end of the hall I see something that wasn't there just a minute ago--my blow-up punching bag with the clown picture on the front. It is a favorite toy of mine because his nose sticks out a little and he is weighted at the bottom so when you punch him he stands back up, which is cool because he's the same size as me. But what is he doing on the top step? Did I leave him there? Wait, he wasn't there a few seconds ago, was he? No, no, he wasn't; I just looked into the hall twice. How is he lopsided and looking around the wall at me? Toys can't lean over! How is he even fitting on the step? Then I remember to close my eyes and breathe; that way bad dreams and things you think you see will be gone. That's what I was told by my mom and dad, so I close my eyes to try and make the scene go back to normal.

When I open them the clown is not gone— it's looking at me and has a different smile. His grin is bigger and his pointy teeth now show. Now I can't get out of bed; I am frozen there, stuck ... and realizing that this is a really bad time to have to go pee. I can't just get out of bed ... what will happen then? Will it disappear? Will it get me? This isn't normal, so how do I know what will happen?

I can't hold it anymore and I pee the bed. I close my eyes and open, them hoping the stupid thing will go away—now I hate that toy! It doesn't go away, and when I open my eyes it is halfway down the hall. Now I know I didn't do that! "Daaaaaaaad!!" I scream at the top of my shrill lungs.

My dad comes in my room. "What is it? What's the matter, honey?" he says. Um, what do I say? I had a dream? I had a bad dream? I have a scary, possessed toy from hell? Even at four you know that just isn't right.

"I had a very bad dream about my toy chasing me because it's just sitting in the hall!"

My dad leans over me and looks in the hall. "There's nothing in the hall. I don't see a toy. Which toy? I don't see it."

I look and it's gone. "It was my punching bag clown, Daddy. It was right there. I saw it!"

"Well, it's not there now. It was just a bad dream," he says softly. "Why is your bed wet? Why is your bed all wet?! Did you pee your bed? Why would you do that?" He is obviously upset at the mess I just made. Surely I can explain that while I was having a bad dream with my eyes wide open contemplating getting out of bed, the scary clown scared the piss out me ... quite literally.

Instead, I just look at him in quiet acquiescence. Knowing he's right, that this is dumb, that there is no way to explain and no way I'm coming out of this in the right.

"You are too old to be making a mess like this, Cali! I just don't under-stand why you wouldn't get out of bed and walk to the bathroom! It's just a door down!"

Surely he didn't just forget about the death clown? (pop!!) *Now his head turns. Oh! I hear it too! "Daddy, what is that? It sounds like something dropped. Or it's a popping sound." I look at him. Hopefully getting in trouble is done with now that there's a new mystery.*

"I don't know," he says. "You get out of bed and take your wet clothes off and put your housecoat on till I can run you a tub. See if you're strong enough to pull your sheets and blanket off and put them on the floor, okay? I'll go see what that was while you're doing that."

"NO! Daddy, I'll come too," I whine.

"Mom is still across the hall and you are soaked—you stay and do what you are told, okay?" he says softly.

"Okay," I finally agree. By the time I have done what he asked I feel fine again—safe and calm. Everything is as it should be again.

Dad comes back up the steps. "Good job, Cali! Let's run a tub and get you cleaned up this morning."

I look at him a moment and ask, "Well, what was the big noise?"

"Oh …" He pauses nonchalantly. "Sorry, honey. It was your favorite toy … the clown … it popped."

Okay, what in the world? Surely he will find this weird. Should I just sit here and stare at him and see if he connects the dots? Well, that's what I do and he does not connect any dots. At least, it looks like he doesn't or he doesn't think it's a big deal. It is a VERY BIG DEAL to a four-year-old. HELLO?!?

Scary clown came upstairs, tried to get me, and then disappeared to go die somewhere on the floor downstairs— ring a bell? Are you not terrified? What is wrong with adults? How does this not seem weird? My toys are coming to get me!

At 3:18 a.m. I was jolted awake by the bizarre memory of the nightmare that was my childhood and the memory of when I was four. I actually woke up afraid. To this day, even as an adult, I could not justify that memory, and I couldn't quite make sense of it—or of most of my memories. It was not the only thing that came up when I slept, if I got some sleep, but it happened often enough that I just couldn't quite shake it.

I looked at the clock on the night table. That's lovely, I thought. It would be nice to sleep through the night once. This getting up at 3:00 a.m. was for the birds! I decided to go to the bathroom and then get a drink of water so I could shake the stupid memory and do what the rest of the world did … sleep. I hunkered down into my blankets with the sleep aid and I was tired enough that it was not long before I got back to sleep. I did not know why I kept dreaming of the same thing over and over when I slept. When I was little I would have the same dream, and as I grew older I still had it almost weekly, if not nightly. As soon as my head hit the pillow for the second time, a dream started:

I am sleeping. I can feel that I am somewhat awake and not able to tell the difference between reality and dream state, a form of sleep paralysis. I learned that was what it was called in my adult years. I feel fully awake; in fact, I am sure I am awake lying in bed. There is something at the foot of the bed. I can't make it out at first because this does not live in our reality; it doesn't make sense. As I focus on what I'm looking at it is just wrong— the feeling of it / him being there is wrong in nature. It is tall, seven feet tall, and I have enough time to see that but I cannot see a face— I just see the eyes glowing red. The body is well built and the bottom is missing … it's just mist or smoke. I am grabbed by the ankles and dragged out of the bottom of my bed, across the floor, down the hall into the kitchen and down the basement stairs where I then stare into the face, the actual face of a smiling, red-eyed demon.

CHAPTER 2
Camping In The Basement

Be-beep, be-beep, be-beep, be-beep ...

"Holy hell!" The morning alarm jolted me from my dream. "Shit, what the hell?"

This was not a dream you got used to having, even if it had become part of an almost-nightly ritual. Some people do yoga before bed, some people listen to music—I dreamed of demons dragging me down the damn stairs. I shook off the memory, slapped off the alarm and got out of bed to start my morning routine of a coffee and a shower. The weird dream left me a little off kilter as I dressed in an aqua-blue, long-sleeve, fitted sweater and light denim with black ankle boots. If I wanted to get to work I needed to move my ass.

Dallas, again, was nowhere to be seen. I didn't know where in this tiny house she could disappear to. I grabbed my book off the shelf for lunch break and remembered I actually had people talk to me yesterday for more than five seconds and they didn't stare at me like I had two heads. It gave me pause, but I grabbed the book just the same for comfort in case yesterday was some sort of fluke.

I remembered to warm up the car this morning— the winter was just too cold for this little car. I turned on the TV and had some of hazelnut coffee with some peanut butter toast I ate quickly while the car warmed up.

I felt a little nudge at my leg and I looked down to see Dallas greet me; odd, but welcome. "Hello, little one. Where have you been hiding?" I cooed at the cat. I picked her up and petted her; this was a rarity in our relationship, so I took advantage if she let me. As I was petting her I saw her fur was a little matted, and wondering what she could have gotten into, I took a closer look at the reddish-brown substance. Now I could see she was all scratched up, and she must have been bleeding—that's what matted her fur. She bit me and ran off. "Ouch! What the heck, Dallas, that hurt! How did you get hurt?" I went to find her quickly before leaving, and she was standing in the hall where I had closed the door to the spare room the night before. Could she have gotten hurt in the room last night and that's why she ran off? What could have hurt her? I tried to get closer, but she wanted to dart away. I grabbed her before she did and picked her up to see if she would let me take a closer look. "I'm not going to hurt you, Dallas, let me see it, okay? I will get you a treat? Does that sound good, a treat?"

At the sound of her favorite word she calmed down enough for me to just take a look. There were some shiny specks in her fur and a slight but long lesion. It looks like … glass? Oh, the mirror from last night … but how would that have happened? Did some of the mirror fall on her? How would she get that in her fur with a cut like that? I had time to clean her up and take care of the wound with antibiotic cream before I was late.

Then I give her the promised treat and rushed to the table to turn off the TV. Just as I went to push the off button the weather man was saying, "It's minus ten degrees Celsius and there is a northwest wind of ten kilometers per hour. The four inches of snow that fell last night will make it slippery as the snow decided to stick around and stay on the roads. Be careful on the roads everyone. Safe driving." The weather man finished his segment.

"WHAT?" I exclaimed in horror. I opened the door and sure as shit there was snow on the ground. "For all that is holy! Damn!" Although Vancouver was in Canada, the snow days, where snow stayed on the ground, were probably less than ten days of the year at maximum. "Shit, shit, shit! Now I will be late." I had to go down to the basement and find the box where I kept all my winter stuff. I take off my cute little boots and exchange them for higher, slightly warmer boots and put on a warmer jacket and toque and gloves. Now that I had done that, I could go do my favorite activity of scraping the windshield and cleaning off the rain and snow mix that fell last night, creating a blanket of ice over the car. I brushed off what I could, but it was kind of crusted on like an extra skin, making it hard to remove. Which made me wonder what the roads must be like. "Oh God, help my tiny car … please be brave and make it to work." I gave a little prayer before I got in and backed out of the driveway to test out the road and see just how slippery the side roads were. Sure enough, everything was slick and no one knew how to drive in the winter, so there are accidents all over the place.

This made my thirty-minute drive an almost hour-long drive and made me twenty-five minutes late. Oh, goody I bet I would be the favorite person today; I just got the raise and now I was late. Back to being the two-headed monster everyone stared at but didn't talk to. Jeez, it would be nice if I could get it together.

I walked in and I was the only person late from customer service, of course. The others probably didn't go to bed at 8:00 p.m. like a child, so they knew about the snow and planned ahead whereas I did not.

"Oh, shit. Is Sean mad? Is he going to ream me out?" I asked Ashley, the other customer service rep and one of Tracy's friends. She was so petite she reminded me of Alice, the short-haired girl in the popular vampire movie *Twilight*. Todd, the fourth and final rep, just eyeballed me and went back to work. He was pretty quiet on the work floor and I didn't know him personally; I think he had said five words to me since I had been here. Tracy just side-eyed me, as she was still on the phone, and gave a wave. Oh good, so *not* the work pariah again.

"No, Cali, you're fine, he's not here yet. Rough start to your day?" Ashley asked as her eyes slid down my wardrobe.

"Shit, yes. I went to bed real early so I didn't know about the snow till I opened the door and now I am wearing the dirt from my car on my jeans— that's just perfect!"

"Don't worry about it, Cali, at least its dry. Just take the dry dishtowel from the kitchen and wipe it off and if there's anything left dampen the cloth. It will come out and you'll be good as new," Ashley proclaimed, and Tracy gave the thumbs up. I allowed my shoulders to release and I took a breath to start over from my hectic morning.

"Where is Sean, anyway? Is he not coming in?"

"He hasn't called in yet," said Tracy as she hung up the phone. "We don't know where he is or if he's coming in."

"We do know, as a matter of fact," proclaimed Mr. Gunderson. I turned around like a child busted for sneaking in. He just looked up and down at the mess I was and then turned on his heel and started to walk away. "Todd, you will be stepping in for Sean for the day," he said over his shoulder.

"Can't Tracy? She's been here just as long and would love the job!" Todd said hastily. Tracy's mouth dropped like her secret had just been outed. She promptly went back to trying to finish her second call.

Mr. Gunderson was already halfway down the hall, but he stopped and said, "Tracy needs training in the position, and you have done the position and can fully do the job. A day at the helm is not going to hurt you. Just make sure things go smoothly till Sean is back. Thanks for steppin' up."

Todd St. John shut his phone down so it would not ring to his desk for customer service calls and stalked into the office and shut the door. He was blond and about my height with an average build, but man, could he hustle out of a room when he wanted to.

I decided to step out of the situation and follow Ashley's advice and get rid of the mud stain on my clothes. When I came back a couple minutes later, the office door was open and everyone was working.

Ashley said in a hushed voice, "Todd will be fine, he just needed a minute to stew. He doesn't like added stress in his life; it's already stressful. He had a service rep manager job in another store. He left and took the internal position to fill a customer service position here as just a representative. Now you're a little caught up." She smiled.

Thank the lord it was almost 10:00 a.m., which meant it was almost coffee break time, though I probably needed to do some work first. When break time came, Todd covered calls while the three of us went to the break room Tracy hurried into conversation like the fifteen minute break would not be long enough for what she had to say.

"So, what are you doing tonight, Cali, any plans?" As I tried to think if I had anything else scheduled later on, Tracy continued, "Let's rephrase—you have plans. You are coming out with us tonight. We're going to Sargent's Pub."

"New band to check out tonight, you in?" ask Ashley.

"Yeah, that does sound good," I said. "I never stay in one place long enough to go out with co-workers. Guess I'll have to change that bad habit now that I'm sticking around for a while."

"It's just the services crew so no one you don't already know," added Ashley.

"We were going to go out later, but I think the plan has changed to go right after work so we're not driving around on the roads. This isn't an episode of *Ice Road Truckers*," said Tracy with a smile.

I smiled back and pondered the new outcome to my day—this was great! I could get to know the other three and maybe find out a little more about Todd; he seemed nice enough. We discussed the plans till break was over and then we headed back to our desks.

"Cali," called Todd. " A Mr. Janssen was here he brought a chair for you to look at."

"Thanks, Todd. I'll be right back." I walked up front and asked one of the clerks to call for warehouse to get the chair and put it in holding in the warehouse.

At the end of the work day, I went to the bathroom to make sure I was at least presentable after the day I had. Not too bad, but a little makeup refresh would do the trick. I smudged some eyeshadow on with my finger and added a little lipstick, ran my fingers through my hair to give some life to it and I was off to Sargent's, which was just five minutes down the road. It was about 6:00 p.m. when I got there, the band didn't start till 7:00. I walked in and tried to locate the trio. Oh, not the trio—there were four. Four people sitting there. Sean was sitting there. Great, he hated me. What I thought was going to be enjoyable evening just got a little tense.

As though they could sense it, they turned to look at me, so I forced my legs forward and put a smile on my face. Everyone was smiling, but Sean was looking sternly at me. Fake it till you make it, right? I was not going to let him put a damper on my evening, I thought as I put my confidence in overdrive. "Hey guys, hi Sean, I didn't know you were coming as well."

"Is that a problem?" Sean asked.

I laughed off his comment. "Of course not, what I mean is, I didn't see you at work today so I wasn't expecting you here, that's all."

The group was watching the exchange in silence till I hung up my coat and slid in beside Tracy. She was sitting beside Sean in the horseshoe-type booth with Todd and Ashley rounding out the table.

Ashley interrupted the silence. "So! We ordered drinks and the waitress said she will be back with menus and to get your drink order."

"Who's the band tonight?" I asked.

"Weird name, Iron Hope, but they're quite good," Todd said. "I've heard them before. I think they're fairly new to the music world." He spoke! I tried not to look floored by the fact that I had finally heard him string a sentence together. He seemed nice enough, but he was unusually quiet. I didn't know much about him other than what Ashley revealed that day—which wasn't much other than he had been a manager, was stressed out and took the lower-level position.

A waitress came to take my drink order and after I ordered a frozen lime margarita she said, "I can get that for you. Take a minute with your menus and I'll be back." She strutted off and Todd watched her over his shoulder. Everyone at the table seemed to notice him eyeing the waitress.

"You could just go talk to her," said Sean.

"And say what?" Todd retorted.

"'Hello I'm Todd' might work," Tracy chimed in with a smile. Todd put his head down and studied the menu intensely.

"So, Sean, you were gone today," I said. "I hope everything is everything okay?"

"Fine, Cali, thanks for asking. I just had a personal day to take care of some things but everything is all good," Sean answered with a smile.

Holy shit, did he just smile? Was it was directed at me? Okay, this niceness was throwing me off a little. I wasn't the only one that noticed the exchange. This didn't feel like the hostile territory I thought it would be. The table fell silent at the lack of commentary on Todd's love life and small talk, and things took a befuddled, awkward turn.

"Soooo, I'm going to the bar to check for drink specials and maybe a shooter. Todd, you want to come?" asked Tracy.

"I'm in, let's go, Todd," Ashley stated, dragging Todd by the arm as if he didn't have a say in the matter. I got up to let Tracy out and they were gone before I could chime in. I guess I wasn't invited. I sat with Sean watching the people set up the band's gear.

"Well, that was odd, they scurried away quite quickly, didn't they? Guess we're not invited," I said with a laugh, trying to defuse the quiet.

"They are quite odd those three," he said. "They have been the unbreakable trio since Ashley started. Tracy has been at Tony's store the longest besides me. I've been there three years, Tracy almost two-and-a-half years, Todd almost two years and Ashley about eight months.

They go to breaks and lunch together when they can and they go out on evenings and weekends. I'm surprised they took you into the fold so fast."

I nodded in understanding. "I was kind of surprised to be invited out tonight myself."

"Not that you're not a nice person … it's just no one can break into the trio. I seem to be the side ornament they feel bad for leaving out of the fold," added Sean. "The person you replaced was just there to work, not to make friends, so they didn't really fit. But you, just like that, you're part of the gang." He smiled, and I smiled back.

I felt like I was flirting. Maybe because I didn't know what to make of him and I was forcing a smile while waiting to be stung.

"I'm happy to be included and have people to go out with. I am from Toronto, so everyone I know is back home. I came to the West just looking to find a different opportunity and strike out on my own to see a part of the country I haven't seen. So I have been temping, trying to find a place I fit. I must admit I wasn't sure about being permanent at Tony's. I've been temping for the last year in Vancouver and have not found anything I like or that I'm really good at. But I am good at this job, and the people I work with are great. So I took the leap." Smiling at him, this time for real, I felt like I just let out the secret of the century—stupid, I know, but this was Sean. Hard-to-read, hard-to-know Sean.

He was very good looking, but I couldn't get past the dislike he had shown me. Maybe I was not as good as I thought at work and he was frustrated with me there. Because this Sean right now seemed relaxed, smooth and friendly.

"Well, I'm glad you did take the job." There was a long pause as I stared at him in shock. "I mean … we needed someone there and you are more than capable," he amended.

"Honestly, I'm glad to hear it any way you want to state it. I thought you really disliked me or just didn't think I was good enough to be offered a permanent job."

Sean stared at me, but not with the 'you're a two-headed monster' look, more of a look of intrigue. I needed to interrupt his gaze before it burned into my soul, so I blurted out the first thing I could think of for small talk.

"The certificates, the ones on your wall—I didn't read them closely. What did you go to the University of Victoria for?"

He cleared his throat and broke his gaze. Finally. Now I didn't feel like a deer stuck in the clear-blue headlights he uses for eyes. "I took global business, and a secondary course in global economics and finance. I also did a minor in art and art history. I was in school for a few years and when I got out I didn't know what I wanted to do, where I wanted to go, or what I was willing to do to get there. So I took a position at Tony's till I had more of an understanding of who I was and where I was going. Kind of like you, I guess."

Great, I was blushing again and I looked like a deer caught in the headlights ... again. Was this how every girl felt and acted when he talked? Wasn't I sure we were, like, mortal enemies or something just a few minutes ago? I had been sure he disliked me, and I was ready to make the feeling mutual.

The gang made their way back to the booth and scooted in as the waitress followed just behind. "What can I get for you?" We each ordered the special, which was wings and. Hot n' spicy wings for me and, ironically, Todd, and teriyaki for Sean, salt and pepper for Ashley and Tracy to share with a salad. Wings are not exactly a sexy food to eat in front of co-workers that you've just been invited out with for the first time. When they came to the table I tried to negotiate them with a fork, which was painful because I was starving and I just wanted to shove them in my mouth and clean them to the bone. I couldn't help but chuckle to myself at the thought and it didn't go unnoticed.

"What's so funny?" asked Tracy.

"Oh, nothing I was thinking like a Neanderthal, sorry." I giggled, blushing with embarrassment.

"I think I know what you were thinking—you can tell a lot about a person by the type of wings they eat," Sean said with a devious smirk. Everyone laughed.

"Great, Sean is the wing fortune teller," said Tracy.

"No, no, serious." Sean Added, "I bet you're dying to just dive in instead of pick at that with a fork like a glass doll, aren't you?"

I laughed at Sean's remark—it was pretty close to the truth. I told them I was thinking the exact same thing about popping it in my mouth and sucking the bone dry, but I had an image of me trying to do it all sexy and failing miserably.

We laughed at me trying to portray my sexy eating habits. "You wear mischief well, Sean Stock, calling me out like that." I smiled at him again with a side glance. I was not expecting Sean to be so easy to talk to—I actually didn't think he would talk to me all night and that he would make this a very painful experience for me. But it turned out to be quite the opposite. Going forward, maybe things would be different with our interactions at work. He was rather good looking, I thought … shit, I figured I'd better not finish this margarita; it was screwing with my brain.

I drove home and it was later than usual for me—almost 11:30. When I walked in my house was fully lit up like a church. Every light in the place was on. Surely I didn't leave the lights on this morning, did I? I was in a rush but this … this was too much. I almost backed out of my house and closed the door.

Then I thought I was being stupid—burglars were not so imbecilic as to turn on every single light to rob the place, right? And I had nothing to rob. I rolled my eyes at my brain's constant need for drama. I must have left everything on. I went around the house and turned the lights off. I tidied up stuff that needed putting away and put a lunch together for the next day while watching Dallas eat the kitty food I laid out. Then I headed off to bed. It was such a hectic day that sleep hit me like a ton of bricks.

I am a six year old sitting in a tent in the basement of my parents' home. It was nice of my dad to set it up so I could play with it. I have made it up inside like a tiny house, with a little sleeping bed at the back and my play tea set for eating and drinking along with my pretend food and a high chair for my dolly. It feels like I have been playing there for hours. I am just thinking about how long I must have been playing when I feel like I'm not alone … like someone is in the basement with me. I stop playing and listen; maybe it's my mom doing laundry? But I hadn't heard her come down the stairs, which I definitely would have; she wears these wooden clogs that look like wooden sandals with a strap, and they are very loud. Come to think of it, everything, including the upstairs, seems quiet now that I am actually listening for noise. I can feel something coming closer; whatever it is, I know that I am not alone. Now I know I'm dealing with something that maybe not everyone would see or feel.

I seem to be on my own in this. My parents don't see things or hear things, and adults in general think I have a "great imagination." I feel the cold and I am getting colder; I feel like someone just entered my space, my tent. I feel it, like someone is staring right back at me waiting to see what I'm going to do. Then a cold puff of vapor comes out of my mouth. It's not my imagination, I say to myself—why would I imagine my breath turning to ice-cold vapor? Cold, sure, that's possible, but even at six years old I realize I can't physically manifest vapor from my imagination. It did get cold; the temperature has dropped. I figure if I can't see what's in front of me then whatever is there won't mind me running through it to the tent door and up the stairs.

I count to three, unzip the tent and run to the steps and up them as fast as I can. I get to the top, on the second stair, and I look back. The tent just sits there in silence. "Maybe I imagined it?" I say to myself. As soon as I say it, the tent shoots up towards the ceiling of the basement and flattens on the floor in disarray. I run to find my mom. It's quiet because she's feeding my new baby sister.

"What's wrong, you came flying into the living room so fast it's like you were being chased. You have to be quiet. The baby is eating."

I tell my mom exactly what happened. This isn't the first time things like this have happened and I have told her the stories. This is the last straw for her; this is where I am coined a storyteller and a liar. "Quit making stuff up like this, Cali, enough is enough! If you can't handle being able to play by yourself in the basement, then don't. Stay up here!"

I never do go back down there by myself; this is where the fear of the basement starts for me. It was so weird though; my mom always talked to me like I was full of shit and couldn't get out the truth if it bit me in the ass. But her eyes, they said something different, like she knew—she knew what I was talking about and was afraid for me. When she said "If you can't handle being in the basement alone, don't go" I think she really just didn't want me to go there by myself—she wanted me to stay where she could see me.

I woke up with a start. I was startled once more when the bedroom light was on as well as the en-suite bathroom light. Evidently I fell asleep with the lights on? No that wasn't right.

I shut off everything when I came home, and I couldn't sleep at the best of times, never mind with lights on. What time was it? I looked out the window and it was still dark. 3:18 a.m., the clock said. Of course it was. I had been waking up at the same time of night since I was a child. I got up, still feeling eerie from my memory in the dream. I stopped short of entering the hallway. The hall lights were on. I walked past the other two bedrooms and the lights were on. I hadn't cleaned up the room full of glass like I meant to the day before, so the door was closed, but a light shone from under the door. Wait, didn't the lamp break in the room catastrophe? There was no ceiling light— that's why I had a standing lamp in the room. I hurried past; if there was a light coming from a lamp that shouldn't exist that was fine, but I wasn't dealing with it now.

The hall bathroom light was on, as well as the light in the living room, the kitchen and the stair well light. Dallas sat by the front door like she was waiting to leave if she could just grow arms and hands long enough to unlock the door and run. This I didn't like; I never knew what to do when shit like this happened. Option #1, someone *was* in the house and I didn't check well enough and now they were screwing with me and I was about to get jumped. Not a good option. Option #2, the electrical was faulty in this old house and I was either going to have a house fire or have to replace all the wiring. Either way, that was a very logical, expensive option. Option #3, I had been found. This shit just loved me, and wherever I went this oddity followed. People literally hated living with me because of all the weirdness that went on when I was around.

My sister said things got so much better at home when I moved out on my own; most of the weird stuff just stopped. I'd had roommates that said the same thing, which was like confirmation that I was not just undoubtably insane. I mean everyone was a little, right? But this shit be crazy. In this option I had no help, I just deal. I couldn't tell anyone, or they would try to medicate my insanity. I didn't have anyone but my sister, who understood, but the clock on the microwave now said 3:30 a.m. so I couldn't call. I went around the house and checked if there was anyone in any closet and crawl-space or anywhere that someone could hide just to rule out Option #1. Nine-one-one was already on the cell; I just had to push send. Nothing. I imagined some entity laughing its ass of as I checked the windows and two doors.

Good, Option #1 was ruled out, meaning no serial killer. I smelled for smoke or burning wire, which smells like copper when it first starts. That's the part when you run, because momentarily your house could burn up. There was no smell and the breakers seemed fine from what I could tell. Excellent, that left Option # 3, which meant I was either a bucket of crazy or I was dealing with shit the most others do not have to deal with. I shouted to the empty room, "I AM GOING TO LEAVE THE LIGHTS ON! YOU WANT THEM ON … THEY ARE ON! I'm going to bed, Dallas. Come with me." Dallas did not remotely hiss at me or even cry or complain; she just snuggled up when I picked her up. Okay, another confirmation— no way this cat would cuddle anyone. She was scared and needed me. I get to the bedroom, where it felt like I left the window open, it was so cold. Knowing I had just checked it and the curtains were not moving in a breeze, I didn't give the satisfaction of checking if it was open again.

I just put Dallas in my bed and wrapped up into a quilt cocoon, with blankets all around me and covering my head. I had been sleeping like that since I was little as well; like my blankets were impenetrable. As an adult, I knew if something or someone wanted to find me this was not the best option, but it did help me go back to sleep.

I am sleeping. I can feel that I am somewhat in that state of sleep paralysis. I feel fully awake; in fact, I am awake, lying in bed, and at the foot of the bed is something I can't make out at first because this does not live in our reality—it doesn't make sense and I cannot move.

As I focus on what I'm looking at I can see it is just wrong, the feeling of it/him being there is wrong in nature, dark in nature. I can see it is seven feet tall, but I can't see a face; just glowing red eyes. The upper body is well built, but the bottom is missing—it's just mist or smoke. I am grabbed by the ankles and dragged from the bottom of my bed, across the floor and down the hall, into the kitchen and down the basement stairs where I then see this demon crawling low to the ground on all fours with my ankles in its hands. It now has legs instead of mist, but they are moving in unparalleled movements, unnatural movements jerking and twisting about. I look into the face of a smiling, red-eyed demon. Its face is scrunched up, its features contorted.

The alarm assaulted my ears at 6:00 a.m. and I smacked it off. I got up groggily and it didn't take me long to realize the memory of last night was real and then the second nightmare paralyzed me enough that I almost couldn't get out of bed.

I felt feeble and frail— that's why I feel so tired. I got up and Dallas followed me into the bathroom. I went to pet her and she hissed at me. "Well, glad to see you're back to normal."

I felt much better about getting into the shower, and after a shudder-some night, my senses started to go back to normal instead of being in hyper-drive. I hopped into a deliciously warm shower and washed my hair with coconut-scented shampoo and conditioner, my favorite. I got out and dried off, pulling my wavy brown hair into a messy knot after blow drying the hell out of it. I didn't want to be late so there was no time for a flat iron or setting my natural waves nicely.

I pulled on a long, blush-pink sweater made from the softest material ever and a pair of leggings. I would look stylish enough for work and it would be comfy—I just needed to be comfy today. After turning on the TV to make sure there were no surprises weather-wise today, I got Dallas her breakfast and made myself cheese and toast. Minus four degrees … well, that was not as bad as yesterday, and by the looks of the sidewalk it was barely a dusting of snow—nothing a broom couldn't handle. I would get coffee on the way this morning. I felt like I deserved a special coffee, like maybe a vanilla-bean latte.

I was feeling bad for leaving Dallas in the house. I went around and turned off all the lights again, and even I didn't want to be here. No point bothering to warm the car this morning— I just wanted to get the hell out of the house and get to work on time. I couldn't be late today. As I pulled into the parking lot I could see everyone in customer service was there already.

Trying to navigate the icy spots in the parking lot was not fun with the new pumps I was wearing. New bottoms on shoes and fresh ice don't mix, so I did my best not to do a Bambi impression. I walked in, put my stuff down behind my desk and headed to the coffee room where I found the whole service team. "Hey there! Everyone having a morning meeting?"

Sean spoke up first. "Actually, that's not a bad idea before we go into this morning, since a third of us will be missing from rotation. Cali and I will be heading into a meeting with the rep from the manufacturer. Sorry, Todd, that leaves you to cover my desk, but don't worry, we shouldn't be more than an hour." Todd just nodded and went back to mixing his coffee.

"The hardest hit will be what's left of the representatives. Instead of having three to answer the phones, that leaves you two, Tracy and Ashley. Just do the best you can and let the other management know you are shorthanded so they can deal with it accordingly."

"I can do that right now if we're done. I'll head to my desk now," said Tracy around a bite of muffin.

"Yes, I think that's it. We'll have a more formal meeting later in the week to announce a few changes coming up, but right now we should head to the desks," said Sean.

The first part of the morning flew by, mostly quick calls with easy fixes—just what I like. It didn't normally go so smoothly.

"Ready for the meeting?" Sean asked from the side of my desk.

The guy was like a panther; he was just all of the sudden right there beside me and I could never hear him coming. A little startled by his quick appearance, I collected my statements and things I needed for the meeting.

"I am now. Let's head over to the warehouse," I said.

"So did you have a good evening out?" asked Sean.

"I did, it was really nice to get out. I can be somewhat of an introvert if I let myself," I said with a smile. "It was nice getting to know you better, too," I added.

"I ... ah, was thinking we could go for dinner later this week. I have some things I would like to discuss work-wise with you, but that will only take a few minutes, then we can just have dinner. What do you think?" Sean asked. His voice didn't sound confident, but the way he held his stance said otherwise. According to the heat coming to my face, maybe it did suggest confidence.

"Umm, yeah, sure, that would be great. Do you have a place in mind?"

We were almost at the warehouse, and I needed this conversation to be over so I could put my boss attitude on and take care of business for my client.

"There's a quiet little Chinese place around the corner, Ming Diamond Palace, have you been there yet? Do you like Chinese?" he inquired.

"That will be fine, I haven't been there yet. Why don't we iron out the details later? I'll come to your office when work is over, okay?" I needed to put an early end to the conversation.

"Sure, that's great. Let's get in there and see what we can do in this meeting. Shall we?" Sean opened the door to let me in first.

"Good morning, Mr. Stock and Ms. Stenson," came a rumbly bass voice from the left of the room.

"Good morning, Mr. Gunderson," Sean and I said in unison.

"Sean, Cali, I would like for you to meet the manufacturers rep, Deacon Hall. He would like to hear what you have to say on the matter at hand for Mrs. Janssen." We prattled off our greetings to each other.

"I'd like to say that from the reports we have gotten this should be open and closed and I should not be here, so I am very interested in what you have to say, Ms. Stenson," said Deacon, the more-than-a-little-too-smug rep. Confidence or ego, it was a fine line sometimes, but I didn't mind knocking him off his high horse for a little bit.

"That's great you got the reports; however, if you did read them you would see the discrepancy I would like amended. Although the warranty is up by a few months, I would like to think that the kind of companies that Tony's Furniture Giant chooses to work with are not the kind of companies that would leave people high and dry. In the charts it is indicated there is a clear specification problem with a chair," I said matter of factly, with as much in-your-face confidence and boldness as I could muster in to my 5'7" frame.

Whether we liked it or not we are usually being people that we are not in reality, but as I glanced at Sean he did look a little impressed. Not that the glance went unnoticed by Deacon, which kind of did undermine me a bit, so I just held my head higher, stood straighter and did not let my eye contact waver from Deacon's as I silently dared him to push me further, I felt like this was a pissing match and he was just waiting for me to falter. That ego exuded from his body as well as his confidence, stating we should know damn well he was above this and he shouldn't be here.

"Are you saying we didn't build it right? Where on earth did you get an idea like that?" Deacon said like I was a child making up stories for fun.

"Actually, I got it from the workers' report; the fact that no one else seemed to notice is beyond me," I said, trying to show him that just because he towered over me and didn't think he owed a minute of his time, he was going to give me more than a few minutes. "The worker report clearly states that the frame is bent, which for a tiny, 140-pound old lady might be hard to do unless she was jumping up and down on it." Deacon was about to challenge when I held up my hand and continued, "Before you say anything else, yes, someone else could have damaged it or dropped it or whatever the case may be for breaking a chair. That is not the defect I speak of." Deacon squinted his eyes at me, trying to figure out what I was getting at. "The defect is how those two pieces of the frame are held together.

"This part of the frame where it is twisting is held with a quarter-inch bolt, when what is needed and what is on the other side of the chair is a half-inch lock bolt. Now, before you say it was probably a home fix …"

Deacon interrupted before I could finish. "We bake our parts in navy blue paint and not the customary steel or black steel components so we can tell the difference." He was surrendering to my argument.

"That's right, Mr. Hall, you paint them navy blue—all the parts were intact and they were all, including the wrong part, navy blue. It was built wrong in assembly."

"Ms. Stenson, do you mind if I talk to you in private for a quick moment?" he said.

"Sure, I can give you a moment, Mr. Hall." I let him lead me away from the group and looking back I could see that Mr. Gunderson was visibly relieved that I got my point across and this was not going to be a matter for the store. Sean shook his head slightly with a questioning look as to why we would need a private meeting. I just shrugged and turned to face Deacon's tall linebacker frame.

"So Cali, what do you think about having dinner with me tonight? I'm in town a few nights and I hate eating alone. Would you care to join me?" Deacon asked questioningly.

I'm sure more than a little shock lit my face. What was this guy doing? The ego attitude had been dropped and though his confidence shone through, it wasn't overpowering. He seemed softer somehow … as soft as a 6'4" linebacker could be.

"Uh … I … um … sorry, you caught me off-guard. I thought we were going to talk about a chair," I said, trying to keep the conversation professional.

"Yes, the chair … well, you stated it was in the report from the worker, so if that lines up then it looks like you're right. We can make it a partial business dinner and discuss our options— mostly I find you beautiful, confident and pragmatic, and I dislike eating alone."

I blushed hard. This guy had knocked me off kilter so quickly I felt like I had to scramble to get a grip. Deacon wasn't the only one that noticed the more-than-uncomfortable situation with me acting like a schoolgirl. The other gentlemen from our group noticed the exchange too.

"Mr. Hall, I don't think…"

"Ms. Stenson, how about we replace the chair, as it is clearly our problem at the manufacturer. Now all you have to contend with is a lovely dinner with me at, let's say, 7:00 p.m. at La Boheme revolving restaurant? I promise I don't usually bite," he said with a full-on grin.

"You know, you have a bad habit of not letting me finish my sentences. Just dinner?" I asked almost nervously. This guy really threw me off my game.

"Just dinner. It would be lovely to have company."

I thought for a moment. "I suppose I could, but please, let's get back to the others. They are staring over here and I would rather not do this with an audience, as I am obviously out of practice with this type of banter." I laughed nervously at my comment and he chuckled back as we turned to walk toward the others.

CHAPTER 3
The Boogie Man In The Hotel

TRACY AND ASHLEY WERE BURIED UP TO THEIR NECK WITH PHONE CALLS. Todd tried to help when he could, but it would be hard going till the other two came back. Finally, around 10 a.m., the phones died down. "So what do you think?" Tracy asked, wiggling her eyebrows up and down.

"I'll tell you if you stop doing that weird thing with your face," Ashley countered.

"Well, I'll tell you what I think. I think Sean is more into Cali than he said he was. I mean, after last night and actually getting to spend time with her there was more than just the vibe he spoke of."

"Tracy, I told you not to meddle; just let it be," exclaimed Ashley. "If they figure out you set up the pub thing and you knew he had the hots for her and used the pub to get them together to see what happened, *if,* and that's a big if, anything happens between them … we are all implicated in your little set-up scheme."

"Yep, I have to agree with Ashley," said Todd from the office doorway. "I want no part in that. Keep it buttoned and let it be."

"I hope they get back here soon. I'm getting eardrum blisters from talking on the phone all morning. A break would be great," sighed Tracy.

"Why don't you go get the two of you coffee and a muffin from the break room, Tracy? I'll cover your desk while you're gone," offered Todd.

"Don't have to tell me twice," exclaimed Tracy.

***

The atmosphere seemed to have changed on the way back to the group. Sean's face was stern-looking, his lips held in a thin line as he glanced at Deacon and then glared at me. "Well, we seem to have an agreement. I will have a company pick up this chair, Cali. I'll call you when I have the new one in place for delivery. If we don't stock it anymore then we will redo the entire frame and put in new seating. You'll hear from me one way or the other tomorrow. I head back to Calgary the next day. I'll try and confirm details before I leave. Good day, gentlemen. Cali, nice to have met you. Talk to you later tonight." With that, Deacon just left me there with the two onlookers and exited the warehouse. I'm pretty sure he knew I didn't need our dinner plans announced to these two—what was he playing at?

"Well, thank you, Cali. Job well done. The owner will be happy to know that the matter is settled and it has no cost to them or the store—I love that part," a gleeful Mr. Gunderson stated. The expression on Sean's face said it all. He seemed pissed, but I didn't understand what I could have done since we entered the building. I was back to being the two-headed monster, I could see that clearly.

He said nothing as we walked the long hall back to the office—a big difference from before. He walked slightly ahead, and even when I tried to walk beside him he seemed to just walk faster to stay ahead. We got there in a record sprint and Sean went to his office and closed the door. "What happened? It didn't go the way you thought and now he's pissy because Mr. Gunderson is pissy?" inquired Ashley.

"No, actually I was right, and it will be dealt with. Mr. Gunderson seemed quite pleased. As for Sean, I have no idea. We walk there and everything is like it was last night—easy and comfortable. We walk back and I'm like a pepper kernel stuck between his teeth. He wanted nothing to do with me. He didn't say a word to me on the way back." I sat down and was bringing my computer logs back online and signing my phone back in when Sean showed up beside my desk again. I hoped he wasn't nearby to hear what I said; we needed to put a bell on that guy. I could never hear him approaching.

Everyone got busy and he turned to me and said, "I implore you to get your time management figured out. Your call specs are not what they should be if you want to work here with permanent status. I mean, you might as well do your job." Then he simply strolled back into his office and shut the door.

Everyone stopped what they were doing, even Todd stopped mid-call. Their jaws dropped to the floor. My cheeks heated. I didn't know what was up with him, but he was going to learn that job or no job, no one talks to me like that without cause. I stood and went barging into his office.

"What the hell was that? One minute you asking me to dinner saying there's business stuff to discuss and the next you're telling me if I don't smarten up I don't have a job? Did you and I attend different meetings? Mr. Gunderson was quite okay with my performance. Why aren't you?"

Sean scoffed at me. "Yes, that was quite the performance. I'm thinking we did attend two different meetings. Well, actually, I guess we did since we were barred from your little side performance!"

"Sean, what the hell are you talking about?"

He just glared at me a moment as if searching for the right words. "What was that little side meeting? It couldn't have been about no damn chair with you blushing and flirting like you were in a bar laughing it up with an old chum!"

It was now my turn for my jaw to drop. Oh my! He was jealous! What a brat. That had to be it, with this childish behavior. "Is this how you always act when a person asks out one of your co-workers?" I asked with one eyebrow up, daring him to continue on his little tirade.

He opened his mouth like he was about to say something and stopped. "I don't have time to deal with this right now. I need you to leave my office."

Did he just try to scold me? Oh no, he didn't! "Listen here, big and mighty, if you're going to be all up in my face because someone asked me out, then own it!

If you have time to scold and reprimand me, in front of coworkers I might add, then you can deal with me and my so-called work problems now!" Sean stood up from his desk and I braced myself for what he was going to yell at me. But he slowly sat back down, took a breath, bowed his head like he couldn't look at me and said, "Cali, I am sorry. You're right, that was very unprofessional of me."

"You're damn right it was, Sean!"

"I fear I have some explaining to do. Can we please just put this on pause? Can you still meet with me after work today?" I could feel my eyes narrowing and my jaw set as I tried to decide if I could let this go or tell him where to go and how to get there, job be damned. "Please, Cali, I am sorry, truly. Just meet me after work, please. Let's not hash this out now. I was wrong with the way I handled things."

"Okay, Sean, I'll meet with you after work. We can talk then, but as you know I have plans, so if you go all "I Tarzan you Jane" on me, I will take you down!"

"Fair enough Cali, after work, then?" I strode out of the office, closing the door hard and leaving him sitting there.

Sean watched as Cali strode out and slammed the door, and he couldn't help but grin. Then, frowning and unable to shake the conversation, he felt like he had to focus on the meeting after work, which was interfering with the work he needed to do now. Great, if she wasn't stuck in his head before, she sure as hell was now.

Cali came out of the office and everyone's head turned. Thanks Sean, she thought. I'm back to being the two-headed monster. "Cali, the other girls already went and got themselves coffee and a muffin to bring back to their desks," Todd said. "If you would like to take a moment before you start and do that as well, we should be back on track soon with everyone here now."

"Good idea, Todd. Thanks, I won't be long." As Cali disappeared around the corner to the break room, Todd scooted into Sean's office.

"What the hell, man? I thought you had a thing for her. I didn't know that thing was to rip her a new one. Dude, you are so screwed now!"

Sean put his hands through his hair, then his head in his hands and looked up at Todd from his chair grinning like a schoolboy. "What a fireball. Boy, she is damn cute when she's mad. She's also smart enough to keep her wits about her and make a few good points ... I'm an ass," he said as the smile was wiped off his face.

"Yeah, you are! You better go fix it like right now, as in pronto!" said Todd.

Sean hurried passed Todd and opened his door but jolted to a stop. It was his turn to feel like the two-headed monster. Tracy and Ashley turned from their desks, glaring at him. Phones at their ear in mid-conversation. This gave Sean pause, and he backed up a step and shut the door. "Yep, I'm the asshole, shit!" he said. "I guess I'll just hole up in my office till the meeting today. I should be grateful she doesn't call Gunderson in on this meeting ... Oh my hell!

She wouldn't call Gunderson in, would she?" Without waiting for Todd's reply he exclaimed, "Jesus, now I'm all worked up. I need coffee." He walked back out of the office.

In the break room, Cali picked up a blueberry bran muffin—not the most exciting choice, but it was actually her favorite. She knew she felt upset, but what was she feeling? Angry, hurt, sad? She was angry with Sean and it had served her well to get her point across and shut him up at the same time. But this residual energy felt off, and she didn't like it. Did she feel like crying? Hell no! Not at work!

Maybe it wasn't about the fight but was more the fact that he would think so badly of her. She hoped people thought she was at least a nice person and that she tried at the very least to be an upstanding person. Were the things he was saying about her work process true? Was she slow, were her volumes on the cue slow or incomplete? She didn't think so; her reports, as far as she knew, were thorough and complete. She did a bang-up job with Janssen's case. Where could she have gone wrong?

"I was a jerk," said Sean from the entranceway. Cali turned, almost spilling her coffee. "I couldn't wait till the end of the day to say this part. You need to know there's nothing wrong with your work ethic or progress. I am … well, I can't say what I am in the public break room, but you can fill the blank with whatever words you want."

Tears welled in my eyes. I guess it did hurt to think someone would question my ethics or how well I could do the job even though down deep I knew I always gave a hundred percent. Sean crossed the room so fast it was like vampire speed.

"Cali, please don't be hurt because of my stupid words."

"I think I just need a moment. I didn't think I let what you said get to me, but just then when you came in I was questioning myself; you made me doubt myself. That's what I think upset me, not the confrontation. Then you came in and, well, that just set me off. I'll be okay. Coffee will help," I said with a smile.

"Yeah, that's what I thought, and that's why I came in here. I will just get a cup and head back and get out of your hair. Take a minute to yourself. I didn't mean to question your integrity and I definitely didn't mean for you to question you own integrity. That is horrible. Again, I'm sorry. Just a bad day, I guess."

"Yeah, a bad day. Though we now both know that isn't what started this."

"No, Cali, it isn't. Can we talk later if you're still okay with that?"

"Sure, Sean, I can give you a few minutes later."

Sean left and I took a minute to take a few breaths and clear out the negative energy. Whatever people thought, good or bad, I couldn't control that, but I could control if it made me feel a certain way. I focussed on how I felt after I was out with my coworkers last night and how I had so much fun, the energy of the enjoyment of the activity. I started to feel happier, like I could just let go of the momentary lapse in judgment from Sean. Yeah, actually I could and that was easier on me. Feeling better now, I followed Sean few minutes later. I got back to my desk and everyone was busy dealing with customers and phone calls so I hopped in and did the same.

The first call in would be to Mrs. Janssen to tell her the good news. Because of the shortage of staff earlier today, there was no shortage of work, and they were busy until the afternoon.

"Tracy, why don't you and Cali take a late lunch in the lunch room?" Todd said. "Actually, take Ashley with you two. I'll cover. Just turn your phones off so the calls come here. I'll let Sean know so if any extra calls come in he can take them on his phone."

"Thanks Todd, you're awesome!" said Ashley. I, on the other hand, wasn't sure if today was the best day to lunch with the ladies.

"So, your meeting went well?" asked Tracy.

"Yeah, actually. It couldn't have gone any better. I'm getting the client a new chair and if it's not in stock or they no longer carry it, Deacon said he would replace the inner workings and seating," I said, taking a first bite of my lunch. I realized Ashley and Tracy were glancing at each other.

"What?" I asked.

"Deacon? You said Deacon. Who's Deacon?" Ashley said around a bite of apple.

"He's the manufacturer's rep," I said matter of factly. They looked at each other again. "What!" I exclaimed.

"It's just the way you skirted the name so quickly when you said it and your eyes went down to the table. Who is Deacon to you?" said Tracy

"You guys are horrible. You're like hawks striking out for prey," I said, looking at both of them. The silence was palpable as they stared at me, waiting for me to spill. "Okay, okay, jeez! Deacon is the rep, and when we were in the middle of the meeting he pulls me aside and asked me to dinner tonight. As you can imagine, I was completely floored. Obviously it was not expected, and I'm not sure if it's wanted. I was in the middle of a meeting! With Gunderson and Stalk standing there watching the whole thing happen from a few feet away! So yeah, that was my morning, how was yours?"

"Whoa, whoa, you don't get off that easy, missy," said Ashley.

"No wonder Sean had a shit fit." Tracy giggled.

"What? What do you mean?" I asked.

"Back up a bit first. I'll get to that," said Ashley.

This must have been what interrogation felt like. "Ugh, okay you monsters! Yes, I am going to dinner with Deacon!"

"It's not like I know a lot of people here yet, and he is quite gorgeous and he said it was just to keep him company. Neither of us needs to eat alone tonight. Not a big deal, it's not a NASA rocket equation, so I think I can handle it."

"You can handle Deacon? Well, that sounds promising," said Ashley in a full-out laugh now.

"So spill, what do you know? Why would that have caused Sean's little tirade? I mean, I figured out myself it was jealousy. But why? He's acted like he can't stand me the whole time I've been here!" I said with confusion.

"Yeah, it reminds me of a schoolboy crush. You know, when the boy keeps pulling the girl's hair to get her attention." Tracy laughed. "And you! You are so blind! He is sooo into you and your oblivious!" she exclaimed. "He's become a crotchety old man in the office. I don't think he can handle having you around and not being able to do anything about how he feels. It's driving him crazy." She smirked.

"Oh, man, I have a meeting with him right after work! Why did you have to spring this on me now? What am I supposed to do?" My voice was full of anxiety; it couldn't be hidden.

"Relax. Do you think you like him? I mean, not now after he lost his mind, but maybe before?" said Ashley.

"I never thought about it before! I thought he was really nice to me last night and that was great. Now he's a dumbass again!" I said.

"He was acting out. He definitely owes you an apology, but I know he does really like you. Just hear what he has to say.

If he turns into asshole Sean again we will all give him hell," said Tracy. "But if not then I guess you'll have to take it from there. No immediate decision required." Tracy smiled.

"How did you guys know about Sean and I didn't?" I asked.

"He came clean to me. I saw it in him, and the way he acted around you. You just weren't looking for that at the time and didn't see what was right in front of you," said Tracy.

"Well, shit, this meeting is going to be more impossible than I thought," I said. With that, I got up and started cleaning up my lunch stuff.

Ashley walked by and whispered in my ear, "It really doesn't have to be." She kept going toward our office.

Tracy offered her unsolicited advice too. "Just deal with the matter at hand first. Deal with anything else after. If he doesn't say anything about it, just give it a chance. See what he does or says over the next day or so; he probably feels like a real asshat at the moment, so he may back off for a bit."

I could feel my shoulders had set high by my ears and my jaw felt tense. I really didn't know what I was going to do with this information, or if I even cared. I hadn't thought about my personal life much; I was just trying to figure out my career. Sure, I figured it would be nice to have friends and meet people, but I hadn't really thought more about a relationship status change on my Facebook page.

It was good to be busy all afternoon. When I logged off for the day, I really wanted to run for my car and pretend I forgot the meeting, but I noticed Sean in his doorway. I turned and ended up face to face with him. "You weren't going to run out on me, were you?" uttered Sean.

"Well, to be perfectly honest, after lunch with the girls the thought did cross my mind. We really need to get you a bell. Shit, I almost ran straight into you."

His lips pursed. "Well, I'm glad you didn't leave. Come in, I won't take up your time." I walked in and stood at the wall by the door he was closing. "Did you want to sit?"

"No, I think I'll just stand for this one," I stated, not able to keep the nervousness out of my voice.

"I am appalled at what I said. I don't even know why I would say anything about your work! I am very sorry for how I made you feel. You are right about everything." Sean said.

"I am?" I was trying to remember everything I said.

"Yes," he said. "I should own it. I didn't like Deacon asking you out. He just waltzed in and did it just like that! Like it was so easy. While I have been working up the guts to do it myself for a month. I didn't know what to do. I mean, I'm your boss, but that is soon to change. I didn't know if you would even consider going out with me. I had too many questions and I hesitated; it's not your fault I can't get it together. I'm a horrible person," he prattled on as he angled himself between me and the desk and put his hands through his hair, making him look like a supermodel advertisement.

"Hold up a minute. First, you are not a horrible person, you had a horrible moment," I said with a bit of a laugh. "Second, what do you mean you're not my boss anymore? Am I fired? Are you going somewhere? Am I going somewhere? Third, you did ask me to dinner and I said yes." I had a smile on my face. Sean took that moment to cross the few steps separating us. He put his hands through my hair and moved it away from my eyes as if to get a better look at them.

"First, I will never treat you like that again, professionally or personally. Neither of us is staying where we are. I was hoping you would say yes to dinner so I could help you celebrate your new job offer, if you take it. I really wanted to be the one to tell you. I really, and I mean really, like you, and now that you have put me in my place—by the way, you are amazing when you're angry—I fear I will never get you from my mind." Just then he planted a warm and subtle kiss on my lips. It stunned me on all fronts. I had more questions than ever; I could barely concentrate on the kiss.

Then he did it again and if there was a thought in my brain, it left and melted away. I was shocked at the chemistry between us. I really had been blind, and I didn't think I would have looked in this direction without road signs and flashing lights to tell me so. He broke off the kiss but maintained the close proximity. "Please, we have much to discuss. Can I still take you to dinner Friday or are you set on hating me forever?"

"I am a grown-ass woman, Sean. I don't hate, I only wish I had put you in your place right then and there instead of behind closed doors," I said sheepishly. "I don't get it. If you're you going somewhere, why start something?"

"I'm not going far. I'll be around, but I would like to have more time to discuss things with you in private. You, on the other hand, are being offered a management position if you want it."

"What about Tracy? I thought she really wanted your position. I mean, I'd love to but I am not stepping on toes to get there."

"Tracy will be offered my position tomorrow. I will be training her in the week to come. She has most of it down. There are just a few things we haven't gotten to yet. You, on the other hand, are being offered a front-end management position. The one that handles incoming sales. Florence is taking maternity and she has quit. She's not planning on coming back. I recommended you."

"Where will you be?" I asked.

"That, Cali, I would rather show you. Friday, if you will still have dinner with me."

"Well, with all the mystery you've put behind this dinner I can hardly say no now, can I?"

"I was hoping you would say that." Seeming happy, Sean opened the door to let me out. "I know you're … uh … busy tonight. I'll let you get going, just don't forget about what we talked about."

"Okay, Sean, I'll see you tomorrow." I stopped by his desk to give him my phone number on paper. The way he said "don't forget about what we talked about" sounded more like "don't forget about me when you're out with Deacon"— not less confident, just more possessive.

"There. Now you can call me for our date Friday. Is it a date now?" I said with curiosity. "Honestly, you have me so turned upside down with all the news and the kiss. I don't know if I'm coming or going."

He chuckled his reply. "Yes, it's a date. I will see you tomorrow." I left his office barely able to take my eyes off him. My head was spinning with details and also the lack thereof. I had never felt so confused.

***

Sean got on the phone when Cali had left. "Mike, it's Sean. How would you like to make an obscene amount of money helping me out this evening? I got a job that requires your expertise ... it's for a date. I need your help with ... yes, I need it to make a big impact. It has to be a big surprise."

***

I barely remembered the drive home. Dallas was waiting for me in the kitchen; that cat was like clockwork. I was a little late with her dinner, so I cracked open the cat food and fed her and then I was lost in thought again. I didn't really know how lavish the restaurant I was going to with Deacon was. I knew it wasn't a blue jeans place, though. It was something to dress up for, but how dressy? I settled on a navy-blue cocktail dress that was almost knee length. It was body fitting and had spaghetti straps. I picked up a short shawl to throw over top and added my silver pumps and bangles. I pulled my hair down, brushed it out and decided to use a large curling iron to make soft waves cascade down my shoulders. I freshened up my makeup and headed to the door. Just then I heard tinkling bells from somewhere in the house. That's odd, I thought. I couldn't think of one thing I owned that would have bells tinkling. I was told as a child if you heard bells, angels were nearby. That would be a nice thought after the last few days. I still had to clean up the mess from the other day, but I would have to get to that after dinner. I started to the front door again and could hear a conversation in muffled voices. I looked over to the TV and it was not on. The door was not open. It seemed to be coming from the back of the house.

I went in search of the voices, but I couldn't really make out what they were saying. There were at least two of them talking. I made it down the hall going back toward the bedrooms and the voices stopped. I didn't hear anything anymore. I stood there in the hall in front of the bedroom I had closed off because of the glass, but there was no sound.

I was going to be late and this was dumb, so I headed to the front door again and the voices resumed. I headed back in search of the sound, and I got to the same place and the voices stopped. "I don't have time for this!" I said to out loud into the empty space. I walked for the front door and this time I left. I got into the car and was lost in thought. What a mess. First I had a mess of a room to clean up and an injured cat, then the house decided to have a mind of its own with lights going on and off. It was getting harder to ignore.

Also, how exactly did I go from knowing no one to going out with friends and having two dates in one week with two different men? Deacon was from Calgary, which was not even the same province so that shouldn't count; it's not like I was going to see him again. And what about this new job? How was I the last to hear that I was up for a new job?

I didn't even know the details—would I want it? What was with Sean's secrecy? Lost in thought, I looked up and saw my light was red. The next thing I heard was cracking and banging as my car was hit and it spun around. I had run a red light. "Shit!" I rested my head back on my headrest, then looked around. The other driver was already up and out of his car running to my window. I tried to unroll it, but I was a little disoriented. He tried to open the door, but it was locked. It took me a while to figure out how to use the unlock button but I eventually did.

The man cracked the door open as much as it would go and said, "I called 911. Are you okay? Your car was hit by my truck. I thought you would be out cold. Are you all right?"

"Yes, I think so, nothing hurts. I'm just a little disoriented." I could hear the sirens approach. The more they drew near, the more panic set in. The fire department was able to pry the door open more than what the man with the truck could. On the other side of the car, the door was practically wrenched off its hinges by another firefighter trying to get in. The more they assessed me, the more panic I felt. Physically I felt fine, but I think I was in shock. They kept asking questions in rapid fire. They put a neck brace on me, which I assured them wasn't necessary, not that my opinion counted. Then helped me from my car and put me on a backboard and then a gurney and strapped me in.

On the way to the hospital, ironically, the panic subsided a bit. I was able to answer simple questions like my name, address and phone number, where I was going and where I was coming from. They asked me what happened, and that was a little unclear to me, but I told them what I remembered.

While I waited for a doctor at the hospital I shot Sean an email, then a phone call to his work number. I felt I just needed to take care of things while I was waiting so I wouldn't lose my mind. "Hi, Sean, it's me. I just sent you an email. I wasn't sure which you would get first. I, ah, wrecked my car. I was in an accident. So no dinner no date. I can't even call to tell him. I don't have his number." I laughed out of nervousness. "I'm sure I'm fine, just a little shaken up. I'm at the Vancouver General Hospital. I might be late tomorrow. I'm in need of transportation, so I will have to work it out tomorrow morning. I just wanted you to know. I don't have a personal number for you, so I hope the email or this message will find you in time tomorrow morning. Talk soon." I hung up.

I also called my insurance company's twenty-four-hour accident hotline and told them what happened and where I was so they could get the claim started and tell me what I needed next. I was pretty sure this was all my fault but I didn't remember. Just then, two officers came in to my little curtained cubicle and asked me the same things the firefighters did. "Honestly, officer, I'm not sure what happened. The information was swept from my mind … what I think I remember I'm just not sure is what really happened." Confusion was thick in my head, and my thoughts were scattered.

The stocky officer asked with no expression on his face, "What do you think happened, what do you remember?"

"I was driving, and I was a little lost in thought," I said nervously, knowing that would not make me look so good.

"I was more than halfway through the intersection and I looked up at the light. It either went from yellow to red or it was red … I don't know. Then there was the crack and the banging of the accident, my car spinning around and the other driver trying to get me out, but I just couldn't open the door or window myself. Then the fire department was there. That's it, that's what I have from memory, and I don't know what's real."

The second officer spoke up. "If you remember something else you can reach me here at this number on my card. Rest now. If you're in shock a good night's sleep will clear things up. Let me know if you have anything else to add."

I took the card and looked at the name and number. "Thank you, Constable Hogan, I will call if there is anything else."

Twenty minutes after they left, the doctor walked in and said, "You, my dear, are a very lucky lady!" I had nothing to say, so I just gave him a lame smile. He checked me over and asked a bunch of questions. Then he said,

"I'm sending you home for now. You have a mild concussion and a slight contusion on your forehead. I see no swelling or bruising and you seem to have good responses. If you are lethargic or you have dizziness or confusion, you need to come in, do you hear?"

"Yes, I can remember to do that," I responded.

"Now, Ms. Stenson, do you have someone to take you home?"

"No, I don't. I'll call a cab." He studied me a moment and opened the curtain.

"No need. I'll get her home." I turned to see a man waiting in the doorway of the four-patient room.

"Sean, how did you know where to find me?"

He held up his phone. "I was still at work … just leaving the parking lot, in fact. My phone dinged with an email alert. Yep, I am a workaholic … my work email is hooked to my phone. I ran back inside and Susan broke company policy to get me your address. I thought I would come here first, then go to your home. The emergency nurse said you were still here. But I had to wait in the hall. I heard everything." He glanced at the doctor. "Are you sure she's okay?"

The doctor answered, "From what I see, she's fine. She is still in a state of shock so no driving over the next day or anything that requires concentration and safety together, because she also has a slight concussion. From what the responders said of the accident she is a very lucky lady."

Sean drove me home, and the shock actually put me to sleep during the twenty-minute drive. When he pulled into my empty driveway I awoke. "Thanks for getting me home. Sorry I fell asleep in your car," I said shyly.

"Don't worry about that, it's understandable. Do you want me to come in? Do you need help with anything? I can totally stay if you need me to."

"No, no, really, I'm fine. I just need to go to bed. The doctor said … or someone did … I don't remember who …. that sleep will make me feel better."

"I'll come by in the morning to check on you, is that okay?" he asked.

"Sean, you would literally have to pass work to get to my house. Didn't you say you lived in the opposite direction of me the other night?"

"Yes, I did say that, didn't I? Well, I don't mind. I'll be by before I have to be at work, all right?"

"Okay, thanks, Sean."

"Goodnight, Cali."

When I went inside Dallas was waiting for me again. I waved to Sean as I closed the door and he left. I was so tired even though it was only 10:00 p.m. I dragged myself into the kitchen to boil water for tea, gave Dallas a treat and sat trying to go over the evening, but my mind wouldn't work right. Cup of tea and then straight to bed, that should do it.

As I sat there with my head in my hand waiting for the kettle, I heard voices again. Where were they coming from? Maybe I hit my head harder than I had thought. I couldn't make out what was said or where the voices were coming from. A voice yelled, "GET UP!" into my ear. I jumped from the chair. "Shit! What the hell!" Disorientated, I looked around the room, but nothing was there. The room was now silent and the kettle had already clicked off. *I must have fallen asleep at the table*, I thought. The clock on the microwave said 10:16. Deciding not to care, as I was already in shock from the accident, I made tea and went to my room, got out of my dress and, without dinner and with only a few sips of tea in my belly, I quickly fell asleep.

I feel like I am deep in sleep, my body so tired from this evening but my mind very aware— aware of itself and my body's lumbering sleep. It's an odd sensation. I feel myself slip from my body, my consciousness above my physical state. I am aware of this happening but really I have no control. My consciousness slips into the hall and down to the room with the broken glass. The door is open, and my consciousness is still aware that the door has been closed. I slip inside the room and there's Dallas poking around. It looks different. The glass is not broken and the lamp is whole. That can't be. I think to myself. Dallas goes into the closet, climbs up the shelves and finds a box of towels to climb in. I note this. "So that's where she hides."

Dallas snuggles in, and time passes. I am not aware of how long I spend floating at the top of the room by the door. The cat comes down and walks over by the bed. She's getting into something but I can't see what, as it's on the other side of the bed. The cat walks back towards the end of the bed. "GET OUT! GET OUT, GET OUT!" say a female and male voice at the same time; it's like one person. The cat lifts into the air, hits the lamp and then hits the mirror and lands on the floor. She lies there a split second and then makes to run out. I feel like I'm moving fast, and my energy goes down the hall and am slammed back into my body.

I awoke and lay there looking around. What in the hell was that? Was that real? Was that just now? How could it be? The spare room had looked as it was the other day, not how it looked now. I got out of bed, turned on the hall light and went to the offending room. The door was closed so I opened it. The room was a mess, just like I left it. So it was another stupid nightmare. But it felt so real… I went back to my room and took my tea off the night stand. It was barely lukewarm. I headed to the kitchen to heat it instead of making a new one and decided to just sit and shake off the confusion. It must have been the head trauma … that was the weirdest thing I had ever experienced. Coming out of my body and floating around of all things … really? But the storyline was what still made my brain tangled. Where the cat hid, the cat getting into something on the floor, the cat being thrown, everything breaking and the cat getting hurt.

If it wasn't so absurd, it would make sense. Just then I had a thought—to go to the room and see if there was a box in the closet that the cat had been using to hide in. I found flip-flops and put them on so as to not step on the mirror pieces. I got to the room, turned my phone flashlight on and looked in the closet. I couldn't see anything there. I moved the door open a little, and the closet was full of stuff from top to bottom, as spare room closets often are. There on the top shelf was a box that looked familiar. I grabbed a chair and used it to climb up to get the box. Sure enough, there was a box of towels full of black cat fur. I took the box down and was going to leave with it but decided to look by the bed. Was there anything there for the cat to get into? Oh my! A bag of string and yarn billowed in messy knots. Yes, that would grab her attention.

I hadn't really played with her, so this would most definitely keep her occupied. I said to myself, "If this stuff is true, does that make the unreal experience true as well? How else would I have known about this?" It seemed too implausible. "Jeez, I need to get to bed. My head is still too foggy to think straight and I'm talking to myself."

Back in my bedroom I relocated Dallas's box to my closet where she could climb up the wooden shoe cubbies and into the box. I showed Dallas her new closet and let her sniff the box and then put her on the floor. Lazily I strode to my bed and was startled by noise. It didn't take Dallas long to figure out how to get to the box. I climbed into bed again and fell asleep.

I am with my parents at a busy restaurant. It's a neat place with big round tables, floral tapestries and floral carpet. I get up out of my chair, I think to go to the bathroom, and I go into the main hall, which is a wide-open space just outside that joins the restaurant. They have beautiful pictures and a beautiful banister staircase. I have never seen anything like it before. I am so small I barely reach the banister. I imagine this must be what castles look like. I start up the winding stairs. When I reach the first level, all of a sudden I'm not alone, and I'm not on the stairs or in a hallway; I'm in a room with a small floral bed with a man holding my hand. The man puts me on the bed and is taking off my shoes and socks. I look at his face then, but it isn't right; it's like a smudged painting. I can't see his face properly because the smudge is in the centre. I don't know him. He has blond wavy hair and wide-set, deep-set eyes. He smiles tightly, and it's like all his skin is too tight for his face. What does he want with my clothes? Why am I here?

I was startled awake at 3:30 a.m.— the dream ended the same way it always ended. This dream always got to me, because I was not sure if it was a dream or a fuzzy memory … was I abducted? Did something happen? My mind won't let me remember. Later in life, just before my move to Vancouver, I had visited a small town, Jasper on vacation. I happened upon a hotel and it was the same one from the dream where I stood in the lobby right down to the same floral tapestries and carpet and the beautiful winding banister that led upstairs.

I couldn't help but go up and check what was on the next floor. Sure enough, every room was done in gorgeous retro furniture. I don't mean the kind where it looks like you walked into a secondhand store. No, this was more like I walked into a rich grandmother's room, with beautiful antiques and cherry-colored furniture and a floral double bed. This used to be a scary dream when I was a kid. After the discovery of the place that fit into the picture so well, my nightmare seemed like a living, breathing thing. I couldn't even think about it, though the dream was always there to remind me.

CHAPTER 4
Spirit Board

GETTING OUT OF BED WAS EASIER SAID THAN DONE. MY BODY WAS SORE AND stiff all over, and my head, though it felt better, still made my thinking fuzzy. The clock said 5:50 a.m. Early, yes, but sleeping didn't seem to be an option anymore and a nice hot shower sounded pretty good. I looked up at the box and Dallas was peeking her head out. I smiled and said good morning to her before I went and started my shower. I stayed in till the hot water ran cold, and it felt good. When I got out, the doorbell rang, which shocked me as I wasn't expecting anyone. It was just about 6:30 a.m. now.

I felt a pinch of anxiety while deciding if I should make myself presentable before rushing to the door and my phone dinged a minute later. I went to the phone instead. The text read *"You up? I said I would come check on you this morning, but you're not answering your door. I don't know if you are sleeping or if I should bust the door down to make sure you are all right."*

"Don't bust the door down, I'll be right there. Just getting dressed," I texted back. I rushed to put on a pair of athletic leggings, a bra and sweatshirt and I went to the door to meet Sean with my hair still wrapped in a towel. I opened the door and Sean was there holding two coffees and a bag.

"Good morning. I hope I didn't come too early. I know you can use the sleep, but I said I would come before work."

"No, I was up a while ago," I said reassuringly. "Come in, what did you bring?"

"Ah, yes, I noticed a vanilla bean latte on your desk the other day. Did I get that right?" he asked as he handed me a cup.

"Yes, that is exactly what I need right now. Thank you," I said with a big smile.

"No problem. I grabbed some bagels too. I figured you might not have eaten yet. I didn't know how you were feeling so I thought I would grab something."

"Thank you, that's thoughtful, Sean."

"Wow, you sure like your house lit up. I think you have every light turned on."

I turned around and anything and everything that could be on, was. "Yes, well, I think the house sometimes has a mind of its own," I said with a halfhearted smile. "Why don't you join me at the table so we can eat these delicious bagels together before you're off to work. I've got some catching up on house stuff, insurance stuff and locating a rental car, so I won't be in today boss, sorry."

"Don't worry about that. I'll make sure everyone knows. Just rest and heal," Sean said.

"So, while I have you stuck here eating bagels with me, let me know what Deacon says about the chair so I know what's happening when I get back," I said.

"If he does ask, let him know what happened last night, but don't give him too much information please, if you don't mind." I realized I was giving my boss directions.

"I don't mind," he said with a smile, as if reading my mind. Of course I blushed—if I could get through once sentence with Sean without my face turning red, that would be great.

"So what about the job you put my name in for? Was it to get rid of me out of the department or is it a promotion? And what is it exactly?" I really wanted to know what was happening— and if it involved me, why was I the last to know?

"Well, to be honest, I wasn't at all sure if you would want the job or not, so I put you and Tracy in as my recommendation. I know this sounds a little ridiculous, Cali, but it was killing me. It was like sitting across from someone that electrifies every bone in my body and I can't do anything about it. I figured you would like the promotion, and it would be a win. Then something came up in my field that I've been waiting for. I figured if I just removed myself from the situation it would be better for everyone. After I got to know you, I didn't want to just move on without saying something to you. Then I acted like an ass and you … well, when you're angry, you are unbelievably awesome." Grinning at me, he continued, "There was no way after spending a little time with you that I was just going to get up and forget you. So Tracy will take my position and hopefully you will take the other front-end job, which you would be tremendous at. After the other day and the way you handled that case and your amazing work ethic, I felt there would be no one better for the job upfront. I should never have been so childish the other day and attacked your capability out of jealousy of another man. That was quite underhanded.

I was not thinking straight. I hope the vanilla coffee is the start to an amends." Sean's voice was tense, and his face showed humiliation.

"I accept your coffee amends. No need for anything else. You had a weak moment, made a mistake and apologized profusely. We are human, and unfortunately we do stupid things. I just want the weirdness between us to stop. Let's move on." I was genuine about this. "Sean, you were the only one who showed up last night. I had no one I could think of calling for that situation. With my family provinces away, there is just no one I have become close to here. I really appreciated the help. You were there when I thought I had no one. That is a huge deal for me." After I spoke we just sat in silence a moment, staring at each other.

He put his hand on my cheek. "I'm glad I was still at work, and that I found you in time to be there for you."

After a pause, I finally I asked with concern, "Where are you going for this new job?"

"I'll be working for a global acquisition firm just downtown."

"That's the secret? You're leaving the store?"

Sean shook his head. "The secret is something I should have shared with you beforehand, but it is not something I can tell you; I want to show you. Tracy, that damn snoop, is the only other person that knows. I hope you won't be upset with me again. If you can just wait one more evening we will go for dinner to celebrate both our successes and I will show you after we're done. The secret will be out. If you're not mad, you will be amazed.

I'm willing to hang on to the secret in hopes you will be amazed, if you can trust me." Wasn't that the question after all this I conversely thought. He continued, "It really isn't anything bad. You have to see for yourself." I sat there in silence, not knowing how to process everything he was saying. My emotions were all over the place. I was a little worried about what was going to happen Friday and if it was something I could potentially be upset over or, as he said, amazed by.

I knew what Sean was talking about now; the electricity between us was bone-melting. I just never saw it; I was blind, as everyone says, and I didn't want to be hurt or upset. "I think you put me up for the job just to get me away from you, though I probably would have taken it anyway just to get away from my cranky, crotchety old boss who drives me crazy and acts like an a –" My sentence was wonderfully interrupted by a kiss that made my head spin and my knees weak.

He broke off and smiled and I couldn't help but smile too. "If I'm offered the job, I will look at taking the new position. Just no more secrets. Everything from now on is up front, okay?"

"Yes, I agree. If I find out about something that involves you in anyway, you will know immediately." He kissed me on my forehead and got up. "I have to get to work. You are being offered the job; Gunderson thinks you're a workhorse from another planet. Do you need anything before I go? Are you sure you're okay to be here alone?"

"I'll be fine. I'm just going to take it easy today. Maybe tidy up. I'll be fine."

"Okay, see you later. I'll take care of what I can from your workload today. Oh, and it will be my pleasure to tell Deacon," Sean said with a mischievous grin.

I rolled my eyes and shook my head. "You're such a troublemaker. Now go before you start trouble here," I said, literally pushing him out the door. After he left I still had a bit of my coffee, so I sat on the couch for the morning and relaxed. I was starting to feel better, so maybe by afternoon things would be back to normal. I turned on the local news, grabbed a blanket and curled up.

I'm lying on the sofa and at the end of it is something; I can't make it out at first because this does not live in our reality it doesn't make sense and I am frozen, I cannot move. As I focus on what I'm looking at it, I feel is just wrong—the feeling of it / him being there is wrong in nature, dark in nature. It is tall seven feet tall. I have time enough to look at it to see that there is no face. I can see just eyes glowing red. But the body is well built and the bottom is missing, and made of mist or smoke. I am grabbed by the ankles and dragged off the sofa, across the floor, into the kitchen and down the basement stairs where I see this demon in full. It is crawling low to the ground on all fours with my ankles in its hands. Its lower half is no longer mist but its contorted legs move in unparalleled movements, unnatural movements, jerking and twisting about. I look into the face of a smiling, red-eyed demon, and its skin looks melted and haggard. It stops and stares at me as if noticing me actually seeing him. It keeps pulling me. I disappear into the dark.

I awoke feeling like I was being pulled on, and my body slid off the sofa at the same time. I looked around and everything was calm and quiet and the TV was still on. The lights were all off; that was new. I knew I didn't shut them off before I fell asleep on the sofa. I looked at the clock. I had actually been asleep for a couple of hours, as it was 10:00 a.m. I sat on the floor with a blanket tangled around me and decided I would think about the accident instead of the dream to try and get my brain to switch gears.

It didn't really help; I truly couldn't remember more. The accident was still cloudy in my mind. I guess whatever the insurance and the cops decided was going to have to be fine with me since I couldn't remember. I decided to get some work done, call the insurance company to see if there was anything they need from me, and call and arrange a pickup from the car rental place so I could get to work. Spending time at home was less than appealing; I would rather be at work. I made all my calls so then it was time to tackle that room and get the glass cleaned up. I put on runners, went into the room full of glass and closed the door behind me. I didn't want Dallas wandering in and hurting herself again. I needed a bucket, bag, a dust pan with a brush and gloves so I went to the kitchen. Dallas came into the hall as I walked back to the room. I guess she wanted to play the crew supervisor and watch me clean. "Not a chance," I said to her and shut the door again. I started with the easy stuff. I picked up the bag of string and yarn and decided to throw it out , since I hadn't knit since I got here. I walked to the door and threw a ball of yarn out to the cat and left the rest by the inside of the door. There was so many small fragments of glass. I picked up what I could and swept the rest into the dust pan.

I figured the vacuum should be okay for the rest of the mess. Then I heard footsteps across the carpet, almost like someone was dragging their feet. I froze in place, crouched over in fear.

The pressure left the room and my eardrums felt it first; it was like they had popped and I couldn't hear anything. There was a whoosh of pressure against the left side of my head complete with a breeze. I don't think I could have moved if I wanted to; I was too afraid. "You shouldn't be here!" a women's voice said inside my head. I felt like bolting, but what was this? Maybe I should stop to find out. I never had the courage when I was younger, I just got the hell out. But I was a grown-ass woman now. In a soft voice, I said, "I shouldn't be where?" "HERE!" the woman yelled in my head. I got up to head for the door.

I looked back at the fractured floor-to-ceiling mirror, only a third of the mirror still hung on the wall. That was when I noticed a weird outline. I had to squint because it just didn't seem real. There were rays of purple that almost looked like purple light, but inside the light was the shape of people. It looked like a woman and a girl outlined in the purple light. That gave me pause from running. It was a little girl, for Pete's sake.

"Where am I not supposed to be, in this room? In this house? Vancouver? Do you know I have been experiencing this my whole life? Things coming and going, seeing things, I experience things that shouldn't happen. What do you mean?" I exclaimed, hoping for answers but not really ready to hear any.

"Here at all," she whispered. Then the vision, or whatever it was, was on the move. It went around me and through the door. I went to the door, opened it and looked around. The vision went down the hall and Dallas watched it go. Then it disappeared. This seemed to shock Dallas, who got off her rump and went to find out where this thing went.

When Dallas lost the trail of the entity or vision or whatever it was she stopped, turned around and came back. I felt like I needed to get out, leave. But I remembered I didn't have a car yet. I went into the kitchen ... "What the hell?" The clock on the microwave said 1:00 p.m. How could that be? I just started cleaning at 10:00 a.m. There was no way it took me three hours to clean up; all I did was pick up glass, and I hadn't even vacuumed yet. And what the hell did the vision mean that I should not be here at all? Damn cryptic ghost!

I decided I just needed to finish. I needed to vacuum everything and be done with it. Forget about voices, shadows, lights going on and off and nightmares. Just do normal, everyday chores normal people do. I started in that room and picked up the broken lamp and vacuumed without incident. I left the room open and continued to the rest of the house. That took an hour, and time was back to normal. The doorbell rang and I jumped; it had been a freaky morning and I wasn't expecting anyone midday. I went to the door and it was the rental place.

"Good afternoon, are you Mrs. Stenson?"

"Yes, I am."

"I'm from AMC Rentals. I have a crossover here for you. I just need you to sign and give me the credit card number you booked the vehicle with and I will take a picture of your photo ID and put it in your file and you are good to go. Just come by and return the car when you're done, at the end of the week term." Another car pulled up with the rental logo on it. The man at the door took all my info, hurried down the steps, hustled into the car and was gone. "Wow, efficient," I said to absolutely no one. I shut the door. "I have gotten so accustomed to weird things, I now talk to myself more than ever." This time I was speaking to the cat. I really didn't want to be alone, but I had nowhere to go. I turned the TV up loud and snuggled into the sofa.

I was wakened by the doorbell again. Who could that be? I opened the door to find the customer service team outside. "What are you doing here? Aren't you supposed to be working?" I said with a smile. Tracy didn't wait for an invitation to come in, as it was one degree outside.

"It's 4:30. Close enough, and it's freezing. Let me in!" She huffed inside. I smiled and let the rest the group in.

Todd looked around. "Interesting place you have here, quite the energy."

Ashley chimed in, "Todd fancies himself an energy reader."

"That's not what it's called, and I'm trained, jeez," Todd said.

Ashley replied, "Whatever." She smiled and moved further into the house.

"Well, that's an interesting tidbit of information. I wonder what that means." I looked at Sean. "I supposed you led this entourage here?"

"I did, and you will have to ask Todd yourself if you want to know. I don't speak hokum mumbo jumbo talk. They wanted to see how you were and so did I, so we kicked off early."

"Well, now that everyone is here, why don't we order Chinese for dinner?" I said. I closed the door, took their jackets and slung them over the chair closest to the door.

"Is that your spiffy new car outside?" asked Ashley.

"Actually, the rental guy just dropped it off not too long before you all got here. I haven't had a chance to go look. I was supposed to do a walk around, but I didn't feel up to it. I hope it's nice."

"It will most definitely get you from point A to B. It's a sleek and sexy black thing," said Tracy.

Todd was busy snooping around. "There isn't much to see. It's a pretty small place but I could give you all the tour." I showed the group around quickly and came up with a crazy cat excuse to explain the broken mirror and busted lamp when we happened across that room.

Todd just eyed me and went, "Uh-huh."

To which Ashley replied, "You are so weird, Todd. It's a crazy cat who busted a room up, not Armageddon." Rolling her eyes, she walked back to the kitchen and I followed her. The conversation was getting weirder than the house. I wasn't sure I wanted to know where it was leading. I ordered the Chinese food we all agreed on and cleared the table so we could have room to sit and eat.

"So, you seem okay … were you badly hurt? Are you coming back to work?" asked Tracy.

"I'm fine now. I think it was mostly shock. I slept mostly today, so I do feel better and I had a concussion. I'm not sure how long those last, actually." I said questioningly.

"You are supposed to go back Monday, I think, to make sure you're okay," added Sean.

"Yes, I heard your knight in shining armor showed up. How did that go?" Tracy asked, wiggling her eyebrows.

"Didn't we have a pact that you weren't going to do that with your face?" said Ashley.

"She left a work message. I just thought someone should be there to make sure she was okay," replied Sean.

"Oh, you don't have to answer to these jokers; they know exactly what's going on. I was the one who needed the road map, lights and dinging signs to point me in the right direction." I said.

I reached up and kissed his cheek. "Thank you for being my knight in shining armor. It would have been rather pitiful to have to go home in a cab. I would not have had anyone to ask for help, so you kind of were my knight," I said with a smile. Everyone oooh'd and aaah'd and poked fun at our exchange. We laughed and continued the banter and conversation. I was laughing and walked away from the table when the doorbell rang, assuming it was for the Chinese food.

Sean jumped up and went to pay for the food. "The damsel still has a concussion. I will save her from the duty of answering the door and paying for the food if she will only consider me for a kiss," he said, playing like he was in Hamlet while everyone laughed.

"That will be $68.99, sir," said the delivery man, waiting for the production to be over. I helped Sean with the bags of food and we returned to the kitchen where everyone jovial.

"This is nice," I said. "Thank you everyone for checking on me. I didn't realize I needed this, but I really do. I feel much better now that you're all here." We ate and joked around some more and when Sean noticed I was getting a little tired, we moved to the living room for tea where I could sit comfy under a blanket.

"Well, not that it is real late, but you have been through a lot, and since you are thinking about going to work tomorrow, we should leave so you can get rest," said Todd.

I wasn't ready for them to leave. "I guess you're right. I just don't feel like being alone right now. I didn't realize something was bothering me until you were all here and I didn't have to be alone," I admitted.

"I could stay for a while if you want. We took two cars here. Todd, would you drive the girls back in your car if I stay here for a bit?" said Sean.

"Yeah sure, man, I can do that," offered Todd.

"Would you want me to stay longer and keep you company?" asked Sean.

"Actually, that would be really nice, thank you. I mean, if it's not going to be too much trouble ?"

"No, of course not. It will give us the chance to hang out and just relax. No trouble at all," said Sean, smiling down at me from his eyes down to his lips. He really was good looking when he wasn't grumping around the office, I thought.

"I don't even want to know what you're thinking right now. I'm almost positive it would be at my expense," Sean added.

"It would be, but also in a good way I suppose as well," I said, my eyes beaming up at his.

"Yep, most definitely time to leave. See you sickly lovebirds at the office tomorrow. Don't forget to show up!" Tracy said to us.

"Maybe we could hang out later, like this weekend?" asked Ashley.

"Yeah, I would like to do that. Maybe we could talk about other stuff too," said Todd.

"Oh, don't give her the heebie-jeebies. It's getting late. We don't need to talk about your spirit board stuff now," said Ashley.

"I would like to know more," I said. 'Spirit board' sounded out in left field. I had pegged Todd for being completely boring and ordinary, but apparently I was wrong.

"Let the girl get some rest, Todd. You need a whole night to go through a conversation like that. You can't just spring it on a person, jeez," said Ashley.

"Okay, goodnight," said Todd, sounding somewhat defeated.

"Thank you for coming and taking the girls back so Sean can stay with me longer. And I would like to hear more. There's more to you than I realized, and it sounds like fun."

With that, Todd perked up a bit and smiled at me. As they left I could hear Todd snap at Ashley as they walked to the car, "I don't use a spirit board. Those are dumb and they don't even work!"

I smiled as I closed the door. "Why don't I get you a hot drink and you can snuggle in on the sofa and find something you would like to watch?" Sean asked.

"That sounds great. Do you think you can find what you need in the kitchen yourself?"

"Yeah, I think I got this covered. Go ahead and relax."

I went to the living room and then called out, "So what is this new job of yours? When do you start?"

"It's basically money management on a corporate level and fiscal responsibility. I've been waiting for something to open up at this company for a while. This is the one, the job I've been waiting for. So hopefully you'll feel up to helping me celebrate tomorrow."

I waited a moment and then said, "I can't believe you're leaving. It's not going to be at all the same with you not there to grump and glare at me."

He walked into the living room with two hot cups in his hands and a fake glare on his face, which made me giggle. "I'll be there for another week yet getting Tracy up to speed. Hopefully after our first date tomorrow you'll decide I'm an awesome guy to spend time with and we will see each other all the time."

"We shall see, won't we?" I teased.

"Speaking of date, the little navy number you were wearing when I picked you up in the hospital … it didn't get wrecked did it? In the accident?"

"No, it fared just fine." I laughed. "Why, is that what I am wearing tomorrow?"

"I don't know if I'll be able to see straight all night if you wear that dress, but I sure as hell would like to give it a try. Change of plans are in order, I think. There's a restaurant called Top Shelf. Have you heard of it?"

My eyes opened wide. "Of course I have. It's a top chef restaurant. The waiting list is almost a year long!"

"Yeah, well, perks of the new job. The company already has a reservation for me there. I told them I would like to take you tomorrow so we'll go!"

"Oh my word, are you serious? You want to take me? Is my jaw still on the floor? I can't believe this! Are you sure you want to take *me* there?"

"It would be my honor if you would accompany me to help me celebrate, and if you take the new job you have a reason to celebrate too." He kissed the tip of my nose and then forehead.

I snuggled into his side. "This is amazing, but I still haven't been offered the new job."

"I'm sure as soon as you're back that will happen. Gunderson knew I wanted to be the one to tell you."

"This will be great!" I said, full of excitement. Soon we were back to small talk and watching a home reno show. At the end of the program, I was getting really sleepy. I could feel Sean snuggle in to get comfy and stretch his long legs out on the foot stool. He turned the TV down so it was quieter. Sleep came easily.

I can hear Todd saying, "I don't use a spirit board. Those are dumb and don't even work!" Not to me, they're not, I say to myself. My mom took me to the toy store when I was thirteen because I wanted a new toy my auntie and cousins were playing with. They wouldn't let me play. So Mom bought me my very own spirit board for me and my younger sister, who was nine. We followed the instructions, just resting our hands on the planchette, the piece that moves, and letting it do the work. It didn't take long before we were arguing that one or the other of us was moving it. "Watch this" I said to my little sister. Instructing the spirit board, I said, "I want you to entertain my sister. I want you to go fast like a race car."

I put my hands about two inches above the movable piece and said again, "Go fast like a race car!" The planchette backed up to the far edge of the board slowly and my hands followed and then zoom! The piece flew right off the board! My sister laughed and thought it was so funny. She said, "Do it again, I want to see." I did it again and again for her. Then I started to worry. If she didn't touch the piece, and I knew I was not touching the piece, where did the energy and information come from? We were told by my auntie it was spirits and you had to be careful because they could be evil. I didn't know if that was true, but I also knew objects did not move on their own. When my mom came and got my sister so she could take a bath I kept going on my own. "Spirit board, where do you get the information from when asked a question? Can you spell out the answer?" "NO," *the spirit board said.*

"Where do you get the information from?"

"You," *it spelled out.*

"NO, I am the one asking the question. How can you answer my question? Where does the information come from?"

"You."

I was frustrated I wasn't getting the information I thought I would. It got dark in the room like a shadow had descended upon it and I was alone. It felt like I was alone in the whole house— like no one was there except the darkness, even though I knew that wasn't true.

The piece flew in one direction and the board hit the wall, knocking down a frame in the other direction. I couldn't move. I hunched down and froze, waiting for it to be over or for someone to come into the room. If the information came from me, I did not tell it to hit the wall. My mother came waltzing in and saw me hunched on the floor frozen in place and the picture on the ground instead of on the wall. "What the hell are you doing in here, Cali? What did you do? Why is the picture on the floor?"

"I … I was swinging around and I hit it. It didn't break. I'm sorry. I can hang it back up." She walked out of the room saying, "Be more careful, would you!" From that time on, things just started to happen to both me and my sister. In this moment, in this dream right now, *like a movie reel, every demon I dreamed up, everything that ever chased me, crept down a hall or the voices that yelled at me or tormented my younger sister, came into my dream full speed. Voices were yelling, "fuck you!" The air pressure was leaving the room, the nasty hag figure was climbing the wall, there was something that looked like a five-hundred- year-old man hovering directly over me while I slept. I was being pushed out of bed, my sister's bed was hovering with four figures at each corner, doors were slam-ming, there were dragging feet noises on the carpet but no one was there, my sister and I were being chased up the stairs or dragged down them. The movie reel seemed to go on and on. I should have never involved my sister.*

"Whoa, whoa, whoa. It's okay, it's a dream. It's just a dream." I could hear a male voice. It seemed to be coming from a distance as I was coming out of a sleepy fog. I opened my eyes— "Holy shit!" I yelled, and I swung out and tried to clock Sean.

He grabbed my wrist. "Shhh, shhh, it was a dream. It's me, Sean. I'm still here. You fell asleep in my arms," he said soothingly.

"Oh sorry, sorry, I forgot. I'm not used to having someone else here. Sorry, sorry." I breathed out.

"It's okay, no harm done. You're not kidding that your house has a mind of it's own—you should get the electrical checked. I think that's what started your nightmare. The lights just went really dim and were fluctuating. You started talking in your sleep, but you were getting more and more worked up and scared. I maybe shouldn't have tried to wake you."

"No, it's nice having you here, and the dream had just stopped. I just, well … I guess if you want to get to know me, here's some inside information for you. I get nightmares, like, all the time, memories from the past. If you would like to come into the world of crazy with me. You may be right—I might have to call an electrician, but also I think it's me. The lights being played with, noises, broken stuff, it's all me. Weird stuff just happens when I am around, so if you don't like the 'hokum,' as you call it, this may not be the right place or I may not be the right person for you. The longer you know me, the weirder it gets. People have literally moved away from me and said things get better when I'm not around.

I moved here from my family home, and my sister says things are so much better since I left," I said with a laugh. "I know I sound like a babbling idiot who just woke up, but honestly if you think I am acting weird you haven't seen anything yet."

"Well, maybe I should stick around a bit and find out. Honestly, with the car accident and the lights and the nightmares, I really don't want to leave. I could sleep in the spare room and keep you company in the house to make sure everything is okay. I would really hate to leave a concussion-ridden, nightmare-dreaming lovely lady in a burning electrical fire," he said.

"Normally I think I would say no, but I really didn't want to be alone today. When you guys came here to see me, it was a relief. Could you stay?"

"It's settled then, I'll stay," said Sean. He made more tea, this time Sleepy Time to help me relax. He was really good at taking care of another person. It came naturally to him and I didn't think I would be as good at it as he was.

"Why don't you tell me about it? I promise not to say the word hokum." Sean crossed his heart and smiled.

I told him about the whole dream and said that it did actually happen when I was a child— my mom did go and get us a spirit board to play with. "The thing is, as an adult you come to know more, grow up and realize things you don't realize as a child with a heavy imagination. Science and reality can usually explain a lot away. At the same time, I always knew the things I saw were not everyday things and not everyone saw or heard what I did. So even as a kid you know you're not right, not normal, maybe even crazy."

"I knew this at the age of four. As an adult its harder to comprehend because memory plays tricks. I can't tell what's memory, what's a nightmare and what is real. Maybe I do need an electrician, or maybe, just maybe, this is just the shit that is my life and I can't explain it. Maybe I am crazy—maybe I have some sort of psychosis and I'm sick. But then why would the people around me be affected to the point that they can see and hear it too when they're near me? I'm pretty sure you can't catch psychosis. So it's unexplainable at the moment, but if there's a logical reason, you bet your ass I'll look for it." I took a breath after my long tirade of a rant.

"That's unbelievable. I mean, if that's just one dream, I wouldn't want to sleep either. No wonder you say you're tired. I bet you hardly ever sleep," Sean said with total understanding.

"I don't, really," I replied.

"Well, maybe you'll sleep better now that you've talked about it. It's out of your system now. I'm here. Maybe that will help."

"Maybe you're right."

We got up and headed to our respective rooms. "I'll be right back," I said. "I'll get an extra blanket. Would you like me to bring in the table lamp from the living room? The cat broke the light in here and there's no other light."

"It's okay, I don't need it. I have my cell phone if I need to trudge around in the dark," he said with a smile. "Wait you have a cat?"

I laughed. "Yes, I guess I forgot to mention the simple things like my tiny, bitchy roommate Dallas. I forgot you weren't with us when everyone did the small tour, you were in the kitchen. She doesn't like people so she's probably in my room somewhere. The others heard about her when I showed them around, but they didn't see her either." I crossed the short hall and came back with an extra blanket. "You know where my room is if you need anything."

"Cali, I'm here for you, not the other way around. I'll be fine. Sleep well. I'll see you in the morning."

I am sleeping. I can feel that I am somewhat in that state of sleep paralysis. I feel fully awake; in fact, I'm sure I'm awake lying in bed. At the foot of the bed is something; I can't make it out at first because this does not live in our reality it doesn't make sense and I cannot move. As I focus on what I'm looking at, I can see it is just wrong; the feeling of it / him being there is wrong in nature. It feels dark. It is huge, like seven feet tall. I can't see the face, just its eyes glowing red. The body is well built and the bottom is mist or smoke. I am grabbed by the ankles and dragged out the bottom of my bed, across the floor and down the hall, into the kitchen and down the basement stairs where I see this demon crawling low to the ground on all fours, with my ankles in its hands. Its legs are no longer mist and are moving in unparalleled movements, unnatural movements, jerking and twisting about. I then look into the face of a smiling, red-eyed demon, and its skin looks melted and haggard.

Its face is contorted and the skin on his body is not clothed. It is a weird shade of brown/grey. It stops and stares at me as if noticing me actually seeing him. I reach the bottom of the stairs and go into the darkness of the basement.

Shit. Damn. I hated that one. I tried to calm myself. My body was still frozen stiff from being scared, my breathing still erratic. Then I remembered Sean was here and it was just a dream. I wasn't alone. I would be okay. I breathed deeply. I would be okay.

***

Holy hell, I haven't had a dream like that since I was small, thought Sean. *Hell, that was so real.* He gasped for breath, trying to calm himself. *This is stupid, but I am going to go check on her make sure she is okay.* His thoughts jumbled as he went over what he thought he should do. That dream scared the shit out him. Sean looked at the time on his cell, and it was 3:18 a.m. He walked a couple doors down and peeked in.

***

"Sean, is everything okay?"

"Yes. Yeah, Cali, everything is fine. I, uh, was just up and thought I would make sure you could sleep, you know … to make sure you were okay."

"That's nice, Sean. I'm up again. I just had a nightmare."

"Yeah, me too. That's why I'm up. Honestly, I haven't dreamed up anything like that since I was a kid."

"What did you dream?" I asked.

"Honestly, I don't want to tell you. I think it would just scare you; it was about you," Sean said, staring straight ahead like he didn't want to look at her in bed.

"Well, I'm up now. You might as well tell me. I'm curious." I turned on a bedside lamp. "Come sit. I promise to be good and just listen," I said with a smirk.

Sean sat at my bedside and told me his dream. I stared at him in awe, eyes wide.

"See, I shouldn't have told you. I scared you now," he said, looking a little worried at the expression on my face.

"No, it's not that," I said with shock. "That's my dream. The one I always have, almost every night! It's the dream I just had! Just like you saw, I was dragged out of bed, down the hall and to the basement; that's what I dreamed. Good news is I woke up in bed so it was just a dream, not real." I stated it like a fact I was trying to convince myself was true. My lips pinched in a thin line but I was trying to smile through.

Sean rubbed my shoulders—he could only imagine what it was like to go through that every night. "How could that be?" he said. "How can we dream the same thing?"

I just shrugged. "Can you stay, maybe? Maybe get the blanket from the room and stay here in my room with me … in my bed? Would that be okay or would that be weird? I promise I'm not using this as an excuse. I'm just weirded out by this, you know?" I wondered if maybe I was acting a little too forward.

"Yeah, sure, I'll go get the blanket," said Sean as he got up from the bed. Just then a black shadow came from the closet and across the floor "Whoa, jeez! I guess I'm a little jumpy," he said with a laugh. "I don't know who will be comforting who right now." Sean laughed again. "The little black ball of fur who ran out of here like hellfire was chasing it—that was Dallas, your cat?"

Now it was my turn to laugh at Sean, a grown man jumping out of his skin because of a cat. "Yes, yes it was. She probably went to your room trying to find peace and quiet. Try not to step on her or scare her too badly."

"Scare *her*? I'm scared she'll scare me!" He laughed as he walked out of the room to get the extra quilt.

CHAPTER 5
The New Roommate

The alarm woke me up at 6:00 a.m. I rolled over. "Okay, I have to say, waking up to your boss lying next to you is a little weird," I said with a nervous smile.

Sean just grinned back and said, "Well, we are just *lying here,* like you said—we have not slept together, per se. Plus, I will not be your boss for too much longer and with any luck you will be the boss." He seemed excited.

"You don't think I'll be stepping on toes? What about Todd and Ashley? They've been in the office way longer than I have."

Sean waved his hand in dismissal and said, "Todd is not interested in any more responsibility. He has conveyed that to his superiors at work many times—no promotion, just leave him be where he is. He says he has enough going on elsewhere so he would just like to come to work and do his job. Ashley hasn't shown any motivation or interest in doing more. She does her job well, but if she wants a promotion, she hasn't shown interest and she has not said anything to anyone about wanting more responsibility. So at this point, don't worry about what others want, worry about what you want."

"Yes, okay. Thanks for the morning pep talk. You should be here more often. I could use morning pep talks and you are awfully good at them," I said, beaming as I looked up at him.

"Well, I can say I would also enjoy that," Sean said, smiling back at me like he was in the middle of a daydream.

"We'd better hurry. You have to get going so you can get to your place, get your things and change so it doesn't look like, well, what it actually is, when we show up for work. We can't have people thinking we showed up to work together this morning," I said, laughing. "I'll make coffee while you get dressed so you can grab a cup before you go. Then I'll shower and meet you at work. What time are our plans for tonight?" I was a little dizzy from the prospect of how this may look once we are at work.

"The reservation is at seven. Then I have the 'other plans'"— he air quoted—"which is what I've been wanting to show you. That's at eight. I can pick you up at 6:30 if you think you'll be ready in time?" Sean said.

"Actually, I would like to drive myself there. I know it sounds silly, but it's our first date, and well, these are the best parts of dating—the suspense, the anticipation, the unknown."

He smiled at me and said, "You're amazing. I'm glad you think the way you do. You voice it so unequivocally, right on the money as always. I will meet you there at 7:00 p.m. I'll get our table. I'll leave word with the front staff that you'll be joining me."

I walked to the kitchen, grabbed us both to-go cups, poured his coffee and left mine empty till after I showered. Sean had already dressed and he came into the kitchen and I handed him his to go cup. He went to the fridge and added the flavored cream. "I will see you at the water cooler." He gave me a warm, soft kiss and left.

I hurried back to the bathroom to take a shower, and then decided to blow-dry my hair today. That way I would be half done my hair for my dinner date later on. Once I was finished all that, I put a little extra makeup on to brighten my face so I didn't look to tired. Last thing I wanted was to walk in looking like I hadn't slept in weeks. I couldn't imagine handing a promotion to a person who looked like the "meh" emoji. I also didn't want there to be any talk of being tired because Sean was over, considering my office knew he stayed.

I went into the closet and pulled out "the power suit"—the blazer was magenta, and the cut was amazing. I paired it with a white chiffon long-sleeve shirt, black fitted dress pants with a wide belt, and a fine-ass pair of knee-high, stiletto-heeled boots. Oh hell yeah, that said boss, all right. I went downstairs and made some breakfast. I seemed to have forgotten to give Sean breakfast before I kicked him out the door in a hurry this morning, oops, my bad. I grabbed my mug on the counter and filled it. Dallas hadn't been seen since her brush with Sean, so I left her food and went to check out my rental.

It was fun driving a new car. Now I just had to figure out how to afford a new car, or else I needed to afford bus tickets to get to work.

I still hadn't figured out what happened with my crashed car—where was it? How bad was it? I guess I should phone and find out.

I'd put that on the docket of things to do later when I felt I could give a damn. Right now I was in a good mood and more lighthearted than I had been in a while. I was damn well going to enjoy it, and damn, I look good. I was going to work this outfit today! Driving the sleek black crossover was awesome; its options had options, and it was loaded to the max! Man, it was a nice sleek black vehicle. It had plush black leather and the vehicle itself felt a little more sturdy than my car. But my little car was probably the size of a Lego car now. I wondered how much this thing was going to cost in gas. That was one thing with my hybrid; I never thought too much about it. The weather was back to normal today. Not warm, by any means, but nice. It was clouded over as usual but it had to be six degrees outside.

At work, customer service was empty as usual; they must have been having their morning convention trying to catch up with Sean and get the scoop, not that I thought he would give it to them. "Good morning, Ms. Stenson," said Mr. Gunderson. "I saw you come in. How are you feeling after your terrible accident? Are you okay to be back?"

"Good morning, Mr. Gunderson, thank you for your concern. Yes, I'm fine, thank you, it was just a minor event. I'm fine now to be back. Lots to do, as you know." He still looked concerned, darn it. I thought that would be enough for him to leave it be.

"Well, as long as you're okay, we should probably have a note saying it's okay for you to be back, otherwise maybe you should be at home," said Mr. Gunderson, probably trying silently to figure out if there would be any ramifications if I was here and not well.

"I'll see if I can call the insurance company or the doctor on call to get a note. But I assure you, it was not a big collision. I just needed time to get things sorted out before I came back to work. Physically, I am well. Great, as a matter of fact."

"Yes, well, call and see if you can get the documentation and then come to my office, please, if you don't mind."

"Sure thing, I'll be there as soon as I can." I sat down to call the insurance people about the note and to see if they heard anything from the doctor or had any documents that said how many days I should be staying home. I also wanted to find out what happened to the poor little car. After I hung up, Tracy walked in from break room. "How was the lunch room jam session?" I asked.

"Not as informative as I hoped," Tracy said, pouting. I smirked at her, hoping I was conveying my best "na na na boo boo" face Sean didn't give up the goods.

"I was just on the phone with insurance. They have documents, thank goodness, that can clear me to be here, otherwise I think Gunderson was going to send me home. My car looks like someone tried to put a square in a round hole so it sounds like they may write it off." Now it was my turn to pout.

"How are you going to get to work?" asked Tracy as the others walked in.

"Well, I have the rental right now, but that's for the week and after that insurance doesn't cover it anymore. I'll have to figure it out from there.

Anyway, can you all please keep an eye on the fax machine? Mr. Gunderson called me into his office, and like I said, if that document doesn't come in that says I am okay to be back at work, I think he'll send me home."

"We will keep watch, don't worry, hun. Go to your meeting. Oh! And good luck!" Tracy crossed her fingers and smiled. I looked at everyone else and they said their good lucks as well. My shoulder relaxed down. I guess everyone was okay with a promotion if that indeed was what the meeting was about. That made my stress level go down a notch. It was great to have support.

"Thanks guys, I'll be back." I walked into Mr. Gunderson's office and he greeted me again.

"Come on in. So I guess this is just a formality, is it? Sean said he would like to tell you of the offer. Has he?"

"Yes, Mr. Gunderson, he has. I would like to add that the letter you require from my physician is on its way."

"Good, good, that's excellent, we can move forward. First off, Mrs. Janssen sent you something, and I was not going to argue with her. Did you know she smacked my hand with the top of her cane this morning?" I chuckled. I couldn't help it. The picture of this old bitty hitting this big man as if to put him in his place was pretty hilarious. "Yes, well." Mr. Gunderson got up from his chair, left the office and then came back in as I was trying to spy around the corner. "These huge lovely monstrosities for flowers are for you!

I tried telling her we do not accept gifts for doing our jobs. Not, by the way, that you don't deserve one, but that's when she whacked me and told me I was speaking gibberish nonsense. She has got to be twenty-five years my senior, so I am not going to argue with her!" He laughed.

"They are very lovely. I will call her and tell her it was very thoughtful," I said, eyeing the hugest blooms I had ever seen.

"By the way, that was great work you did the other day, amazing. The manufacturer was quite quick with the work, so either today or within the next couple of days she will have her new chair. She was elated!" Mr. Gunderson sounded proud. It kind of made me blush. "Yes, well it was a line problem, so catching the problem in assembly now saved them big headaches and a lot of money and they can move forward correcting any potential further problems. Speaking of which, you're going to love this. They heard from Sean about your car accident. And because you caught the mistake and they did not, off their own assembly line, they have a card here for you. A get-well card, but it comes with a weeks' rental car of your choice, already paid for! That should come in handy," said Mr. Gunderson with a bright happy face. I think giving good news made his day.

I read the card, and it was from Deacon.

"Wow, here I was worried that I got ditched for dinner, and here you were hurt somewhere in a car accident. I really hope you are okay; maybe we can have a rain check on that dinner? The gift card is to help you to get to work in the meantime.

I hope you don't mind if I help out a bit. You really saved my ass with pointing out the specifications. That could have cost me my job or it could have had ramifications for my job.

These are things I should have been keeping track of and this one slipped by. So you saved me big time. I hope you don't mind me returning the favor.
xo
Deacon.

I looked at Mr. Gunderson, and he obviously saw the note, which for sure made my cheeks red. "Wow, that was nice of them to do that. I, um, think I can use that this week to get me to work," I said sheepishly.

Mr. Gunderson sat back down. "On to new business then! Will you take the promotion? I will have Cory train you if you're available this weekend, and you will be set to go by Monday. She's the one that heads up the whole front office. She has been here for a decade. But once trained, your only boss now will be me and the store owner. She will still be up front if you have questions after training. It will probably take you a month before you are completely comfortable, but the job comes with a great raise and two weeks' paid vacation. So what do you think?"

"I think yes, Mr. Gunderson, it sounds like a great opportunity and if Cory is willing to come in this weekend to help me, I will for surely be here. Thank you," I said with glee and I shook his hand.

"Glad to have you aboard the management team, Ms. Stenson. I will let Cory know you'll be in. You'll get your employment package by three o'clock today." He showed me out of his office.

"All right, thank you again, Mr. Gunderson."

I travelled down the hall with my bouquet in one arm and card in the other hand. Mr. Gunderson was right, this was a monster bouquet. Tracy was just coming around the corner from Sean's office. "I thought you went for a job interview or a promotion or something, not the Miss America Pageant," she said.

"Haha!" I said. "You're so funny, Tracy. It's a good thing you're cute because that sense of humor, girl, I tell you what, it needs work," I said with a smile.

Sean came out of his office to see what was going on. He looked a little worried, which was kind of cute and a bit funny. Make him sweat a little, I guess.

"Sooo, stop holding out, who is that all from?" asked Ashley.

"It's from the wonderful, most beautiful … pause, wait for it … Ms. Janssen. She got more than she bargained for, and she is happier than a pig in mud." I laughed. "Side note, did you know she whacked Mr. Gunderson with her cane? That would have been fun to see."

Everyone added their two cents'. "No way!" said Tracy.

"That's awesome," said Todd. Ashley was just laughing at the thought of it.

"He said we can't except gifts for doing our job and she whacked him with a cane," I exclaimed joyfully; the picture in my head was too funny not to share with the others. Finally Sean was smiling, and everyone got a laugh from the thought of this eighty-year-old woman smacking their boss around. "The card is from Deacon," I said quickly.

The smile was wiped from Sean's face.

"Well, what does it say?" asked Todd, apparently now into consuming gossip.

"He thanked me for helping him; apparently I saved his company from a lot of grief. He gave me a gift card for car rental service for the next week. Sean had told him about the accident, that's why I missed the dinner date."

"Stupid Sean," Sean interjected.

I finished my sentence. "He wants a raincheck." Sean's eyebrows shot up and I glanced away as if I didn't notice. "Well, I don't know. How many people does a lady need to go on a date with?" I smiled at Sean. He relaxed at the comment.

"Lots!" said Tracy. "Ladies need to date lots of men!" The glare that came from Sean was unholy and hit right at Tracy. "I'll sit now and ignore that look. I have work to do." She turned around and planted herself in her chair all serious like, but once she turned away from Sean she was grinning like the Cheshire Cat.

"Anyway there's not much more than that. I don't get my work package till this afternoon for my new position. So let's hit it so we can quit it," I said. I was excited for the work package and even more excited for the after-work events. Everyone gave their congratulations.

Just before noon, a front-end manager showed Deacon back to customer service. "Deacon! Wow, what are you doing here?" I asked. I swear, all phone calls were dropped like no one had anything better to do than listen to this one conversation. Even Sean came out to look busy at the filing cabinet. "Good morning, Sean, good to see you."

"Deacon, I see you're still in town. Nice to see you as well."

"Yes, well, I came into Tony's today to see if Cali was okay." He turned to me. "Are you okay, Cali? How are you feeling after the accident?"

"I am quite fine, thank you, but you didn't have to come all the way here to check on me. Or are you here on business at the store? Oh, by the way, thank you for the card. That was very thoughtful. You really didn't have to do that," I added last second.

"It was my pleasure, Cali. I don't know how that connecting part got missed, but that could have caused a great deal of trouble for me. I got lucky that the past many months were not worse because of that missed assembly. I was lucky I had you to catch it and save me from a firestorm. So I should be thanking you." There was an air of silence that seemed like an hour, though it was only a moment.

Deacon spoke up. "I'm not here on business though, I will be leaving later tonight. Would you like to maybe have lunch with me?" Oh boy, this was super awkward. Everyone was watching, and I didn't know what to say. I would rather just run from the room. Then I thought... honestly, when I felt like running I should just tell the truth; if that didn't scare him off then maybe it wasn't what I thought anyway.

"Actually, I missed a day and I was going to have lunch here. But that's not the only reason I can't do lunch. I actually have a date tonight with my soon to be ex-boss, Sean Stock." I looked over and smiled at Sean, who seemed to be standing taller. I added, "See, we have a few promotions in our office today, so he's taking me out. But before I make it sound like a business date, it's not. Sean has made it more than clear that it's a date-date." I smiled shyly at Deacon.

"Well then, that's too bad. I wouldn't want to step on any toes, so to speak. I just wanted to get to know you a little better. Seems like I was beaten to it." He also smiled at Sean. "It was very nice to have met you, Cali." He gave me a short stolen kiss on the cheek and then headed down the hall. "Goodbye, Cali Stenson," he said as he walked down the hall.

We looked like a bunch of choir singers; everyone's mouths were hanging open. He sure knew how to make a point, that Deacon Hall. I shook it off and went immediately back to work so everyone else would too. For some reason he really got under my skin. He was a very good-looking man, tall and broad and built, and he carried himself with confidence, which I found appealing. But that ego, that entitlement, and that kiss was for show, just to get everyone's goat.

You knew on the other side of that luscious head of hair he was enjoying the environment he just created in the room. Ugh! Jackass. How could one man make your insides warm and mushy and your outsides want to find the nearest sharp object to throw at him!

I ate lunch at my desk just like I said I would. I was not actually planning on it, but after that escapade with Deacon, I did not want to be in the lunch room, as I was going to be the gossip. I wasn't going to explain shit to anyone! Coffee break came and I got my employment package. "Do you want some privacy? You can use my office," said Sean.

"Sure, thanks." I got up and went into the office. "By the way, I'm not sure what your plans are tonight, but I do have to be back here by ten o'clock tomorrow morning for training. I don't want to put a damper on things tonight."

"That should be fine. I don't think what I have planned should interfere. I liked the way you handled Deacon; that could not have been easy with eight extra ears hearing the conversation. You just say it like it is, and I really like that about you. I mean, it sucks being on the other side of it sometimes, but it's refreshing to see." He gave me a smirky smile, probably remembering me putting him in his place at the beginning of the week. "I'll give you a few moments alone and I'll go grab coffee. Would you like some?"

"Please, if you don't mind, Sean. I've been sitting all day, so coffee would be great."

"Yes, boss," he beamed, teasing me about the promotion.

"Wow, would you look at this!" I said to myself, as there was no one in the office. My wage was now a salary! I took out the calculator to figure out how much the increase in my income would be. My eyes got big; there was no way Tony's Furniture Giant people made this kind of money. Did they? It was like adding ten dollars an hour to my wage! Was that what Sean made? Wow, maybe in a bit I could afford more than bus tickets to work after all! Now I was excited; I had been gone from knowing no one and being in a new part of the country and hating everything and being miserable to having friends, a man who seemed to want to spend time with me and a second man I had to turn away because of the first man. I had a home that was mine regardless of how glitchy it was. I *had* a car but now that could be remedied thanks to the new promotion. I guessed I could set down roots and make Vancouver a home, a place to settle. A one-eighty-degree-turn in a matter of just over a week. That was divine intervention right there. No matter what it was or how this happened, I was glad it did. All I had to do now was get a set of office keys, have a photo identification and key card made up and I was ready for training. I signed the package and put it back in its envelope. I opened the door and everyone was standing around the desks.

Todd, of course, was at the phones like a workhorse. "Oooooh, I see cupcakes," I said.

"A little celebration for everyone," said Ashley. "Here's to Sean and his new job!" She handed him a cupcake. "Here's to Tracy! My boss!" Ashley chortled and handed her a cupcake. "Here's to Cali, a raise and a promotion in less than a two-week period—unheard of. Cheers!" She smiled and gave me a cupcake.

"Here's to me! I get a raise, so I will train all the new asshats coming in here to properly to do customer service. I'm gunning for the next spot now, though!" she said with a smile and determination on her face. She grabbed herself a cupcake. "And here's to Todd, who shuts up, puts up and puts his head down and goes to work. Plus, he is the bestest friend ever, so he gets the bestest cupcake!" With a big grin on her face she held out the only vanilla bean red velvet cupcake, and yes, it was huge.

"Awww, you're so awesome, Ashley, this is my favorite!" exclaimed Todd.

"I know!" she said, beaming with pride. "Cheers to everyone. Now let's get back to work so we can get the hell out of here."

The day finished pretty smoothly. It was a really good day. I had a bit of a headache, but that was probably left over from the accident and having to work. I was actually really excited for the date tonight; giddy, even. I drove home in my rental, and the roads were way better than they had been all week, so the drive was really nice. I got home to a very dark house—for once, all the lights were not on.

When I walked in and turned on the entranceway lights on, I saw a wave-like shadow in front of the fridge. It looked like it was blocking it and then it moved, which startled me. I stayed standing by the door. It went into the living room, right across what would be my path, and it stopped almost directly in front of me.

It almost resembled a wall of water; it looked like waves or a heat wave on the asphalt, like water in a bucket rippling with rhythm except there was nothing containing it, just a wall of water. Then it moved again and went into the hall, and it was gone! I tried to follow, thinking maybe it went somewhere else, maybe I could see where it went. But it was gone. I went back to where I started to see if it was back in the kitchen or living room. It was not there. It was so odd. I felt like it was trying to tell me something, but I couldn't comprehend what. Not that the water could talk, but like a thought was put in my head. So I went to check the bathroom and nothing was there either. I knew, somehow, I knew it had to do with the hall bathroom. I would keep my eye on that from now on. Out of the corner of my eye I saw an old man walk passed my window in the living room. This window faced the sidewalk on the side of my house, going to the backyard and small shed.

"What the hell, who is in my yard?" I didn't recognize the old man; maybe it was one of the neighbors? He had what looked like a farmer's cap and he was wearing military green except it looked like the overalls janitors used in schools. I ran to look out the window but couldn't see far enough down. I pulled on my boots and went outside to look for him and find out what the hell he wanted and why he was in my yard. I went around back and there was no one in my fenced-off yard. Well, that was just great. Now I had to go into my small shed or wait for him to come out.

Regardless, I was calling 911. I took the phone out of my coat pocket. Thank goodness I hadn't taken off my coat yet. I dialed as I opened the shed door. "This is 911, what is your emergency?"

"Cali Stenson here, I, ah, saw someone in my back yard but I can't find them. There's no one here, so I'm going into the shed to see if they're in there." I opened the door and grabbed the flashlight on the shelf and ignored the operator and whatever she was saying. I looked hard into crooks and corners and saw nothing. "I, I... I'm sorry, it must be my mistake. I saw a man, and I thought maybe it was a neighbor, but I really don't know. I've only been in this house six months. I followed him out here, but he's gone!" I said, all disheveled, to the operator.

"Do you have a description?" asked the operator.

"Yes, he's older ... sixty or maybe sixty-five years old, brown cap on his white hair, and he was wearing military green but it was like a janitor's over-alls. Oh, and he was average built and almost six foot tall."

"Well, it wasn't your imagination. That's a pretty good description. I can send someone out if you like." I was just about to say yes please but then I thought about the floating water in the damn house. I couldn't tell what was real anymore. "Actually, is there somewhere you can keep it on file? In case something happens where I have to call back later? I truly can't see or find anyone here, and I don't want to waste the officer's time. If they were here, they are not now," I said.

"Yes, everything including the time and date, phone number called from and name is logged and in audio comments. It's no trouble to send someone out," confirmed the operator.

"No, I'm alright, thank you for your help." I hung up.

I was still rattled, and I went back up the same path we had both walked on and into the house. I took off my coat and boots and stared out that window. Wouldn't you know it.? "Holy shit, there he is!" I said out loud. This time he was going the opposite way towards the front by the door and by the car—for sure I could catch him now! I threw the door open, but there was no one in the front yard and no one by the car. I walked out to the road in stocking feet looking in front yards. There was nothing. Well, shit, maybe I was seeing things that weren't there.

But usually when I saw and heard things they were malevolent, not just your average joe looking to borrow a shovel or grass seed. That's what this guy looked like. Someone nice, someone you would go out and say, "Hey neighbor, how are you today?" As for the floating water, that didn't make much sense either. But I definitely felt like I was supposed to understand something.

I went back inside. I had a date to get ready for, but it was going to be really hard to concentrate on that when all I could think about were my visitors. No wonder the damn cat was so high anxiety. Poor Dallas. "Dallas, where are you? It's me." As if that would help. I looked in her box and she was there. "Hi sweetie, I just wanted to say hi. I understand now why you are the way you are, you poor thing.

I bet you see lots of stuff go on and you hate people and busyness, this must drive you crazy." She purred—actually purred—at me. Wow! "Maybe we should try one of those pet-sitting places where cats go hang out on the furniture and get treats, and maybe even see other cats?" At the word treat her ears perked up. I got her food out and I brought her treats right to her box. I felt so bad if she was seeing what I saw, that poor thing. I felt much better knowing Dallas and I were on the same side.

It was time to get ready. I found the navy-blue dress and paired it with some navy and white gold bracelets and a necklace and earrings. Since my hair was already blow dried this morning, I just ran a brush through and straightened it, letting it be smooth and sleek instead of its normal wavy bounce. I added punched-up lipstick to give that power-lip look. Then I went for the makeup bag and transformed my makeup into evening wear by adding a smokey eye and mascara and a darker cheek color; just enough to give definition. Instead of the silver heels, I opted for over-the-knee navy suede boots with a diamond ankle bracelet over my right boot. I walked out that door like I owned the world and it felt good.

I parked my car in front of the building and a valet came around to get the keys. The front of the building was done up in lights, and it was big and beautiful with a fireplace right outside. The foyer was a long hall with the best of the best from art galleries and large photographs of famous people and the chef. At the end of this foyer was a single small desk and a coat check area. A young lady dressed all in black with her hair sternly pulled back in a bun asked my name.

"Ah yes," she said. "Mr. Stock is here at a table waiting for you. Would you like to leave your jacket?"

I nodded and she took me to the coat check where another women dressed in black, this time with blonde hair pulled tightly into a bun, took my coat. I was led into the restaurant and up a glass staircase. Once upstairs, just to the left was a man in a cobalt-blue suit, standing and smiling at me from where he stood by a big window. I had never seen someone look like money— if that was a thing? Sean did. He looked like he was made of a million dollars. "I thought it was the man's jaw that was supposed to drop to the floor. You look fabulous!" I said to Sean.

" Ah, yes, well, thank you. You don't see my jaw dropped, because I left it on the first floor when I saw you walk in looking like you were absolutely going to surpass the beauty of every woman in here." He kissed my cheek then kissed me lightly on the lips and sat me down first.

"Well now, Sean, that is absolutely the best compliment I've had, well, ever! You might be trying too hard," I said with a mischievous smile.

"I absolutely am going to try hard. There is no damn way anyone is thinking I'm leaving without you on my arm. They all must know!" he said like a goofy declaration.

I said to him, "If I'm to be honest, I thought this was going to be awkward and filled with a lot of small talk, but so far this is great." The waiter came with two bottles of wine and poured some in two tiny glasses.

"Do you like sweet or savory? Or are you a gal that likes a dry wine?" asked Sean.

"Actually, I don't like really dry wines at all. I prefer less dry." Sean tasted both and pointed to one of the bottles. The waiter poured us both a little bit and Sean waited till I had a sip.

"Oh, that is very nice. You are good at this!" I smiled at him. The waiter topped up the glasses a bit and left the bottle. "This is a really amazing place. Thank you for thinking of me, this is great."

"If it's my turn to be honest, I don't think of much else these days besides you. I find you attractive on many levels. Your beauty is beyond compare, you are intellectual and fiery in a passionate sense. I think you are amazing." Now the silence set in. I didn't quite know what to say to him.

So of course I joked. "Well, if your intent was to light my cheeks a flame red, I believe you have done so. I don't think I can get through a conversation with you without my cheeks going bright red. I feel like a giddy schoolgirl."

"Me too!" He laughed triumphantly at his own joke. We talked about what we thought it would be like at our new jobs, how different it might be, how anxious we were and if we thought this would change our new dynamic. Just then the waiter came back for our order. We both ordered the specials with scallops and risotto to start. "I want to try everything," I said. "I don't know when I'll be back." I smiled at him.

"Well, if my new pay is as good as they say it is, maybe sooner than we think," Sean replied. We ate dinner almost in silence so we could enjoy this meal by an amazing chef. It was a completely understood silence, not awkward or weird—more of an appreciation for culinary gifts and amazing company.

"Sean, darling, you're starting to look a little nervous or piqued," I said with a bit of concern after we had finished our meal.

"Yes, well, it has come to that part of the evening where I pay the bill. Though I'm sure it is astounding and rightfully so after this delicious meal, I'm concerned more with what happens next."

"What happens next?" I asked, a little nervous.

"I pay the bill, we leave and I'm going to take you to an up-and-coming art gallery. There's an opening there tonight."

"Oh, well, that's not so bad. I love art. I love art galleries."

Sean seemed to relax a little and said, "Well, that is great news. Let's head there now so we don't miss the opening. We can go in my car and come back for yours later." I nodded. Sean paid the hefty bill and we walked down the stairs to the coat check where he helped me into my coat. The valet pulled up in Sean's car, but it wasn't his Jag.

"When did you get a sleek black Mercedes?" I said, in awe.

"Company car. I like it too," he said appreciatively. He tipped the valet, helped me into my side of the car and then we were off on our secretive adventure— the art gallery. We parked across the street. The gallery looked full, so it must have truly been a big night. There were so many people there it kind of reminded me of a fancy pub. We went through the double doors and were immediately offered champagne by a waiter. They had turned the foyer into an area for socializing and drinking with tables where you could stand and have conversations. Then there was a bit of clapping, and it turned into a cacophony of clapping and well-wishing. People were clapping and staring at us. "What's this Sean?"

"Well, this is the part I was nervous about, of course. It's my art on the walls. Actually, the art is to the back. To the left is where my work is. But it's a pretty big deal to get your art in here, so I have friends, co-workers, new co-workers and you for support; at least, I hope I have you."

"Oh my gosh, Sean, this is huge! This is what you wanted to show me? You're a closet artist? Lead the way, this is very exciting."

"Well, I hope you think so," he said, "once you see my stuff." He mumbled something.

"What was that? I couldn't hear over the crowd of people," I proclaimed.

"Oh, it was nothing. Why don't we head to the art?" Sean seemed like he was trying to change the subject and he seemed so nervous. I was in awe of the whole thing.

"This is really great. I'm having a good time with you, Sean." Just then someone came up and shook his hand and Sean did introductions. It was like that all the way to the back hall where his art was; people coming up and shaking Sean's hand, telling him which ones they had bought and how good his art looked in a gallery.

"The art won't be here for long. It's selling very well," said an overly portly man, Mr. George, who Sean introduced to me as the gallery owner who had a stake in the sales.

"Good to hear, Mr. George. I'm pleased as well." Sean gripped the man's hand firmly. Sean whispered in my ear as we were walking away, "Well, at least he's pleased. That's half the worry gone." I squeezed his hand to let him know I was there for him. Then we turned the corner, and the gallery was amazing. There were photos of people, buildings and places, and paintings that looked like his soul had come out onto the canvas. I went to the central wall, drawn there by the square set up in the middle of the room with dozens of paintings of various sizes, the smallest being about 16" x 20". The clapping started again, and I looked toward the entrance where I had walked away from Sean.

As I was about to bring my hands up to join in, I looked up and everyone was looking at me and clapping and smiling. One person even mumbled near me "bravo, bravo." I looked at Sean, not understanding what was happening, and I was getting a little nervous and scared. He pointed with his left hand for me to turn the corner of the central block. He started to walk toward me as I turned the corner and saw an almost life-sized painting. I stepped back a good eight feet—it was me. The painting was of me.

I was in shock; my mouth dropped, and my hand went over my mouth and my other hand went over my heart. It was beautiful, the color, the way the paint looked like it was going to jump right off the canvas. The shock of looking at myself on a what looked like a five-foot canvas was bizarre.

"Do you like it?" I jumped, startled out of my reverence, and looked at the worried look on Sean's face.

"Sean, when would you have had time to do this? It is beautiful … well, magnificent, really. It's rather large." I laughed and he laughed too.

"I was so scared you would go running in humiliation, and that I wouldn't see you again. I thought you would think I was a crazy stalker."

"Well, Mr. Stock, I'm not sure about stalker, but crazy is possible. Why me, Sean?"

"I saw you alone after work one day, and the way you sat there contemplating at your table at a quiet coffee shop set the art in motion. Here, do you want to see the very first one? It's called 'quiet contemplation,' and it's the first time I noticed you. I mean, really noticed you—it's the one in the coffee shop. It's a photo." He took me to it nervously.

"You took a photo of me and put it in the gallery?"

"Yep. That's why I am waiting for you to call the cops and have it torn down. See the yellow sticker? It means it sold."

There was a pregnant pause and then he said, "I bought it for you. In case you would like to have it. I also have a sticker on the large painting of you in case you wanted it, and if not I would love it at my new place, if you wouldn't mind. I didn't know how you would feel about this. This could land me in a lot of hot water if you hate it, or if you're really angry about the fact that I hid it from you. Or you could bust my balls for hanging it up for all to see. There are many ways this could end badly for me, but when I said you're in my head… " he paused before he hastily continued, "what is even more scary, is if you hate all of this or are angry, you may be not only in my head but in my heart too. It is going to break, and I swear on all that is holy this was my last secret."

I didn't know what to think. Everything he said made sense. I should maybe be angry, but there was an honest look in his eyes and his heart was on his sleeve for all to see. In fact, a whole gallery of his heart was hung on the walls. I reached up and I kissed him in front of everyone.

"They are beautiful, and yes, I would like that picture. I don't think I could get used to the idea of someone buying a picture of me—that is a little weird, not that I've had a lot of time to think about it. It is a beautiful picture. Thank you for buying it for me." We sat on a bench off to the side in silence for a moment. "You know, it's awfully weird to see yourself in a portrait. I've never had the opportunity to see myself through someone else's eyes like this." I was amazed and awed. This was what Sean's eyes saw of me; how could I be upset? It melted my heart.

Tracy walked up. "What do you think?" she asked.

"Tracy, I'm glad to see you. I think these photos and paintings are wonderful, though it's kind of nerve wracking to see yourself as someone else does."

"Aww, I'm here for you, doll. The viewings have been very positive. If a man looked at me the way Sean sees you, I would handcuff him to a chair and never let him go," Tracy joked.

"Well, you have a weird way of putting things, but I definitely see your point." I smiled. A group showed up to talk to Sean so I excused myself to go back to the main foyer to get drinks. I bought two red wines from the pop-up bar and found a central table. How could someone I used to think despised me see me like the women in the painting? It was warm, full of love and light. I didn't understand the motive for pushing me away while he secretly painted my portrait. Maybe he was ashamed that he had feelings for a perfect stranger, and maybe he was ashamed that he painted me without my knowledge. I really couldn't reconcile the two Seans.

"Are you okay?" said a deep burly voice. I turned quickly around, a little startled out of my thoughts.

"Deacon, what are you doing here? I thought you were flying back tonight."

"Flight leaves at 11:45 tonight, and some of the office staff said they were coming to an art opening and a party at the gallery. I had time to kill, so I thought I would check it out. Your boyfriend is quite talented. I saw your photo. It was amazing, as was the painting." There was a pause before he continued, "Cali, if I knew you two were an item I would not have pressed for dinner dates."

"It's not really like that … well, I don't think. What I mean is –" Sean stepped in and saved me from an awkward conversation.

"Deacon, how good of you to take time to come to the gallery. I thought you were off home by now."

"Yes, well, I'm on my way now, as a matter of fact. I was on my way out when I saw your … Cali here, and I thought I would just say hi before leaving. My flight is soon so I should get to the airport early. Very impressive work, Sean. Have a good night."

"Thank you. I appreciate that, Deacon."

Deacon nodded and walked away. I slid a drink in front of Sean. "You look more in shock now than you did earlier," he said. "Did he say something to you to upset you?"

"Yes … I mean no, he did say something that made me think, but he didn't try to upset me." I tried my best to clarify.

"What did he say?"

I looked up at Sean, searching his eyes for answers. "He thought we were together … what I mean is, he told me he would not have kept pressing me to go for dinner if he knew we were an exclusive item. He called you my boyfriend. I don't know, again, this is a lot of information for me to comprehend. Maybe the car accident turned my brain hazy, I don't know." Sean tried to interrupt to tell me something but I needed to freak out and get my thoughts out. It may not have been the most ladylike thing to do in public, but at the moment I didn't care.

"It was just at the start of this week that I had decided I would give you a taste of your own medicine. I had put up with you disliking me for almost two months. I was ready to dish it back." Sean tried to interrupt again and I didn't let him. I kept going. "Then I find out that's not the case, you actually like me… you're just being a little outlandish about it. Then you went on a tirade at work in front of everyone— a big blowout for all to see—then you saved me at the hospital and quite frankly have been doing a bang-up job of trying to take care of me in your spare time. Then I find out all the while, you have been painting and taking photos of me. I don't know what it's like in your head but I feel like I'm on a roller coaster. Now Deacon throws the word boyfriend out there and it kind of landed like a grenade. I don't know if this is panic or if this is my concussed brain on overload, but I'm pretty sure I have a point in there somewhere."

Finally I stopped my barrage and took a big breath in. "Cali, you are exactly right; there is no one way to go about caring for someone. But I'm pretty sure there is a right way, and I have missed that mark." Sean was about to continue when another group of well-wishers came to the table. We put on our "this is the most proud, awesome moment" faces instead of our "we're in the middle of a relationship talk" faces. Once they left, another group was heading over.

"Sean, I don't want you to leave your opening early, but I think I need to leave. It's been a very long day." The second group interrupted, and my mind was barely present through the congratulations. I was lost in thought. I was really happy for him, and I didn't want to convey that I wasn't or that I was disinterested in him. I just needed time to think without being on the Sean Stock roller coaster.

After the group left I finished what I had to say, "Sean, I am very happy about the gallery, the pieces—all of them are wonderful. I'm proud to be part of such a big moment with you. Also, just so you know, the date was amazing. I'm not trying to be a hater here and scurry home. I'm just tired, and I do have a lot to think about and it's hard to do in a room full of beautiful, bustling people. I'm just a little out of my element today." I smiled at him and put my hand on his.

"That is completely understandable. I have gone about this in a very odd manner and it has left you full of wondering and confusion. On top of it all, it was only the other day when you were in an accident. You probably aren't up for all of this just yet. Let me take you home."

"No! I mean no thank you. Please stay. This is your big moment. I can get a ride. I just want to go find the others from work and say goodbye." I kissed him and left him standing at our table as I went back into the gallery to find my friends. When I looked back another group was there with Sean. He looked at me while trying to hold a conversation with the congratulators. I turned the corner, almost running straight into the gallery owner.

"Ah, Ms. Stenson, how are you enjoying your evening?"

"Fine, thank you … Mr. George, is it?"

He nodded then said, "The paintings are wonderful, his work is doing very well."

"I'm glad to hear it," I said.

Then I saw the painting of two people; it was just their silhouette under a tree on a grass hill with bikes and a picnic set out, The man's arm were around the woman. "Mr. George, I would like that painting there," I said, and pointed to the eye-catching piece.

"I will have it sent with the other picture of you." He called a lady over and she took my information into an iPad. Mr. George put the yellow sold sticker on the item.

I didn't normally spend that kind of money, but there was something about it. I just needed to have it at home. Plus, the bonus was that I could support Sean. "That's a really beautiful painting. Did you buy it?" inquired Ashley.

"Hi, Ashley, yes, I did. I was actually on my way out. I saw the painting and just had to have it. Plus, with a new raise at work this will be my gift to myself," I said with a smile.

"Did I hear you're leaving early?" asked Tracy.

"Yeah, I think I've worn myself out. It's been a long day and I'm really starting to feel it. I think I'm just going to go get my rental at the restaurant and then go home.

"I can drive you to your car," Tracy offered and ushered me out without waiting for a reply. These were a good group of people. I liked the way they took care of each other, and me too now, I guessed. We gathered the group at the door and said goodbye.

Sean came over, kissed me on my cheek and whispered in my ear, "We can talk later if you like. Take care of yourself. If you want I can come by and see how you are tomorrow?"

"I have training tomorrow, remember? I won't be around. I'll be fine. We can talk sometime later." I kissed his cheek and left with Tracy.

"You sure you're okay? You look a little dazed and confused." Concern lit Tracy's face.

"No, I'm fine. I just think it has all been a bit much, you know?"

"Yeah, I guess I can understand that. It's a lot to take in." We were halfway down the street when I spotted Tracy's car.

"I'm a little tired. I guess I have to heal more than I thought. I didn't think the car accident was a big deal, but I took a lot out of me." Tracy looked at me with understanding as we got into her car. "I'm just a bit floored, first he dislikes me and I feel like a pariah for two months! It was the same day we went out to the pub that I thought 'if he dishes it out, then I will dish it back.' I don't understand why he pushed me away if he felt another way for me."

Tracy waited for me to be done and said, "Well, first, we aren't supposed to date our co- workers. It causes trouble and then someone gets fired, and that would have been you because you are, or were, the temp. No one is going to argue with you that he went about it the wrong way. He was as mixed up as you're feeling right now."

I looked at Tracy; she had a point. Everyone was allowed to have feelings, and we didn't always know how to handle them. We drove down the street.

The restaurant was now just a few blocks east. "You're right, Tracy, it's just that after that, I find out he likes me, which was a weird way to show it. Then he yelled at me and tried to embarrass me in front of everyone."

"Yeah, that was not his hottest moment. That one is most definitely on him," Tracy interrupted.

"Also, he was my saving grace at the hospital. He has been trying to take care of me when he can, which is very sweet. That's just in one day!" Tracy pulled her car over behind mine. "We went on a date, a really amazing date, the best one I've ever been on, and then to an art gallery where I am a muse for his art and I didn't know about it!"

"That's pretty up and down and hard on the emotions," Tracy agreed. "Really, I don't know how I would do in your shoes. I don't think it's just your car accident that has you reeling."

"Right! Then Deacon is at the gallery and is calling Sean my boyfriend. He said he would not have pushed if he knew how serious we were. Are we serious? I mean, I didn't really know the whole story till tonight."

"I think you need some rest, truly. I also think the accident plays into the fact that your head is spinning in circles. Take the weekend to think about it all. It has been a pretty weird ride, but I do think Sean means well. Maybe now that things are changing, so will the weird dynamic. You can have a healthy and enjoyable relationship with him if you choose that route."

"Maybe you're right. I just need time. I thought I heard him say something about his new place at the gallery too. I didn't even question him ... is he moving too? I really do need some rest" I laughed off my rant.

"I don't know if he is ... maybe?" Tracy said. "You'll have to ask him. For the first time I'm out of the loop." She scoffed like it was a huge deal, and pretended to be upset about it.

"Thank you for leaving to get me to my car; that was really nice of you. Actually, you're all really nice. I like the way you all take care of each other and I'm glad to be a part of that. I hope to return the same kindness you all showed me. You have been amazing."

"Aww, you're a doll. Really, it's not a big deal, hun. I'll see you Monday. I'll tell Ashley you're out for the weekend plans and that you need some rest." She grabbed my phone and put in her phone number as well as Ashley and

Todd's information. "There, now you have all the pertinent info in case you want to get together or talk."

"Thanks, girl, and thanks again for the ride." I took my phone back and got out. I drove slowly, eager to just relax. When I got home, everything was just as it should be. I got a cup of tea and sat on the couch, watched TV and relaxed. The only thing out of place was Dallas; she was sitting with me. It was nice to have furry companion company. I finished my tea and went to bed, where I slept without waking or dreaming for the first time in a long time. It felt really good.

CHAPTER 6
Friends And Benefits

I WOKE UP EARLY, EVEN THOUGH I DIDN'T HAVE TO BE AT WORK UNTIL TEN. I still wanted to have somewhat of a calm Saturday morning. I made flavored coffee and got dressed. At least today would be a short day. The store was only open till four, and because I was just training I would only be there from ten until three, and it was the same tomorrow. Dallas and I ate breakfast together. I think the abnormally normal night did us both some good. She was acting like a normal cat and it was nice to have her around. I felt more grounded and rested than I had in a long time. After coffee and breakfast, I locked up the house and drove to work.

The training went well, and by the time they stopped for lunch the day was pretty much over. It was not hard to grasp. The key was to be someone who could do all the paperwork in an office and handle conflict resolution when it could not be done by another staff member. I basically looked after all the sales information on the computer, handled the management of the front end at point of sales staff and resolutions. That was it. I mean, I was sure it would be an ongoing major job, but the concept was easy. I drove home at the end of the day and got a text from Tracy, who was still at work, that said, *"I gave Todd your number, hope that's okay that we all trade info?"*

When I pulled into my parking space, I texted, *"no problem."* I just got in the house and had just hung up my coat when I received a text from Todd. *"Hey, I know you're trying to relax and take it easy. Tracy said you may not come out with us tonight. I thought maybe I could come and chat with you sometime this weekend. You said you wouldn't mind hearing about what I do and what I have to say…unless you were just being polite?"*

I left the text to sit there a moment. I wanted to have a bath and think about what my next steps were and what I wanted with Sean. Everything over the course of the last two weeks were happening fast, in my career and with Sean, and even with what Deacon had said. It gave me a lot to think about. *"HI! Ya, I'm not sure if I am going or not. I kind of want to but I don't want to exhaust myself either. Where are they going? And what time?"*

Todd replied right away, *"They are going to the blue light lounge, it's a hopping place with lots of people, great ambience and awesome music. They are going around 9:00 p.m."*

I texted back, *"Well, it is only 3:45 right now, did you want to come around 7:00 and hang out? We could go together, if I get to tired and I don't want to go, you wouldn't have missed anything. What do you think?"*

I didn't hear a response right away, and then a text from Todd came in, *"That sounds good. I will be there at 7:00 p.m."* I texted Todd back the thumbs-up emoji. I thought if I was going to have time to myself and relax I better hurry up and do it, which kind of defeated the purpose. I fed the cat early, grabbed the wine and several scented candles, and went to run a tub. I got to the bathroom and it looked like there was already rippling water in the tub.

I put everything down on the counter so not to drop it and watched as the water wall came out of the tub and turn itself over like it was standing in front of me. There was not a lot of room in the bathroom, and I felt like I had to move out of the way. I backed up into the hall then realized I didn't know which way it was going to go, so I went into the kitchen and living room area. The water wall phantom followed me in. "What is it you want? I don't understand, but I feel like you are trying to tell me something. I have a friend coming over later. I don't really know what he does, but it sounds like he deals with this stuff, so maybe he can help if it's in his wheelhouse."

It wrapped its way into the kitchen and I followed and it was gone. "And now I'm talking to … well, whatever that was. That's just great." Just like the other day, one weird thing happened and then the next. The janitor neighbor guy crossed my sight at the window. This time I didn't go to the window, I ran through the house and went to the back door onto the small porch. The older gentlemen went through the door into the locked shed. After the water wall I didn't have to check the shed; I knew he wasn't real either. I went back into the house to the bathroom, and I looked at the tub. I kind of felt weird using it now, as I felt like it already belonged to someone. I grabbed my stuff and went into my bedroom where the master bath was. It wasn't as nice a tub, and it wasn't as big, but I didn't want to feel like I was stealing someone's space. I ran a tub and got in, poured my wine and put my phone loudly on spa music. I wanted to try to go over the changes in my life. First and easiest was the new job. It wasn't every day a promotion just fell in your lap, and with a great raise. I really needed it.

After the car accident and buying that painting I decided whatever nerves I felt about the new job, I had to put them aside. I would just go in like I was going to rule at my job. I would try my hardest, double check the work I was doing the first couple of days and make sure everything I was doing everything right. All I could do was put in my best effort. It's not that I didn't think I could handle the job— I knew I could. The training was going very smoothly, so the nerves were for nothing. Change was just hard to adjust to for some, and it wasn't like I was going far— I was literally moving down the hallway. With that settled, there was the glorious roller coaster that was Sean Stock. I didn't know how I felt about everything. It was rather confusing, and my emotions were up and down. I felt like a little kid in a school yard. (I don't like that boy!— I do like that boy!— No, I don't like him at all, he's mean!— Ooooh, I really like that boy!—That boy is nice to me.— That boy does really weird things behind my back.— That boy does nice things for me.) I felt like I was wading through mud and not getting far. Maybe it was plain and simple if I didn't think about how I got to this point with Sean and I just thought about how I felt now, how Sean felt right now. Sean was the most confident man I knew, except when it came to me, and when his confidence got shaken, he didn't know how to handle it. I thought he did really like me; he said I was starting to get into his heart. He was just waiting for me to figure out what I wanted—not that I had a lot of time to think about it. Did I need a lot of time? No, I didn't, if I thought about how I felt and forgot the roller coaster ride.

When we were together he was genuine, good hearted and funny. He treated me well, and as he said, the chemistry was bone melting, and I had to agree. After that first kiss I knew that.

Was it weird that he painted me while he acted like he detested me? Yes! It was weird. Did I understand it? No, I didn't, but I didn't have to, If I gave him a chance I could probably get to the same place he was too. I knew how he felt, and I could also see it in his beautiful talent, in his art. I did really like him and the chemistry was there and all he was asking for was for me to forget the previous weirdness. Why not? What did I have to lose by doing as he asked? I had nothing to gain from hanging onto it. If shit went sideways, just like any relationship you either dealt with it or you didn't. I wasn't going to give up before I got started. Sean was a nice and kind person, so why wouldn't I give him a chance? Just like Tracy said, if a guy saw her like that, she would chain him to a chair and never let him go. At least I could give a guy a chance.

Now that that was all figured out there was one more thing weighing on me— the goings on in this house. I didn't know what "hokum" Todd was into, but maybe help was on the way. I figured I should get out of the tub. I got dressed and blow dried my hair. I didn't realize how much time I spent in the tub, but I still had enough time to get ready. I decided on a fitted pair of jeans and ankle boots with a pattern that looked like printed newspaper in black and white. I put on a metallic silver and black tank top with a light leather jacket over top that had cloth hanging lapels that made it look like I was wearing a scarf.

After ordering pizza, I did my hair and makeup. Just like clockwork, as soon as I was done setting my natural curls the doorbell rang and it was the pizza guy. I ate in a silent house while the cat ate her dinner too. I cleared everything and there was a knock at the door.

I planned like a genius—that must be Todd. He was early, but that was okay, everything that had to be done was.

I went to open the door and was surprised. "Hi Sean, what are you doing here? Aren't you going out tonight?" I spoke too soon ... so much for planning genius.

Sean said, "I am, actually, but I thought I would come here first to see how you are."

"Come on in. I have company coming in about a half hour. Todd is coming over. I may or may not be going out tonight, but I thought I would dress just in case."

"I can leave if you like, I shouldn't have just barged in on you like this."

"No, it's fine, Sean. I have to talk to you anyway."

Sean paused and looked me up and down. "You look wonderful, by the way."

"Thank you. Would you like something to drink?"

"I'm fine, Cali. I just wanted to see if you were okay, both from the accident and from the barrage of information and the highlight reel that was literally painted on the wall."

I smiled at Sean's quirky remarks. "Sean, I've been thinking today. Things have been a little unorthodox, but I don't think that really matters. The journey of how you get there is the story you tell everyone when you are together and you, sir, have made it quite the story. I think what matters is how we feel right now, in this moment. If you still feel for me how you put it yesterday, that I was getting into your heart."

Sean came over to me. "I feel that way. I absolutely do." He held my shoulder and put his hand through my hair.

"Well, I haven't had much time to think about it the way you have, but I know now that the chemistry is there, *that* is undeniable, and I know that you are sweet, caring and charming. I know that I like you. What I'm saying is, if you want to, I want to see where this goes based off of what is now in this moment."

"Wow, that's great. We can finally be on the same page ... never mind, we can be in the same book." He kissed me and then stopped as if remembering something else. "Should I leave? Todd should be here soon. I'm going out later with everyone. We can see each other then if you want or I can stay too."

"Well, that is up to you. It doesn't matter to me, and I don't think it matters to Todd, so long as you don't talk against his, and I quote, 'Hokum Talk.' That's why he's coming over, I think."

"I promise I will be open minded and stay out of his way."

Just then the doorbell rang. Sean opened the door.

"Oh. Hi, Sean, didn't know you would be here."

"I stopped in to check on Cali. She told me you were coming. I can leave if you like and see you guys later?"

"Well, it's just ... I wanted to tell Cali stuff, you know, the stuff ... you don't like ... that stuff."

"Come in, don't stand in the cold. I told Cali I would be open minded and stay out of your way and not jam your spidey senses. I spent a night here, and it wasn't the most pleasant and that wasn't because of the company. Ooops … cat out of the bag. Sorry, Cali."

I just rolled my eyes. Todd interjected, "Oh. Well, I'm afraid that's exactly what it is. She has company, or rather maybe she *is* the company, to this house. I'm not exactly sure, that's why I came by. People can suffer all kinds of things when they don't know what they're dealing with. Hi, Cali, didn't see you there standing behind tall, dark and ugly here," Todd teased Sean.

"Hi, Todd, glad you could make it, please come into the kitchen. I've made coffee, but if you would like anything else, just let me know."

"Actually, while I'm here I will have water if I am going to help you out. Anything else messes with my senses and my nerves."

"What is it you do, Todd? I've been very curious after the tidbits of conversation I've been picking up on."

"I am an intuitive and an empath. I can use auras and energies and do card readings, but I don't really need them. That's just for show or if I am nervous. I was raised by a friend's dad, and he raised me up just like he did his boy. His boy wasn't interested in learning to be a shaman, so I also got to pick up on that.

That part is more spiritual, but he could do pretty much anything dealing with spirits, energy and herbal medicine. If I can't figure out your situation, he is who I would go to."

"That is very interesting. You don't say much, Todd, but when you do you blow my mind with information. I had no idea you could do that or that you grew up with another family. Thank you for coming back to check out my home."

"That's no problem, Cali, I just noticed bit of extra energy here and there, and a few extra friends I didn't think you knew you had. I was hoping on top of it all, I could do a reading on you. If we have time."

"What do you need to do to start?" I asked.

"I already have … it is important you know I'm not what I would call a shaman. I do a few things differently. In my friend's family and their friends' families they pass down through generations the teachings and that way of life. I learned different because I started at age eight on my own, not really knowing what it was or what I was doing till John, my friend's dad, helped me channel myself so I could do good things and help people. Anyway, I guess I'll just jump in and ask the obvious—have you noticed any oddness around the house?"

"Yes, honestly, the oddness in this house is if it is quiet and normal like today. Normally, there are voices, people with purple auras, lights that dim or turn on, nightmares and just recently a walking wall of water and a friendly neighborhood janitor."

"Interesting. Well, it's probably quiet because I was just here the other day and said prayers and incantations in the house. I noticed your two entities that had lived here prior to you, but nothing else. They are here all the time, like roommates, I guess. However, it doesn't sound like you're able to see them all the time."

"Which are the two that are here?" asked Sean, now concerned. So much for the hokum, I guess.

"Your wall of water, that is … Janice. No, no, sorry … Janet, she lived here in the early 2000's. I can't pinpoint when she died. But she keeps trying to tell you she is here and she is trying to tell you what happened."

"What happened?" I asked, nerve-wracked to know there were things there all the time and I was not alone.

"She was a suicide, Cali. She was very sad. I think she had a child die and I think she thought it best to go too. She realizes now that was not a great idea. Hindsight and all that. She got stuck here, but her baby went up to a better place, moved on."

"Oh my, that is so sad, can we help her?" I asked Todd.

"I think so. She managed to drown herself in that bathroom," Todd finished.

I said so quickly I almost interrupted him, "That's what I saw! I went in to take a bath, and it was like water was already the tub but I could tell the water wasn't really there. It got up and went into the kitchen like an oval of a wave, almost like a heat wave, and disappeared.

I felt like I was trying to occupy a space already occupied, so I moved to the master bath. How did she do it?"

"With great determination," Todd said. "She got in the bath brokenhearted and drowned herself. It takes major determination to die like that, because you can easily just get up out of the water. No one or nothing held her down. She just lay there till someone found her a day later. That's when I think the realization hit that maybe it wasn't a good idea, because the baby was not here. The baby was somewhere else. I get the feeling the baby is fine, happy even, so there must be a better place to go to where someone looks after children when they die." Todd was talking to the thin air. Well, at least to me and Sean that's what it looked like. "Janet, I know this is home to you." Todd said loudly then mumbled something with his eyes somewhat shut. "We need to send you on your way, this is not home anymore." He repeated the process of talking low, eyes closed. "The baby is not here! The baby will never be here, she is gone, yes, to heaven, if that was your belief system. All I know from down here is it is better than where we are and it's better than where you are stuck. We need to get you there, Janet, so stay put. Don't disappear anywhere. I can help." Todd mumbled something again with his eyes closed.

He said some prayer called "the white light." It only took a minute, and then he had us all read from the white light prayer together. He laughed and said he needed more juice, as in more power, so we all read together. Then he disappeared to find the four corners of the house and put a drop of oil in the baseboard so it couldn't be washed out. I think it was bamboo oil. Then he got out a metal urn from his pocket.

It fit in his hand, and he put some white leaves in it, burned them and said something else three times that sounded like chanting. "There," he said. "Usually you do the whole house, but I'm not done yet. There is the matter of the auto mechanic, and I don't want to just send spirits into oblivion unless they belong there."

"That's what he is! I thought he was a janitor. I called the cops on him the other day." I laughed and Todd laughed, but Sean did not; he just stood there stupefied, looking back and forth like Todd and I had eaten the same bad nuts.

"Hopefully I can keep them gone for good. These are usually the easy kind. Are you two okay with this? I know I just walked into your house and started spouting all sorts of weird, but this is my job, this is what I do. Really, I don't know anything else. This is my normal. I forget this isn't everyone's normal."

"Well, my normal scares the shit out of me," I said. "I will take any help anyone is able to give me, and if you want to spout all sorts of weird, as you said, this is as good a place as any— my weird home is your weird home."

"Do what you got to do, man," Sean said. "This is crazy that you two see the same things. I'll just sit and ignore; I don't want to see anything."

"Don't worry, not everyone can. Oops, the janitor just walked by. We've got to get to the shed and beat him there before he hangs himself and starts over again. It's like talking someone off a ledge."

Todd ran out the front door, and I ran out the back and caught him before he got to the shed. I unlocked the pull latch as the mechanic walked in and got on what appeared to be a chair. Todd was almost at the shed.

"Stop!" I yelled. "My friend is here and he can see you and help! Stop!" The old man jumped off the chair.

"Shit," Todd said. "I am going to have to try and call him back, or wait till 4:00 p.m. tomorrow. That's when he did it. But if I wait, I don't know if what I did for Janet will last that long. I'll have to start over."

Sean caught up and joined us outside the shed. "So what is his story? Who are you chasing?"

"This man fell on hard times and lost his job when he already could not provide for his family. The family left him here and went to go live with relatives. This was back in the sixties, so he's been here a while. He hung himself here in the shed after realizing he probably would never, ever settle his debt and find work. Again, hindsight—he keeps hanging himself every day after 4:00 p.m. like something will change and it is obviously not going to change. His family never did come back here, and I don't know where they are. I know they're not dead, so I don't know if I can find them. The best way to persuade him to move on is that if he goes to a better place he will finally be able to look out for them."

"Did he hear you? Because he's coming back!" I exclaimed.

"Mr. La Clare! Mr. La Clare!" Todd called. Again he closed his eyes and said something in low, mumbling voice. His hands were open, facing up to the sky at waist level like he was trying to explain something. Then he spoke aloud and quietly told Mr. La Clare what he told us—that he could finally look out for his family if he stopped dwelling and moved on.

He repeated the process of what he did for Janet, and this time he put oil on the four corners of the property line and in the outside wood of the house and shed. He said the white light prayer and we helped again and he burned a bigger pile of the dry white leaves. He got out what looked like a big wand of white leaves, which he said was for smudging, and he went around the entire property.

After we went into the house, Todd said, "I don't think I'll have time to do anything else. Plus, I'm quite drained. If it's okay with you, I would like to smudge again and do every single room in the house. Usually you let them burn out on their own. But I can cut the burning part off and leave it in a pot to burn out on your front step. That will protect for a while from anything getting in. I can come back and finish up another day. Let me know if you see anything else or especially if you see Janet or Mr. La Clare." Whatever he burned smelled wonderful, and he left some out on the step in a pot.

"Are you coming out tonight for a while, Cali?" asked Todd.

"Yes, I think so. Just for a bit. I have training tomorrow, so I'll just stay a couple hours. I'll take my own car so I can leave when I need to."

We all jumped into our vehicles and headed north for the lounges. When we parked and walked in, we found Ashley and Tracy already goofing around on the small dance floor. "Wow, so it's going to be that kind of night." Sean said, he looked compelled to walk back out the door. Then he looked at me and seemed to decide to hunker in for what could be a shit fest if we couldn't reign the girls in.

"It'll be okay. Just wave and head to the bar for drinks and I'll find a table. They'll either settle in and hang out or they'll go off their rockers and be puking by 9:30," I said to Sean.

"Oh, it's not that bad. They're just letting off a little steam," explained Todd. "There's hardly anyone here yet, so they're just taking advantage so they don't have to slap the hands off the salivators waiting to sink in their hooks while they dance."

"Hey, guys and lady, didn't see you come in," said Ashley.

"I can't stay long," I said. "I have training tomorrow, and something tells me this booming music isn't great for a concussed person. I have to say, though, this place is awesome! I like the ambience and the music seems pretty good too." I noticed Todd slide close to Ashley. I raised my eyebrow a little and stared into Ashley's eyes in a silent message: (Seriously, you and Todd?) She got the message and raised her shoulders, but her eyes softened as she looked toward him. I smiled back as if to show my support for the two of them.

Tracy chimed in. "Oh, hell, you couples are making it feel like a love fest in here. Ashley and Todd, and assume Sean and Cali have figured out your … well, your whatever you have between you two Sean?" Blunt as always, Tracy didn't mess around with the facts. I loved her for that.

"We decided we were going to make it official and date exclusively. Try things out."

"Well then, Sean, guess you're not the outsider you thought you were in our group. Looks like you two fit very well. I'm happy you figured it out. Honestly, keeping his weirdo crush a secret was exhausting," Tracy exclaimed.

"I would also like to try out Tracy's blunt but factual way of speaking," said Ashley. "I say we stop harassing Todd for being an intuitive person. He helps people—that's why he just wants to do the job he does at work because he puts all his energy into helping people."

"People like me," I said. "And if he is going to help me, I would like to speak about that openly with Todd without getting harassed. You don't have to agree, you just have to let him be."

"Hear hear, cheers to that," said Ashley of her new man.

"Elephant in the room, let's speak of that! The other couple, Ashley and Todd? Are you sure about this fuggly guy?" said Sean. He was teasing Todd for calling him ugly earlier.

"I think so. I have known for sometime about his passion for helping people. I find that very attractive, plus he's quite attentive." Ashley wiggled her eyebrows and bit her bottom lip.

"Okay, okay, I've had enough. I'm going to the bar." Tracy twitched and wiggled away.

"She is too funny," said Ashley. "She will never admit to having lovey dovey, mushy feelings for anyone. We've been coming here every weekend for three weeks and it isn't for the drinks. Unless she lands that tall, smokin' hot guy at the bar. She doesn't like to be the chaser; she likes to be the one who is chased, swooned after, so to speak."

"Huh, Tracy and the bartender? He looks like he could be a professional fighter. The guys is huge!" I said.

Ashley added, "He must be pretty smart too. Tracy doesn't go for someone who isn't all brains; if he has the muscle too, that's just a bonus."

"I'm glad you two are trying things out," I said, and Sean nodded. "Yes, you two seem to fit together like a beautiful puzzle. Two kind souls who found each other."

Todd kissed Ashley's forehead as she snuggled into his side.

"Well, you all, I told you I would stay for a drink or two, but I think I will stick to just one and go," I said just as Tracy was getting back to the table after a lengthy chat with the bartender.

"Why leave now?" she said. "You just got here an hour ago and we haven't even danced yet."

"Oh, well then, I'm glad I'm leaving. I don't dance," I said with a smile and continued with my explanation. "I haven't been exactly following doctor orders, and that's probably why I still don't feel right. I think I'll head to bed. I have to be at work tomorrow and I can't be flaking out there." I said my goodbyes to my complaining co-workers and left with Sean in tow.

Sean spent the night after we left the club, for other reasons than just to make sure I was okay. I think he needed to make sure I felt great. I wasn't planning on a little tryst, but one could rarely plan these things. I was in my mid-twenties, so of course I was prepared if anything did happen. Though Sean beat me to it with the good old "I have a condom in my wallet" trick. I know we had just decided to move ahead with the relationship, but our bodies had been on overdrive with each other all week—it was just a matter of time before this conclusion was inevitable, so why delay? It got heated fast, and his mouth explored mine with great urgency and with heat deliciously licking up my body every time he caressed my skin.

He made sure he found the time to explore every inch of my body. While I writhed in the agony of my heat, Sean finally put me out of my existential need of this moment of relief, and he plunged in giving me the release I was looking for. Together we found rhythm; he took his time with me, caressing, kissing and licking and bringing heat to the core of my body, building and building. As my back arched high off the bed we ended the night on high. The time with Sean went into early morning; so much for an early night.

Things seemed to be moving fast with Sean, but my body had other thoughts. What I needed, I got in the moment. I could figure the rest out later when my brain wasn't so twisted with hormones.

It was nice waking up with him there. Since work wasn't till ten, we got ready and went out for breakfast. Then of course I went to training and Sean went home. So far his job was giving him everything; he was looking to be the new up-and-comer. His job provided a fancy new car, gave him perks like the restaurant he took me to, support at his art opening, and indeed a new place to rent, which we talked about. It sounded amazing. It was a suite below the penthouse on Marina Side. Man, isn't that where rich people live? I wouldn't know, I just figured with the pictures of the place he showed me it must be. I was worried it would be farther away, but it was not any further than his house now, and it was closer to the new job. I would jump on the offer to move there too. I couldn't blame him. With his new income, he could afford it.

My training went really well over the weekend. Now that it was Monday, I was putting it to use. It was odd not being around the same people. It felt like I was somewhere else, but my friends were just down the hall. If I could call over in time maybe we could catch lunch together. I didn't bring a book, as I was used to having people now, so I hoped I would catch them. The job was just like the training—the only difference was the pace, which was ten times faster. So I missed the lunch hour and decided to eat my lunch in my office. There was a knock and I looked up, thinking I had to deal with a customer relations thing on my break.

That was not it at all; it was Sean. With relief evident on my face, Sean came in and closed the door with his heel. He offered me a coffee and a bottled water from the break room.

"How's the boss's first day?"

"It's going well, I think. I haven't exactly taken a survey out front, but I hope everything is good. I miss you guys, though. I thought I would be able to time my breaks better, but the pace up here is super fast."

"It will take some time to work out a system so you don't feel run off your feet. Every newbie goes through it. It will come, and you will be able to come and go more easily."

"How is training Tracy?" I asked, as Sean rolled his eyes.

"Did you know she's a very honest person?" I laughed at his sarcasm. "Very blunt and sarcastic too," Sean added, and I laughed some more.

"Well, I'm telling you, enjoy the sarcastic banter while you can because soon you will be elsewhere." After a lofty pause, I added, "You'll be missed here not being part of our regular water cooler convention."

"Speaking of being missed, it would be a crying shame if we didn't have an office tryst in your new office when we have the opportunity—soon the opportunity will not be here." Sean came around the desk and pulled me to his body and kissed me devouringly.

"As wonderful as that sounds, if someone barges in here, the whole front office is part of the action. I don't think I'm ready for a twenty-four-way relationship," I joked, trying to feel and look less disheveled.

"Do you feel like company tonight?" asked Sean.

"I can't. I have to go back for my recheck at the doctor's after work, and then I have to get chores done that I ignored for the week."

"Okay, well, I'll see you tomorrow anyway. Maybe we can get together." I smiled at him, leaned in and kissed him deeply and then he was out the door and gone, just like that. I was left all heated up with nowhere to go. Jackass, I thought. I hope he felt the same. Then I smiled to myself at the thought. Man, I could not wait for the day to end. I seemed more tired than usual.

I arrived at the office of the doctor I had seen at the hospital. "Hmm, we may need to do some further digging," he said. "Everything seems okay, but I think I should do a scan just to make sure."

"Okay, thank you," I said as worry flooded into my body "Is everything okay?"

"I am just doing a scan to be on the safe side, Everything looks fine." The doctor explained.

By the time I got home, it was about 7:00 p.m. I did my usual routine of feeding the cat and then cooking and cleaning up after dinner. I also checked in with the car rental place, gave them the gift certificate voucher number, and rented the crossover for another two weeks.

With that done, I called the insurance twenty-four-hour hotline for existing claims. As I guessed it, the accident was my fault and the vehicle was written off. So that meant I had to pay for a new vehicle myself with whatever the insurance company gave me for the written-off vehicle, which probably wouldn't be much. Screw the tea, I was heading for a big glass of red wine. The wine was good and it helped me relax and warmed my insides.

I decided to throw in laundry and then read for an hour. By then I was good and sleepy, thanks to the wine.

I feel like I am out of my body. Before I know it, I am looking down at myself sleeping and then I'm out of my house and in the streets. It's like I am conscious of the fact that I was dreaming, but I am capable of being aware, having control of my own thought process. But I can't control the dream. I am on the streets of Vancouver. I recognize the street but I am in an alley I don't recognize. Then the bartender from the bar the other night comes out the back door with garbage. He walks a little ways down to deposit it in the bin, and on his way back there is a person behind him standing next to the wall. The man looks like he jumped out of an 80s denim fashion show. He comes up behind the bartender, and the hulking bartender turns around but it's too late. The man is wielding a very long sharp knife. The bartender that Tracy had been fond of has just been stabbed. It's like my spirit runs, because the next thing I knew I am hiding behind a green dumpster

I woke up in silence, in awe of what had just happened. I didn't even make it to 1:30 a.m. this time before I woke up from a seriously weird dream. It must have been the wine. It felt so real that I could call the cops and give them every detail. I was sure something had happened and

I was also sure the bartender's name was Jack. But what was I going to say to the police — *excuse me, but while I was dreaming I was floating out of my body I dreamed someone I met got stabbed. Can you please check this address?* Not only would they think I was a crazy lady, but if by chance something happened and they did check it out or got word of it, I was sure they would be calling right back and I would be implicated … this one really kept me up. I thought it was real. I took a sedative and it still took till 2:30 a.m. to go to sleep.

I am somewhat in that state of sleep paralysis. I feel fully awake; in fact, I am sure I am awake. lying in bed. At the foot of the bed is something I can't make out at first because this does not live in our reality—it doesn't make sense, and I cannot move. As I focus on what I'm looking at, this time I see it truly for what it is. This thing is wrong in nature, it feels dark. It is huge, seven feet tall. I can see the face of a smiling, red-eyed demon, and its skin looks melted and haggard. Its face is contorted and the skin on its body is not clothed; it is a weird shade of brown/grey.

The body is well built, and this demon is crawling low to the ground on all fours, its legs moving in unparalleled movements, unnatural-like movements, jerking and twisting about as it grabs me by the ankles and drags me out of the bottom of my bed, across the floor and down the hall into the spare room. Everything looks whole again; there is no broken mirror, no disarray. It's a freakish thing to notice in a split second, but I feel like I am aware of what is going on and I am trying to judge if it is real. It stops and stares at me, as if to notice me actually seeing him. It smiles and then contorts its features in to a monster's sneer.

It still has my ankles, and with no effort except for the features on its face, it throws me into the mirror and I crash to the ground. The mirror breaks and the lamp knocks over and breaks too.

I woke up screaming; that was just too real. The adrenaline coursing through my veins had me shaking. The house felt darker than usual, and I couldn't see a thing except the alarm clock. I quickly turned on my bedside lamp and nothing was there. I was safe; it didn't actually happen, because I was still here in my bed and not bleeding out on the spare bedroom floor. I took a deep breath. It was 3:18 a.m. That was just great, absolutely no sleep at all tonight. I rolled over to turn off the light and noticed a tiny bit of red on my bedsheet, then some more. "What the hell?" Turning around, I saw my sheets were full of blood. There were cuts down my arms. I ran to the bathroom and looked in the mirror. My entire back was sliced up and bleeding. I start crying, and I didn't know what to do.

Then I decided I didn't care what time it was. I picked up the phone and called my sister in Toronto—it was early morning there now, anyway. "Hey, Cali, I haven't heard from you in three weeks, what's up? It's pretty early."

"Sorry, Angie, I have been really busy. I know, I usually talk to you a lot more," I said, still crying.

"Oh, honey, what's the matter?"

"Well, Angie, would you believe I'm calling because I had a bad dream … dreams in fact. But this time I woke up and I'm bleeding everywhere. I don't know what to do," I said, crying into the phone.

"What? What happened?"

I told her about the man being stabbed and about the other dream where I was thrown into the spare-room mirror. I also told her about what I thought happened to Dallas and how the mirror was already broken. She knew what these dreams were like because she got them too. But this was different; he was more real somehow, and this time I got hurt in my dream. "Honey, I am going to treat this like it is real, not a dream," she said. "Get in the shower and rinse your skin, just in case there's debris. Get into a soft cotton shirt you don't mind wrecking and get to the hospital. That's probably all that's open right now, right? It's early there."

"What am I supposed to say to them?"

"Just find an excuse. Is there anything you can think of that would work for falling really hard into glass?"

I thought for a moment. "I had a glass of wine. I'll tell them I had half a bottle and tripped backwards over something on the floor and hit the mirror."

"How you going to get there?" Angie asked.

"I'll drive but tell them I cabbed. I think I'm okay to drive."

"No, you're not. You're very upset and rattled, which screws with your brain and if any of the above of your excuse is partly true, call a cab!"

"Okay, Angie, thanks for being there for me." I sniffled my goodbye into the phone as Angie told me to hurry up and said to call later.

I did call a cab. I felt a little distraught, and my sister, as usual, was right. When I got to the hospital it wasn't busy. There were a few drunks, a car accident and a heart-attack victim. I didn't have to wait long; they'd just pile me in with the drunks after the story I fed them. That put me at number seven in line unless someone was injured worse than I was. I finally I got to see a doctor. Dammit, it was the same guy I had seen for the car accident. I told him my story, though he looked at me skeptically, probably because I wasn't drunk or drugged at the moment except for one sleep sedative that probably wore off with the adrenaline.

"Are you sure you don't want to tell me the truth, like maybe you are having dizzy spells and fell?" I thought *ooooh, that's was a better excuse.* It angered me that he was looking at me scornfully, especially after what I had just been through. Of course, he didn't know what I had been through.

"No, that's not what happened, so I'm not going to say that."

"Well, what did?"

"How about a demon dragged me from behind and slammed me into a glass ceiling-to-floor-length mirror and I cut up my back—does that truth work for you?" I said, perturbed.

"Well, it's better than the first excuse and more colorful, but if this is a domestic thing I will have to call the police and have them press charges against your boyfriend."

"Well, that's great. Do that, but first find me some hot guy to be my boyfriend, then you can call the cops." The doctor looked at me all ornery-like. "Look, I have been up all night I am tired and I am hurt; can you please just fix me and I'll be on my way? I promise you seven ways till Sunday that no one beat me up."

"Okay," said the doctor, and added, "I can see that part is the truth. When you have been in emerg as long as I have, you usually can tell when people are lying. That did not seem like a lie." He started to take a look at my back and clean it up as I winced along. "What about the gentleman that came and picked you up after the accident?" he asked.

"He's a co-worker, and if I am being honest and keeping it real, we did start dating, but this is a recent development and he was not with me, though I wish he was. I had to cab here."

"Well, it's about 5:00 a.m. now. Do you think he would come get you again?"

"Oh gosh, I'm too embarrassed to ask. Plus, we have to work at eight."

"Oh no! There is no work for you for two days. I will write a note. I can even fax it in right now for you." the Doctor said.

"Damn it all to hell! Even when I try to get my shit together, I can't catch a break! Just before meeting you, doctor, I have gotten two raises and got into a car accident and now have a back full of glass and have missed work already."

"Yes, well, you should not have been working at all up till this point. Maybe if you took time to slow down, things wouldn't keep happening to you." That hit home. I couldn't think why a demon throwing me into a wall was a thing that had to happen for a reason, but it did feel like the harder I pushed ahead, the further I fell back. Maybe this guy was right? Maybe there had been too much change in my life and I had not been focussed or coping with that change. This was why weird things were happening.

"I'm going to give you an anti-bacterial cream and dress your back up for you. You can remove it in a day. Also, you can take 800 milligrams of an anti-inflammatory if you are in real pain for a couple days, then cut it back to 400 milligrams for a couple more. If you still need something after that, just regular strength is all you will need for a few days. You can pick that up in any pharmacy."

After he left I got out my phone. "Sean, it's me Cali."

"Hey there, this is a nice surprise to hear your voice early in the morning."

"Well, I thought you might want a repeat of our first morning date—you know, the one where you pick me up from the hospital and we eat bagels for breakfast? Do you want to come get me at the hospital?"

"Are you kidding? You're at the hospital again? What happened?" Sean said. It sounded like he was talking while running around the room trying to find clothes.

"I'll tell you when you get here. Take your time. I'm fine now. I just need a little help, if you don't mind, or I can take a cab. I know you should be getting ready for work now.

"No freaking way. I'm already dressed. Just let me brush my hair and teeth. That's ready enough for work, and I'll be there in a flash."

We disconnected our call. Maybe I should have told him, but I didn't know what to say. Now he sounded really worried. I should have said something to him, I guess.

Sean showed up, and I started to sob. "Hey, Cali, it's okay now. I'm here." He went to hug me.

"Ouch! Ow, ouch!" I tensed up from the hug.

"What's the matter?"

"My back and my arms are all sliced up."

He pulled me back towards the curtained rooms, hustling me into the stall. "I want to see," he said. I kind of felt childish, but I turned around and told him to be gentle with the already bloody shirt.

"You can't see much anyway. I've been bandaged."

"What the hell, Cali, how did this happen?"

"Don't get mad at me! I didn't do this!"

"Sorry, I know you didn't. I'm just worried, not mad. What happened?"

"I had a dream, and at the end of the dream I had the injuries from the dream. Can I finish this talk in the car? I don't want to talk here." Sean cradled me into his side. I gave him my note to give to Mr. Gunderson, and I hoped I wouldn't get fired. I took my prescription to the hospital pharmacy and then we preceded home.

Sean did stop and pick up bagels like I asked, as it was on the way home anyway. When we got to my place Sean bounded through the door like he was expecting someone to be there. I smiled at his concern. We went into the kitchen, and I told him everything that went down. "That's it, we need to call Todd," he said. "He needs to come here. No, actually, you need to leave, that's what. You can stay with me." Sean on a rant was endearing, and a bit funny.

"I think what I need is some tea and a sofa and some of that medication. I feel like I've been whipped. My back is so lacerated."

"I'm afraid to leave you here. Just don't go to sleep."

"I've been up all night, unfortunately, so that's probably what I will do. Just go to work, Sean, and please apologize to Mr. Gunderson. I feel bad that I can never keep on top of my life; it always comes crashing down on top of me."

"Don't worry, I will do my best to handle it. I'm going to ask Todd about this too … is that okay if we come over?"

"Well, I sure as hell don't want to sit here alone all day by myself."

"Okay, I'll see what I can do and call you later to let you know. Maybe by afternoon coffee break I'll give a call to make sure nothing has changed."

"Thanks for all you're doing, Sean."

Sean left, being careful not to touch me and cause me more pain. Every movement seemed to hurt me. I understood his fear of me falling a sleep. I drank as much caffeine this morning as a person could just to not fall asleep. All that did was give me the jitters. A few hours later, sleep came at me hard. Before I knew it I was dreaming. It was a regular old dream about work, how my day went and the hospital. I wasn't aware I was dreaming, though, until it just switched.

I am out of my body again, floating down a road I recognize as Granville. It's very weird, because I'm floating towards an oncoming car. This particular little beige car is driving down the wrong side of the street as he comes up to the Granville Bridge. How did he do that? He is driving all erratic from lane to lane, not to miss cars but just out of control. The driver looks stunned, but there is no panic or worry in his face. He hits a car and it causes a reaction of several cars being involved in an accident. A small car is turned around and is now facing the wrong way.

Another car comes careening along, trying to slow in time so as to not be involved in the accident, and it hits the turned-around car, which acts like a ramp and the car goes over the side of the bridge.

When the car goes on top of the other car and starts to go over the side of the bridge, this is when my body switches views. I go over too, faster, faster, till the cold plunge of the water. I see the person in the car. It looks maybe like a lady, but I can't tell. The hair is long and dark. The jacket is a man's down blue-and-red winter-type jacket. I can't see the face. I can't breathe; I am running out of air.

I woke up gasping for breath like I had truly run out of air. I was not in the disaster, but again the dream felt so real. I needed to know. I turned on the TV and watched the news. After an hour of watching, there was nothing about an accident. Good, something like that would probably be on the news. I decided I wanted a shower, as the bandages were really bothering me, and they felt wet. It felt really gross. I was hoping it was from the ointment and not blood, yuck. I was going to have trouble getting them all off, and I was supposed to wait till later, but it was noon now so they had been on since 5:00 a.m. I figured it was good enough. Man, it was going to hurt to shower, but a bath could cause infection so I would just change the shower-head to the lightest setting. After the shower I would make lunch. I still hadn't fed Dallas, either, but she was not complaining yet. The shower was very painful at first, but as I figured out spray and temperature and took more anti-inflammatories, it started to feel better. I stayed till I ran out of hot water.

Once I was dry, the real question was how to put the bandages back on. I didn't have the same stuff as the doctor, but I thought I was going to be able to do it myself. There was no way. I would have to wait till someone got here. I put on a clean cotton tee and wrapped my hair in a towel for now. I was starving. "Dallas, kitty, let's go get a treat," I yelled a couple times as I walked down the hallway. I never knew where she was. She came out from hiding and I fed her, and as promised I put a treat right on top her food. I loved that grumpy cat. I made lunch for myself and went to hang out in the living room.

"WHY DO YOU STAY CHILD?" I turned and saw the woman and child again, glowing in their purple aura.

"I don't know why I should be the one to leave. I don't deserve this!"

"THEY BOTHER YOU BECAUSE OF WHO YOU ARE, TO TRY AND LESSEN WHO YOU ARE."

"Who are they? What do you mean because of who I am? And why do I need to be less than?"

"THE MAN THAT PUSHES YOU AROUND LIKE YOU ARE A CHILD ... HE IS NO GOOD."

"What, Sean? He's been taking care of me. I was a little thrown off by the way he handled a conversation at work and the way he pulled at me at the hospital today as he worked me into a room. I think he was worried, and you're a ghost, so I don't need to explain myself to a hallucination!"

"YOU DO NOT NEED HIM TO TAKE CARE. YOU NEED TO GET OUT. YOU DON'T BELONG HERE IN THIS WORLD."

Just then the doorbell rang. It was a little early to be the gang. I looked into the corner and of course the lady and child were gone. I went to the window and looked. It was a flower delivery service. "See, Sean is awesome," I said to the empty room. I opened the door, signed for the flowers and put them on the table in the kitchen where I spend most of my time. They would be visible from the living room. I opened the card.

I heard you were hurt. I was at Tony's today ... flight delay and change of plans. I was there to introduce my replacement. I am leaving the furniture world and moving into a different career in Victoria. I hope you are okay. Sean said it was a bad fall. I am very sorry you are going through a difficult time. I'm also sorry I lied. I don't think I can give up just because you and Sean are a couple; there is something there, Cali, I feel it. I don't mean to be disrespectful. I only want to say the truth. If you tell me to buzz off, you will never hear from me again. I just wanted you to know I still would like to get to know you if you let me pursue whatever this feeling is.

xo

Deacon.

My mouth dropped at the choice of his words. I didn't know how to feel about it. I thought, *Wow, the guy is ballsy … I'll give him that.*

I didn't think Sean told him the part where we had only know each other for a couple months and dated for two days; but then again, neither did I. We were not exactly an item, but the fact that Sean was there for me when no one else could be held a lot of weight.

Though that damn ghost got into my mind about what she said about Sean, now I felt conflicted. If that ghost was a hallucination, then that would mean I felt that way about Sean—that he was pushy and dominant over me. But I didn't think I felt that way, and plus, I was not convinced that the apparition wasn't real; she said other comments about things I didn't understand. What was she talking about?

The flowers were gorgeous. If Sean saw them, what would he do? They were so beautiful. I didn't think there was any harm in keeping them. The flowers cheered the place up a bit and made me feel lighter, happier. My phone started ringing—like his ears were burning, Sean was calling. His picture was showing up on my phone. "Hey Sean, what's up, are you still coming over after?"

"Hi, yes, we are. Sounds like the whole crew is coming over. Is that okay?"

"Yes, see you all in a few hours. Hey, do you think you can pick up some 4x4 quilted gauze pads and some first aid tape? I need to replace the bandages. I don't have the right stuff here."

"Sure, we will be there as soon as we can." After I hung up I went in search of a new restaurant menu for supper.

When 6:00 p.m. rolled around a group of cars came in together on my street—looked like everyone took their own cars here today. The neighbors were going to think I was having a party. Mind you, the only people on the block I had met were already dead. My co-workers and friends had bags with them with the family Italian restaurant logo on them. Looks like I didn't even need to think about supper; everything was taken care of. I greeted them at the door. "Hey everyone, I saw you pull up through the window. Come on in."

CHAPTER 7
What The Cards Say

"Hey girl, just came to see how you are and have diner, but then I have to bounce," said Tracy. "I want to go see if Jack is around. He's the bartender from the other night." She winked at me and wiggled her way in. I didn't think Tracy was capable of walking without swaying her curves. The color drained from my face, and not without notice from both Todd and Sean. "Jack? That's his name?"

"Yeah, he's a sweetie. I'm going to go ask him out. I figure if he won't, I will." With determination in her stance and a glittering smile, Jack wouldn't stand a chance—he would have to say yes if he was alive.

"What's the matter, Cali? You look like you're going to throw up," Ashley said as she peeled off her jacket.

"I think I just need my meds and some help with changing my bandages," I weakly stated; I was feeling a little green at the mention of Jack from the bar.

"I've got them, and I saw how the doc taped you up. I can help you re-bandage," said Sean. "Why don't the rest of you dig around the kitchen and get what we need out for supper? We won't be long."

"Ever the boss," said Tracy to Sean. But she strutted to the kitchen just the same to help out. Sean and I went into my bedroom and I undressed and used a towel to cover my front.

I knew we were dating, but I just wanted to get this done with after what Tracy said. I didn't want all of me showing when I felt sickly ill and torn up—quite literally. "Is it about the bandages and meds, or is there something else that's upsetting you?" Sean got out the ointment and bandages and started working on me. I took the medication again and winced every time he touched me; everything hurt.

"Jack is his name—that's what threw me. The guy Tracy likes. I saw him in a dream this morning, and from then I knew his name was Jack I was hoping I was wrong. Sean, he was stabbed in my dream. Now I feel like he won't be there tonight. I feel it was real."

"That is a very horrid dream. I knew his name was Jack, though, maybe you heard me say it."

"Maybe that's it," I concurred, but that didn't feel right. Once we were done, Sean helped me into a hoodie. I couldn't wear a bra and it didn't feel right in a room full of people to be in a t-shirt with my boobs out. It just wasn't that kind of day.

Everyone was in the living room watching the news and waiting for me. That's when it came on— the news anchor said, "Take your time out there today, and if you're headed out near the Granville Bridge you are going to be in for a delay. An accident happened just a couple hours ago.

A car went the wrong way on the bridge and caused a seven car pileup with an eighth car going over the bridge. Police are still trying to get divers and searchers to the area. The delay will be a while. There is a truck rolled over on Highway 14 and spilled logs are the cause in that delay. Police are asking you to find alternate routes. In other news, multiple stabbings happened last night. Six people were taking to hospital in a neighborhood drug dispute in front of a Richmond apartment, and another stabbing took place in behind Blue Light Lounge. No motive has yet been determined."

Tracy and Ashley spoke at the same time. "Oh dear God,"

"We were just there; that is super scary," said Ashley. Then I went down like a felled tree. I fainted, hitting the side of the sofa before hitting the floor. When I came to, I was in my bedroom with Ashley staring at me and Sean sitting in the chair by the side of the bed.

"Are you okay?" asked Ashley.

"Yes, I think so. Maybe I just need to eat. All those meds on an empty stomach."

"You weren't out long. Just a couple minutes. I'll tell everyone you're okay and to start plating. I'll get one made for you too. Spaghetti or Fettuccini Alfredo?" Ashley asked.

"Spaghetti, please."

Off she went, leaving me with Sean. "Are you okay?"

"No, I think we need to eat and get everyone the hell out of here. I need to talk to Todd alone. I don't want to scare the other women."

"Are you not going to tell Tracy your dream?"

"No! What if I'm wrong? If she goes there and he's at work, then everything is okay. If not, well, I will tell her then … maybe."

"I think you should tell her instead of her going there to find out on her own. That's cruel when you have information she could possibly use. It's on the news. You can't be wrong; by the sounds of it, you're very correct."

"Sean, please, this is my freaking disaster, let me handle it how I see fit. I have no choice because I have no proof. I'm not going to upset her for no reason. Not only that, but she will think I'm a freak. Now, if your done telling me what to do, I'd like to go eat." I got up and left him to follow behind.

"Hey everyone," I told the group. "Sorry for my little interlude. I'm good now … better if I can eat. Hey Todd, do you think I can speak with you after everyone leaves and when you're done eating?" I tried to convey my wishes in one sentence hoping the others would get the gist and leave after the meal.

"Sure, no problem. I wanted to do a reading, remember? Maybe we can do that too."

We sat down to eat, and I told everyone my back injury story. I decided to tell the truth although I was ready to run with the "I fell" story. The group just balked at me in disbelief. "I know, my weirdness is a bit much."

"It's okay, Todd is weird too. We're used to it," said Tracy, filling in her two cents. Gauging from the way they handled that story I thought maybe I could tell them the rest.

"That accident on the news … I was there, I saw it."

"Which accident? Are you okay? Oh, for all things holy, did you get hurt in that too?" said Tracy.

"No, here is some more weird for you. I was sleeping, and I astro-projected out of my body. That's right, I had to look it up. I didn't know what I was doing till I looked it up on the internet. A piece of me just up and leaves my body while I'm sleeping. That's how I got hurt. I went out of my body somehow and the demon was there and he threw me against the wall. I have absolutely no control over when I leave my body or why. I saw the lady drown when she went off the bridge. She hit a spun-around car and it lifted her front end up and over, and she was driving too fast. She just fell, and I fell with her. I know where she is. I didn't know it was a women at first, but I'm pretty sure for some reason now. I know where she is, but I can't tell anyone. Am I supposed to call the cops and say I had a dream and I dreamed of the car accident and the lady flew off the bridge, hit the water, the window broke out and she got sucked out of her car and is stuck on a sweeper branch in the water? No one would believe me!"

"That is just incredible," said Tracy.

"I don't think you will think so after my next story." This time everyone just stopped what they were doing and Sean stared at me and nodded for me to go on. "Tracy, if you go to Blue Light, it would be safer for you if you took Ashley with you. That is, if Ashley can go?" I looked at Ashley to confirm. She nodded yes, and I continued. "Please don't be upset at me; it's just a dream. I don't know if it's even real."

"What do you know, Cali?" Tracy said calmly. We all just stared at each other and I was looking back and forth from Sean to Todd, looking for what I should do or if I should say anything. Sean nodded for me to continue again. "Cali, damn it, what do you know!" yelled Tracy.

Shit, I knew this would happen. "I saw Jack in a dream. He went to the alley to take out garbage and got jumped." She didn't even let me finish. She jumped up and left the house in a huge hurry.

Ashley scrambled to catch up to her. "Don't worry, I'll talk to her, Cali, this isn't your fault. Besides, it might not be him, right?"

"Absolutely right, Ashley. I wasn't actually there. I was here at home."

"I'll calm her, it will be okay," she said.

"Well, she's gone so you better follow and make sure she is," said Sean. With that, Ashley left.

"Hey, I would like to talk to Cali," Todd said. "Do you think we could have an hour? Maybe you could go with the ladies, Sean, and check in with them and come back?"

Sean looked to me.

"I know we just started dating," I said, "but I too would like to do this in privacy. You are more than welcome to come back if you want, but don't feel you have to on my account. I'll be okay."

"That's what you always say, Cali. I don't think that has been accurate once yet. If you want me gone for privacy, that's fine. I'll go catch up to the others. But I'm coming back." He left somewhat huffy, but with concern in his eyes and in his words. That left me a little confused, and I felt like I had more than one red flag raising.

"Well, now that the news is out, we can continue with what you wanted to talk about." said Cali.

"I didn't know you can do those things, Cali, you must have the same natural abilities as mine."

"I don't know. I don't know what I'm doing. Trust me, I don't want to be out flying around when I should be sleeping. I'm a freaking nervous, tired wreck. I just want to be normal."

Todd laughed. "I think you missed the mark on that one; no chance in hell you're just average or normal." I grimaced and started cleaning up after supper. It wasn't a big job; it was just a matter of throwing away containers and plasticware.

"Look, normal is highly over rated. You don't want to be normal. You're just going through a lot right now. We can figure this out. I wanted to do a reading. I thought I would need my cards, but there is so much energy here, I won't need them.

"Let's sit down and have tea and you can tell me what you would like to say." I got the tea ready and poured and we got started. He started speaking like the information was going to burst from him. I just let him keep going and going unless I really needed to stop to ask a question. "I wanted Sean to leave because I didn't want his energy affecting what I say. There is more than one protector in your life; they are here to share the truth with you no matter what happens to them—they are here to help you. They are on their way to you or they have already put in a foothold and you know about them already. Two different parties, and from what I am seeing they don't travel together, and both groups have different energies. I am starting to think one group may not be of this world. This is where I get scrambled. It's like the universe doesn't want me having the information. I can't see past the static. There is also one man who is your saving grace. The other is your tormentor—two men in your life, not one. You will have nightmares because of one of them and they or just one will make your life more than a little uncomfortable. I really can't see who is who, although I would like to stick up for my friend and say he is outstanding." Todd smiled and I meekly smiled back, though I was concerned. "There are yet more obstacles in your way. You are heading down a path and you are not supposed to be on it.

Until you have a realization, these so-called life fiascos are just going to keep coming till you change course. The one you are on is not right; you are not supposed to be here on this path."

"Stop! That's where I need to ask you a question. What do you mean I'm not supposed to be here on this path?"

"Literally your life path is wrong and the more changes you make to adhere to that path, the more painful and heart wrenching this journey will be for you. Why, is there something you're not telling me?"

"I don't know, Todd. I'm not sure what I haven't told you. Wait, have I told you about the woman and the child in the purple light that came to me just this afternoon before Sean called and they ask me why I stay?" I explained the other things they said as well. "What the hell does that all mean, Todd?" I was breathing heavily after my long rant trying to remember everything.

"I don't really know. Maybe we should figure out who *they* are first, then figure out who it is that's bothering you intentionally. As for the 'you don't belong here in this world,' that is a new one to me. If I can't figure out the first few questions I have, I may have to ask for help from the shaman. Let's go back to the reason I came to talk to you first; we will handle this sequentially. It sounds to me like these light beings with the auras are trying to share information with you, so maybe they are the ones helping. If they come back, try and treat them with respect and listen to what they have to say. They always speak fragmented and beat around the bush. Nothing is ever straight forward. But if you listen well, maybe we can figure it out together. Maybe they are one of the groups looking out for your well-being. I know Sean has been, so maybe he is the other group. Any ideas on who else it could be, Cali?"

"No, not even a little. I treat all ghosts, demons and apparitions the same because they are unwanted. Maybe you're right about the purple aura ghosts, or whatever they are—maybe they are trying to help me. I refused to listen because of their riddles. I'll do better and listen if they ever show up again. I'll try and figure out what they meant this time too. As for the party who looks out for me, I mean, I have family—maybe it's my sister. She was very helpful the other night."

"No, like I said, this is another male energy. Who are the flowers from? Sean?"

I blushed. "No, they're from Deacon. He said he heard about my 'fall' and wanted to give me flowers with all that has been going on. He said something about moving? That's it I think. Well that and he likes me, but that is not new."

Todd looked pensively at the flowers. "He could potentially be the other person who cares about your wellbeing and is taking care of you." I looked at Todd like he was out of his mind.

"I hardly know the guy. Met him twice for five minutes, as a matter of fact. That is not our other person."

"Well, Cali, maybe he will be. I mean, he is changing from law at a manufacturer to civil and criminal law right in Victoria ... a hop, skip and a jump across the way."

"Law?" I said questioningly. "I thought he was a representative like me and you."

"He fills in when he's in town and is the closest person to deal with a matter, but he is their lawyer and bills them as such. That's why he's grateful to you for finding the errors within the company; it could have caused him quite the headache later."

Someone knocked on the door and Sean walked in. "You guys done yet? We got to talk."

"Yeah, I think so. What's up?" I asked.

"It was Jack. Tracy is beside herself. She didn't really know him that well, but she wanted to, and she was into him. It really freaked her out and I think it made things worse that you knew beforehand. Ashley managed to make the point that if you didn't know or warn her then she would have just thought he was not at work that night and he was at home or something. Instead, she knows he's at the hospital. What about Cali; is she going to be in danger again?" Sean asked.

"Truthfully, tonight I don't know," Todd said. "I can do a few things to help, but from what I know, whatever it is bothering her is determined and strong willed, well, very strong in general. I hope I'm a strong enough match."

"Is Tracy going to the hospital to check on Jack?" I asked.

"I don't know. She thinks it may be weird if some girl just shows up there out of the blue from the club. Ashley told her if she was really concerned there is nothing wrong with checking to see if he is okay, even if she doesn't see him."

"What a mess this all is. You're right. I'm on the wrong path. Everything I do just makes things worse."

"Don't be hard on yourself," said Sean. "I kind of pushed you into it, so I'm sorry for that.

Hey, more flowers … those are new. Who are they from?" he asked.

"I guess you told Deacon I fell or something and I got really hurt and would not be in. He sent flowers and said he was leaving his post at the company and moving to Victoria."

"That guy just doesn't quit, does he. He is like lice you can't get rid of, yuck. No does not mean no to him. I don't get it—why'd you keep them?"

"Well, they're pretty, and they go nice with Ms. Janssen's on the next table. Also, the flowers I got this week make me happy."

"Well, I guess if you need is another man's flowers to make you feel better while you go through hell, then I guess its fine by me."

Well, that was a snub if I ever heard one. While trying to disregard the situation with cool dissatisfaction, Sean's "trying to be cool" was not working. When he walked into the kitchen to get a drink, Todd and I both sniggered.

"Maybe he just feels bad 'cause he didn't get you flowers. Maybe he should stop pouting and get you flowers."

"I'm good, really. He has been really off today; maybe this is all too much for him. Maybe this 'hokum,' as he calls it, is just the reason why he couldn't tolerate talking about it."

"I'm right here and yes, the hokum is a bit much. And yes, I'm tired of the person I'm dating being a punching bag for whatever is going on. It is non-stop. Yes, I think it is stupid you keep flowers from another guy." Sean seemed completely off his wheel. "Am I wrong to think this is all a little nuts! Did she show you her back, Todd? Have you seen your girlfriend look like someone whipped the hell out of her? Yeah, I'd say I have a right to be worried and upset."

"Sean, maybe you should go," I said. "You obviously are very upset about what has been going on. Take some time and just do normal for a while. I totally get it, just go." He kissed my forehead, but he stormed out the door like he had lost his mind.

"Are you okay here? I'm sorry about Sean. I don't know why he's acting this way."

"Tell you the truth, Todd, I haven't known him as long as you and this is the only way I have seen him act other than when he has been my knight in shining armor a couple times and at our lovely dinner," I said with a grimace. "Don't you worry about me. I can take care of myself. Plus, you have a girl-friend to find. Go see if everything is okay."

"Okay, Cali, I'll check in tomorrow. If I think of anything else to help you I will try to get hold of John. If I can't help anymore, maybe the shaman can."

I was relieved to be alone, but then not. That visit did not go well. I wondered if I would have friends tomorrow. I was not at work again, so I could give them a breather from the crazy that was my life. This was why I didn't keep friends or jobs. It was too hard to have all this going on and still live a normal life. It was hard not to be exhausted from it all. I was so tired of my life being this way. I felt done. Not caring what time it was, I decided to go to bed.

***

Tracy had made it to the hospital parking lot with Ashley. "I don't know what I was thinking coming here. He doesn't even really know me. I can't go in."

"Don't worry about what it looks like. This was made more personal for you because a friend knew about it first. That's the part that's bothering you—how you found out."

"How did she even know? I mean, how does that happen? Things like that just don't happen! You don't just know the future or the present or whatever."

"I think some people do, Tracy. More people than we think. I think it's more prevalent in our society and people are just afraid to talk about it because it's a faux pas. I mean, look how upset you were at her, at the situa-tion—would you want to be on the receiving end of that? Cali would have been way better off if she just kept her mouth shut and let you find out about Jack for yourself."

Tracy looked up from her lap to respond. "I know, what she did was prob-ably hard to do and now she regrets it because we all ended up storming out."

"Todd stayed behind; he understands her better than any of us. They have a lot in common. Sean just came to find us because Todd wanted to talk to her alone," suggested Ashley. "Tracy, we don't have to go in. We can just talk to the nurse and see if he is okay and leave. It will put your mind at ease. I have to ask you, though, not to prove your point or anything, but do you know his last name? I'm only asking because we can't find out anything without it."

"Ugh, yes, you just proved my point. I don't know him well enough to be doing this. Maybe we should just leave," Tracy declared.

They sat in silence a moment, then Tracy, in a soft voice, uttered, "Hollander. That's his last name." She side-glanced at Ashley.

"Then let's go in and see what we can find out," replied Ashley.

They asked a nurse in emergency if they could locate where he was. He had already been admitted since it had happened in the middle of the night, which was about twenty or so hours ago. The emergency nurse directed them to a unit to go and ask in general admittance. By this time, Tracy was pale and nervous. Ashley spoke to a unit clerk to find out where Jack was, and as they were talking to her a voice came from one of the rooms. "Tracy?" They turned and two doors down from the unit desk they could clearly see Jack. He saw us walk in.

Tracy nervously looked at the nurse and then walked toward Jack. "What are you doing here? Are you visiting someone?" asked Jack.

"Hi, well, you … actually, I came to see you, Jack. I know it's a little weird. I honestly just meant to find out from a nurse if you were okay. I went to the bar and … "

"It's okay, Tracy, thank you for checking on me," Jack interrupted. "Actually, the food sucks and I am bored out of my mind, so company is good."

"I … I don't really know what to say. How are you, are you okay? What happened?"

"I'm fine, really. I should get out tomorrow or the next day. The dumbass missed anything vital, so I just got tore up a bit. I need healing time. I got jumped. I guess he figured I had money or something. I didn't know the guy, and I don't think I have ever seen him in the bar. I'm pretty good with faces. I don't really know why me or why this happened, but I'm going to be just fine."

"While I'm here would you like me to get you anything, sneak some food or some magazines or something?" Tracy offered.

"Why don't you sit and tell me about your day? Keep me company. For as long as you wish, or however long the nurse will let you stay." Tracy looked at Ashley and Ashley nodded and headed to the cafeteria to get coffee.

***

I looked at the clock on the bedside table and it said 9:48 p.m. Good, time to take a sleeping pill and hopefully sleep peacefully through the night. Not that I didn't know I was asking too much. It took a while to fall asleep with my mind racing around all my live events.

But sleep came to me finally.

I am with Sean and I can't tell where…we are in a gorgeous room, so not my house, and we're having a drink. He leans in and kisses her, she kisses back. He rubs his hand along the side of her arm and takes both their drinks and puts them on the glass table in front of them. They're sitting on a dark-grey-colored leather sofa, plush and gorgeous and comfortable. He leans in again and lays her back a little. He kisses at her neck and nibbles by her earlobe and makes his way to kiss her mouth.

She has her hands on the front of his chest and can feel the corded muscle working underneath; he is a handsome man. He decides to get up off the sofa and pulls her up too. Her feet hit a long, shaggy white carpet and then she is lifted off her feet. Sean picks her up and her legs wrap around his waist and her hands around his neck. He's walking with her facing backwards so she can't really see where she's going. Out of her side vision she can see the one wall is covered with windows and has a view of the city. The other wall is a dark grey. He kisses her and kisses her to get her attention back to where he wants it, to where she wants it, as he walks her toward the bedroom. She's enjoying every minute of his attention. She crosses the threshold into another room. She stops kissing him to turn back and look around.

His bedroom is done in creams and dark and light grays as well, sleek, like him. His bed, over-sized, takes up a good portion of the room. She turns back to look at him, and his shirt is already off. It disappeared at the door, and she looks down and something is very wrong. His feet are hooves, his legs bent like an animals, and are like fur and human skin, ripped, corded strength running through those legs. She looks up to see the demon. He throws her on the bed. "Now you see what I can do, what I do." He snarls an ungodly snarl ...

I woke with tears in my eyes, unable to move. I was safe at home, not wherever I was before. Why would I dream Sean was the devil? Where the hell was I, in that place, in that room? I couldn't help replaying the dream over and over in my head. Trying to go over what I saw, what I thought happened. My mind was not able to think right for a long time, and I felt violated. The clock said 4:00 a.m. Good enough. I needed to get up. I couldn't stay in that bed a moment longer.

Once I was up, I took the bandages off. Should be time to go without them anyway. I jumped in the shower, which was a bit of daily routine to help get that nightmare out of my head. Then I got dressed and towel dried my hair. I was not going anywhere today anyway, so jogging pants and a hoodie would be just fine. Although if I need my bandages redone, I may have to go to a doctor. But I didn't think so; they were healing well. I walked to the kitchen. I figured tea instead of coffee may be the better option this morning. As I made the tea I was already able to think a little more logically.

Although I couldn't explain the place or where I was in the dream, I could technically decipher the dream. There was no doubt there was chemistry between Sean and I; a chemistry that both of us would like to explore.

Sean playing devil's advocate yesterday and being miserable about everything made him a bit of an ass. My subconscious just turned him into the ass of all asses, the jackass from hell— hooves and all. I would rather think that as the cause than any other hocus-pocus nightmare situation; it made logical sense, even though my dream took it to the extreme. That nightmare was one I would not soon forget. The way he talked right to me was too real. Thinking about it had me frightened all over again. I didn't feel alone in my house. I now felt like the presence was with me. That darkness was there in the house and now inside of me. I couldn't shake it. Anxiety crept in, my feelings electrifying my body. I could not think straight anymore.

CHAPTER 8

Life Sometimes Goes Up In Smoke

Being at home for the second day in a row was definitely not fun, but considering what Todd said yesterday, maybe it held merit. Maybe everything was moving too fast—could that be what he meant? What this all meant? The job, the two promotions, the instant friends, not to mention instant boyfriend who has a super crush, a house and permanent job, all in the space of a year, most of it in the space of two weeks. I mean, that was bound to cause a ripple in life, right? I don't get it, though. This has been happening my whole life, not just two weeks of it. I do notice that when things get normal and I do what everyone else calls day to day, my life seems to go up in smoke. I can't seem to do normal without shit hitting the fan. I find it impossible for me to continue doing the normal things in life, like full-time work, friends—anything that would require permanency never really exists for me because the oddities I deal with and live with can keep that from happening. I can't just get a promotion, no, I get in a car accident too.

I get an unheard-of second promotion and I'm kept home for two days with the excuse "I fell" attached. I guess that's better than *Oh, sorry, Mr. Gunderson, I had a bad dream, and in my bad dream a demon threw me into a mirror and the funniest thing happened. I woke up soaked in blood ... funny, right, Mr. Gunderson?* Even in my thoughts I am sarcastic. I spent some of the morning reflecting on what Todd said. I knew it made sense, but I didn't know how to connect the dots.

I spent till early afternoon contemplating what the apparitions said: were they helping me? What they said couldn't hurt me, well, except that I didn't belong in this world. That sounded rather threatening.

120

It was 6:00 a.m. I decided to get breakfast and find Dallas and feed her; she had been hiding for quite some time. As I was finishing breakfast, the doorbell rand. I already know who it was. Only one person showed up this time of day, but I checked the window to make sure. "Hello, Sean. Come on in."

Sean opened the door with a greeting: "Hello, Cali, I bought an apology vanilla bean latte. It got me out of hot water before, so I was hoping it would work again." He handed me the coffee and then tried for small talk. "Its already warm outside … well, warmish. It's supposed be plus ten today. You should get out of the house for while while it's nice this afternoon."

"Sean, it's nice of you to bring coffee, but really, if you're going to argue with me every other day, well, that's a lot of coffee. I don't need the calories, and though an apology tastes better with vanilla, it starts to lose its effect if it's all the time. I get that you're jealous of Deacon, but he is not here, you are. I get you're mad I kept the flowers. Maybe you have a point on that one. I just thought they were too pretty for the garbage." I delivered my point again.

"You know what, Cali? You're right. Well, I don't know about being jealous about Deacon, but I can see you think the flowers are pretty and pretty does not belong in the garbage.

I'm just maybe overwhelmed a little and overreacting. I don't think I knew what I was getting into. I like you Cali, but the stuff that happens to you hurts you, and it is a hard pill to swallow."

"If this is too much for you, I totally understand. It's too much for anyone, myself included; there is no reprieve. It has been a little worse now than it usually is. It's not normally an everyday thing, but it certainly has been since I moved to Vancouver. I'm exhausted from it too. I understand if you made a mistake in asking me out. You didn't know the whole truth about me. Though I would appreciate it if you didn't share this information about me with anyone."

"I don't want to give up, Cali, unless you want me to. No, I didn't know about all of this, but you are still you, Cali, and everything I said in the past about what I see in you I still see. You are beautiful, smart and driven. I like everything about you. I don't like seeing you hurt, I don't like competing for your affection so maybe I can admit to that much. Look, I will let you be today, unless you need me. Don't hesitate to call. Just think about what you want. I know what I want, Cali Stenson." He stared at me a moment, backed out of the doorway and he was gone.

Shit, maybe he was right. He acted like an ass, but what he said made sense. No one could get used to this. I was twenty-four and had been dealing with nightmare situations for twenty years. How could I expect Sean to be okay with it in a week? He may never be okay with it. What kind of future would I have with any man? I mean, really, who wanted to deal with this shit? I sat on the sofa depressed for a while. Which was a good thing, because it ended up kicking me in gear. I needed to get things done to deal with everything.

I needed to see about a new car, I needed to see the doctor to see if he thought my concussion was still a problem. I needed to get out of the damn house and go for a walk. Maybe I needed to see my regular doctor to see if he could get me into a psychologist or psychiatrist. Maybe I was not a freak for paranormal stuff. Maybe I was sick. Maybe I was causing stuff to happen. Maybe I was crazy for real, and if that was the case maybe it could be medicated away.

I made few phone calls and then I pulled my hair into ponytail and put on a nice fall jacket to cover up the fact that I look like I was going to the gym in loose clothes and left the house. I went to my same dealership where I bought my car and purchased a new crossover that I had been looking at online. I had done a lot of my research prior to actually coming in to the dealership. No more little cars for me; I loved my little hatchback, but this Rav4 was going to give me exactly what I needed. I thought insurance processing my claim would take longer than it did, but they had already had adjustors out to the vehicle and they wrote it off, gave it a dollar amount and when I called that morning they said the cheque was ready; they hadn't had time to call, considering it was only 10 a.m. So I went, picked up the cheque, signed it over to the dealer and the first payment was secured.

I didn't get much for the totalled vehicle, but I was prepared for that burden. I kind of felt like I deserved that. I drove off the lot, and was off to the next thing to cross of the list. It was now afternoon and I went to my general practitioner. I told him some of what was going on. I said I was stressed and I'd had a car accident, and that I hadn't been doing well, and I wondered if I could see someone for that.

As he was looking for counsellors for me, I blurted, "I see stuff, like, I think hallucinations. That's the real reason I'm here. It's nonstop and it controls my life and how I live." He looked at me a minute and asked me to describe what I see. Of course I didn't tell him every single thing, as I would have to write a book. But I told him about the wall of water, mechanic, nightmares, poor sleep and the demon monster thing. I could barely speak, but I gave him the important points. He wrote a prescription, and he said he would send a referral and let me know when he heard back. I thanked him and got the hell out. I couldn't believe I just did that.

I went back to my vehicle, relieved and happy at its newness. It took some of the burden away from what I had just done in the doctor's office. I might have to find a new doctor. I felt so embarrassed about going in and saying those things. He must have thought I had lost it. I decided to have lunch and then I would go for a walk. I stopped at a local diner for a sandwich and soup and then headed home to see how the new crossover looked in the front drive. It was nice out, and the sun just made a rare appearance. I wasn't going to let that pass me by. I decided I would walk to the grocery store and fill two weeks' of the prescription and try it out. Then I could get a coffee on the way back.

It was not far, only ten minutes to the store, it would give me time to think everything through. Doctors like to prescribe, and side effects of these types of medications, if the television commercials were any indication, could be horrendous, but I could find out once I got to the pharmacy. What if it did get rid of all of this?

What if it was all in my head and I took medication and it was gone or even just diluted. Wouldn't that be better? But then what did that mean? Todd had seen them too … did he need meds? Why would I need meds and he wouldn't? I mean, he was the one that clarified that the dead guy was a mechanic, not a janitor.

I looked up and the sidewalk had vanished, turned into a park. I turned around. Nothing looked familiar; how did I get here? I walked to the store all the time, so how did I get into a forested park? I wasn't paying attention, I would have noticed walking into a wooded area instead of on pavement! Not only that, but there was no park in the direction of the store, and definitely no wooded area. *"I am glad you came to see us so we do not have to come to you,"* announced the lady with the child in the purple light.

"Where am I? How did I get here? What do you want?"

"I brought you here. you did not get here on your own. I warned you, I am trying to help you, listen to me!"

"Listen about what? I'm on my way to go and get medication to make this all go away."

"Medication will not change who you are, just defuse and confuse who you are."

"What does that mean? Who am I? Who am I to you? And why do you want to help me?" I said, trying to control my frustration.

"I cannot divulge your path early. That is against the rules. I am no one to you, child, but I came to help."

"Just like Todd said, but why so cryptic? Why not just say what you want from me and be done with it?" I was getting frustrated and wanted out of wherever I was.

"That is finally the right question. I want nothing, but they do, the others who seek your attention, the others who keep you up through visions. I can only say and do so much. It takes every scrap of energy I have just to be heard by you. I can do no more for you. Find out who you are, why the others want you, why they torment you. That is where your truth is."

They faded away with their last cryptic message. "Wait, how do I find out? What do I have to do? Why can't you tell me more?" I was back on the street yelling at the newspaper box. There was a guy two doors down mowing his lawn and trying to pretend to mind his own business while the lady walking her dog crossed to the other side of the street. Great, that's just great, now I look like the crazy lady. What do I do? Do I get the pills? Do I listen to the ghost who says "don't get the crazy pills?" Or do I keep walking and go get them because as of right now the newspaper box isn't talking back, and I do look pretty crazy standing here deliberating. I decided to go to the store and fill the prescription. I don't have to take them if I didn't want to, but I'd have them.

I laughed when I got the prescription and read the side effects. *May cause drowsiness, may cause, in some cases hallucinations, may cause restlessness or nervousness, may cause sleeplessness, may cause weight gain.* Great, so the side effects of the medication were what I was trying to get rid of. Sleepless nights, hallucinations, and restlessness or nervousness? No problem, I do that every day, but gaining weight on top of it? What the hell, man? Was I not going through enough that they had to make me gain weight too? It said people had gained up to fifteen pounds! Awesome, that was the only word that came to mind. Oh, and the price tag for two weeks of the pills—forty dollars! What a system, curing crazy causes crazy and you get to go broke doing it while you get fat! Now I needed to add liquor to the coffee. Those facts had strained my brain and I couldn't get over what I was possibly going to try.

Not only that, but I had enough of a crazy day on the way over; did I really have a choice? No, I didn't think so. I grabbed the coffee, the prescription and raced home so I didn't have to go back to the watchers in the woods. When I got home, the UPS man was coming back down my driveway. "You live here?" he asked.

"Yes, this is my place."

"I have a couple packages that need signing for."

"Oh, okay, sure." I signed and then proceeded to the house to unlock the door. The man brought a large package and a smaller one into the house. I thanked him and shut the door. I opened the boxes' the art from the gallery had arrived.

I had totally forgotten about it in all the hubbub. I decided the picture of me would hang in my room, so I went and lay it on the bed so I could go find a hammer and nail.

The picture of the couple would hang over the sofa instead of the ugly sunflower picture I had there from the thrift shop. I put that by the sofa and proceeded to get them up on the walls. Once finished, I looked at the clock. I'd a pretty productive/weird day. It was already 5:00 p.m. and I hadn't heard from anyone all day. That was okay. I just wanted to be reclusive and turn off the phone and hide in my bedroom and watch the small TV in there. I needed to be alone, crawl under my comfy rock, so to speak—no more peopling for me today. I checked on Dallas and she seemed okay.

I decided to leave a message on my cell that just said I was home and taking me time, and that I was fine so please don't knock my door down, as all was well. I thought I should do that or one of the crew, particularly Sean, could potentially come here and do just that, thinking something happened to me. I didn't want to be bothered right now. I was excited to tell them of my news about the new car and such, but that would be the water cooler talk tomorrow.

Silence and peace and quiet was nice. My back was feeling better, but I couldn't really lie on it; it still itched and in some spots it was still stiff and sore. I finally had a good dream; it was a memory I shared with my sister. Of course, it was changed around a bit in my dream to keep it fresh, I guess. I wish these were the dreams I always had.

It was our first time in Mexico, the excitement and joy was in the air. Angie and I were walking the far side of the beach, the ocean starting to come in, the evening tide getting higher and higher. There were so many buildings for a small place and they were colorful. Looking at the way others lived life was so interesting. Watching others on the beach, looking at local cultural art, was a delight. My dream changed, and I was fully aware of the change. This time I paid attention, like I knew I had to. I was outside castle walls in olden time— if I had to guess, I would say the 1300s. I was where the regular folks were farming just outside the walls. I felt I needed more time to process where I was and why ... why did my dream change and how was I aware of my dream changing? I ducked into a building, and it had a hay floor and slatted boards that made up the walls. The spaces were almost big enough to put my arm through.

I went to the back of the small building and peeked between the boards, trying to figure out what happened to my Mexico dream and why I was in this one. Where was this place? When was this place? I could sort of see the castle on the other side of the very large grey brick walls. The people were gardening just outside the wall, dozens of them, like a group community effort. I kind of felt like that's what I was supposed to be doing too—helping them garden. Maybe this was a past life dream. Maybe this was how I grew up? Why was I so aware of the dream changing? Why was I so aware of what was happening even though it was clearly a dream? I turned around, extremely aware that someone was behind me. I could feel the presence. The first thing I saw were sandaled feet. I didn't feel like I was in trouble...I felt calm, like maybe I knew the person. Like they were there to give me a message. I had a chance to talk to God, that's what it felt like. I looked up slowly, knowing I wasn't supposed to see their face. I looked up his cream-colored robes to where a rope belt was tied, and I thought I would try to look at their face. The light at face level was so bright I couldn't see. I put my hand up to shield my face and to look towards the person who just showed up, in this tiny barn or what seemed to be a place where the people cut wood. Why were we here? His staff came out and it cracked against the chopping block. Lightning struck out; the lightening went down and went up and blasted into the sky.

I woke up scared out of my mind, and instinctively I knew I had just received a message. I went over the dream in my head, and as I did the message got clearer and clearer. Not that it had anything to do with what I saw or felt in the dream. The message didn't make sense to me, but I knew it to be true. The higher being who created all, who in my belief system we call God, maybe He sent His son to me to deliver the message, he who goes by many names. I knew in a single instance what the message was when I woke. When the staff cracked against the wood, the message was delivered.

He said He was taking back what He had given to me to watch over me, that He needed her back home. It was someone he had given to me to help me through the pain and process of what I was going through, because I was going through it alone. I was no longer alone; I had friends and family. I was not alone anymore. He was taking Dallas, his watcher, his gift, my elusive furry best friend.

She was there to keep an eye on me and report back, and he was taking her home. I cried. That couldn't be right. Why take a cat? I knew I could have treated her better, I knew I could have cared more. But I didn't want her gone, I still needed her here, he had to be wrong. I said a little prayer and begged, "I know I haven't been around a lot and things are kind of a mess here, and she is always hiding, but I do need her, don't take her." I felt like I was having a conversation, because in my head it was like someone had told me that Dallas was not just a cat; the spirit inside her was something more. I argued that they could not take her, knowing no matter what I did it was a fight I would not win.

I got up out of bed and got into the shower, trying to clear my mind, trying to clear the vision I had. I didn't have to listen if I didn't want to, but even as I thought it, another thought came into my head that told me I had no choice. I instinctually knew it to be true. But it was just a dream. I got angry. "I will fight for her. You can't have her, I won't let you take her." I could feel there was no use trying to fight a supreme being. I wasn't going to win. Then came the bartering. I got out of the shower and I sat in the chair by my bed wrapped in towels. "If you are going to take her, before you do, I need to say goodbye. You can't just have her. She is someone to me too, I love her, grumpy cat and all." I got up from my chair knowing I had been heard. I wasn't going say goodbye now, because I knew instinctively it wasn't time and I didn't want to face it, but I knew she would be gone, taken from me, and soon. I had no say. Saddened by what was happening, I tried to put it out of my head. It was just a dream. Maybe I was just getting carried away.

I was trying to get myself together long enough to get through the doors at work. I felt like I walked in, did my work day in a blurry haze and walked out at 5:00 p.m. none the wiser to actually being at work. I just droned on like a robot.

I remember being excited and glad to be back, thinking getting into my work would bring some normalcy into my life. I didn't really leave my office all day. I had not heard from anyone back in customer service. Maybe Sean said something about giving me space to the whole group. Which really wasn't what I meant, but it was nice to have yesterday and I really did not feel like speaking today. I was off my game.

I got back to my car.

"New car, huh?"

"Oh hey, Tracy, yeah, just yesterday I got the cheque from insurance in order to get a new car. What do you think?"

"Lookin' good, love the color choice. Sean said you needed some space, so we thought to just leave you be today. I wasn't ignoring you."

"Actually, Sean said *he* would give *me* space. It wasn't a group thing. Honestly, though, I'm tired of talking about my antics and circumstances in my life. I had this one good thing and that's the car, which I meant to come by and tell you guys about. I just never got around to it."

"Well, Cali hun, if you don't want to talk, you don't have too, but please don't ever feel like you bothering me. I am here to talk, listen or whatever."

"Thanks, Tracy. It's just been a lot, you know? Thanks for offering your support. Hey, maybe we can do a night out on the weekend"

"That's a plan. Okay, I will talk later, see you," replied Tracy.

I got home and I could feel that things weren't right. I felt down and out, like a punching bag that has been hit too many times. I could feel something settle deep within me that I didn't like or care to keep around, a sadness, but it felt deep-rooted, like it wasn't going anywhere soon. Dallas came from the hall and was meowing at me. I picked her up. "Hi there, lovely lady, what have you been doing today? I was thinking we should get our dinner and watch a movie together. What do you think? Actually, I'm having leftover chicken. Would you like some in your dish?" I got a meow in return and took that as a yes. I took my dish and Dallas's cat food into the living room.

I settled on a movie with Cameron Diaz, something fun and light where she played a teacher. Dallas and I ate and then she settled on my lap instead of beside me. That was unlike her. It made me think this might be my goodbye time, and I wasn't going to miss it or lose it. I watched the movie and petted Dallas and loved her up and enjoyed her company. I fell asleep during the movie and awoke to the smell of smoke and something coppery. Suddenly I started coughing, and it turned into a hack. I opened my eyes and they started to water with the smoke that filled the top half of the room. I looked around and Dallas was nowhere to be seen. I got off the sofa in a hurry, looking in the kitchen, which was also half full of smoke. I went down the hall but couldn't go any further. There were flames coming through the floor and walls already.

I ran in the other direction. "Dallas, Dallas, come kitty, come kitty! Dallas! Dallas, come right now." I lost my capability to yell as smoke filled my lungs and choked me out.

I crawled to the door and ripped my coat from the chair and with the other hand grabbed my boots and opened the door. I put on my jacket and boots and gasped for breath and tried again. "Come on, Dallas, you have to get out. Dallas! Dallas! Dallas!" Now the neighbors were out, some running into their houses and back out with cell phones. I pulled my keys and phone from my jacket. I was going to call 911. But I realized that's probably what everyone on the block was doing as flames shot from the back of the house. I screamed, "My cat! My cat!" begging for mercy in hopes that somehow my Dallas would make it. The firetrucks came from around the corner. I hadn't moved back, and the firefighter that got out of the truck came and dragged me away from the house. The flames and air were so hot, my face was red with heat burns.

I was stunned into one position. My neighbor came and sat with me and was talking with me. I had no idea who it was or where they came from or what they were saying. I was in shock … again. By the time the flames went out I was sitting in the back of an ambulance trying to get some semblance of reality. I had an oxygen mask on and my smoke-filled face was streaked with tears that I didn't remember crying. The back half of the house was completely gone; only the kitchen and living room would be left, maybe. I stared ahead and picked up my phone. I dialed and Sean picked up. "Sean, I think I need a place to stay. Can you help?" I dropped the phone to the floor of the ambulance.

I was told minutes later that I passed out, either from shock or oxygen loss from smoke inhalation. The paramedics had picked up the phone and filled Sean in. I came to moments after. I wasn't out long, but they retook my vitals and made sure I was okay. A black car came screeching around the corner, slowed down for the onlookers and parked. Sean ran out of the vehicle fast. The paramedics released me to his care. He had brought an extra blanket from home and coat. I guess he wasn't sure what I ran out of the house wearing. He put me in the car and drove me to his new apartment. It was downtown in a building that kind of looked like it was made of mirrors. It was beautiful on the outside, so I figured on the inside it must be amazing.

He parked his car underground, and we took the elevator up almost to the top. His place was shockingly amazing and oddly familiar. The door opened up to a small entranceway, which looked out to the full living room. The whole area was open concept, with the wall that I faced almost all windows. The furniture was dark gray with a long white shag rug and a beautiful octagonal glass and silver table; it even had a centerpiece. This guy had style. I wondered what he thought when he came to my house, as it was not as put together as this. The walls were also gray and art hung on every one. The floor was a tiled charcoal grey, almost black, and the kitchen was to the left opened to the living room. It was done in beautiful bright whites.

There were what I assumed were two bedrooms and an open office area only divided by a wall. On the other side must have been a bathroom, which I was going to definitely need before I went anywhere in this house.

He saw me looking around and said, "Why don't you take as long as you need in the bathroom? I will get you a robe before you go in and then while you're busy I will see if I can come up with anything for you to wear for tonight."

In the bathroom the sight of myself in the mirror almost put me in a state of shock. A few minutes of being in a burning house equaled looking like I had been lost in the woods for a month. I took off all my clothes, and they were a mess. My scarred-up back was a mess too, and it hurt. My medicine was at my burned-up house.

I ran the shower and got in, and the smell of smoke filled the air and grime ran down the drain. Once the water was clean my emotions correspondingly welled up. My heart felt like it was going to well explode and then the subsequent pain of the evening hit. Dropping to the bottom of the shower, I could no longer stand. The tears came at the thought of it all and the loss of Dallas.

I was trying to sob quietly on the floor of the shower as my heart broke. Sean didn't knock before he opened the door and called, "Cali honey, can I come in?" I tried to stop but the sobs couldn't be contained. Sean came to the shower and got inside, clothes and all, and held me for a moment. He kissed my temple. "Just get comfy for a moment," he said. He grabbed the shower head and slid it lower on the pole so the water kept hitting me and keeping me warm but didn't spray my face and head. He grabbed the shampoo and washed my hair, scrubbing out the smoke. Rinsing it off, he stood me up and carefully put me in the robe.

I stared at him a minute and broke the silence. "Now what? What do I do? Everything is gone. I just had everything and now it's gone."

Sean pulls me close and replied, "We will figure it out together, okay? I have some things for you in the kitchen. Do you think a glass of wine would help you relax?"

"No, it feels too celebratory. Do you have whisky?"

"Of course. I will get you some. I have ginger ale if you would like mix."

"Yes, please. Equal amounts. I think I need the whisky more than the soda."

Sean sat her on the sofa and brought her bag of clothes from the kitchen. "What's all this?"

"I figured you only have what you had on, and we will have to throw those clothes out. There are stores downstairs as well as a nice café. I had couple stores bring clothing up that I purchased while you were in the bathroom." She slowly dug into the bag and brought out a sage-blue pair of yoga pants and a black-and sage-blue matching shirt.

"You didn't have to do this, Sean, this is very thoughtful." She put her hand in the bag again and found a gift card.

"That's for if you want normal, business-type clothes. I didn't know what you would like. I thought it would be nice to be able to pick something out yourself." Lastly she pulled out a black pair of leggings and an oversized shirt.

"I saw those outfits hanging on the back wall through the window, so I just had the saleslady ring up mediums. I figured that way they're not too small or too big. But if you need something else, I'm sure she will take them back at the store."

"These are fine, Sean, thank you." Oddly, going through the clothes did help calm her a little.

Sean handed her a drink. "Before we left I went to your vehicle and looked inside for keys. I was going to ask you for them but I found them on the front walkway. I moved the car to park it on the neighbor's driveway. He said to do so. I locked the car up and brought the keys here. They are in the dish by the door. I'll leave you a key to the apartment as well. For tomorrow, though, if you want in and out just ask Charles; he's the doorman. Give him your name and tell him you're with me, and he will let you up no problem. He knows you're here."

"Thanks for taking me in, Sean. I, I just automatically dialed your number. I didn't really know what I was doing. I can find somewhere to stay if you give me a couple days."

"It's okay, Cali, you will be fine and comfortable here, it's not an imposition. Did you want to talk about any of it?"

"I don't know, I don't think I can. My thoughts are spinning in my head faster than I can spit them out into a sentence."

"I was thinking just to make things easier for you, for just a little while, we should call the temp agency and have them send someone over to Tony's. I think it would be best if you slowed down just for a little while."

I filled with fear for a moment but then relaxed, remembering what was said in the forested park by the apparition of the woman and girl about too much change. There had been an awful lot of loss and too many phenomenal circumstances. I might not have a job when I got back, but I nodded yes.

"I will help you with forms at the Employment Insurance office, and we will get you a note saying you're off for medical reasons or do a lay-off or something, just to give you time. I know it takes a while for that to kick in, but it's better than nothing, and I can help out too."

"Sean, we only just started dating. This is too much. I will figure something out, I promise, this might be the whiskey talking, but I think I can handle this."

"That, my dear, is most definitely the whiskey talking. I brought out the good stuff." They finished their drinks and he helped her up off the sofa. "I made a bed for you in the spare room. I, um, didn't know what to do there. I didn't think tonight was a good night to play old married couple, so I thought I would make up the spare so you could decide."

"Thanks, Sean, I could use a place to decompress if it is okay with you. I will take the spare room."

"Sure, of course it's okay. I'll bring your new clothes into that room. If you need more blankets they are right across from your room."

"Okay, thanks. I will see you in the morning, and maybe we can talk more then when my thoughts are not so jumbled."

"Okay, I will be up early for work and I will fill in Mr. Gunderson on what has happened, and you can fill in the rest of the group if you wish. I won't say a word till you do."

"Thanks, I will probably come in sometime just to talk to the boss and see everyone. I have to say, I can't get over how familiar this place looks. So odd. Goodnight, Sean, see you in the morning."

"Goodnight, Cali."

We each went to our bedrooms and shut the door. I didn't realize how late it was. 2:00 a.m., the clock said. Poor Sean had to be up in a few hours for work. I was grateful he helped me. I really needed someone there to literally pick me up when I was down. The whole relationship had all moved a bit fast, though. There was a romantic side to Sean and there was the tentative side to him, but he was a little overbearing and he was thrust into some weird protective caretaker roll because of my situation. This was why I hated the life that I knew. On the outside it was normal, plain and even boring. But sometimes my peculiarities affected other people directly. It made my life hard, this otherworldly/paranormal business— or maybe they were just hallucinations that also affected the people around me.

It was harder than just normal everyday living. It was not for the lack of trying… I had tried to stop, pull myself together and do as society did: go to work, make a living, take care of a home, day-to-day errands and chores, and cars with car payments, bills, extracurricular activities and friends. It always went up in smoke. It was always a mess. I was always starting over. This time my life literally went up in smoke. Hint taken—normal wasn't for me.

CHAPTER 9
My Future

SLEEP DID NOT COME EASY; IT WAS A WAKEFUL NIGHTMARE. I HAD LITERALLY lost everything except the new car. My cat, my home, most likely my job, and my relationship with Sean was in a weird space and going at a super fast-moving pace. There was no joy to having a new relationship; I had been robbed of that and so had Sean. He took care of me and seemed to always be where I needed him to be, but it was out of necessity and need. The relationship was odd the moment it started, and I thought I could make something of it. My life and the way it smashes everything to hell was making it hard to have a relationship of any kind with anyone. The spirit was right—it was like I didn't belong here. I wished I knew what that meant. I felt so bad. I wondered were Dallas had gone, why I couldn't find her in the house when I called out to her. I guess I got my moment with her before the Creator took His guardian back, His watcher. Tears rolled down my face. It didn't make it easier knowing in advance; at least I got what others did not and that was time to prepare and have that special time beforehand. That was what I prayed for, and that's what I got. She left, and because I was told it was going to happen, I figured there must be a place to go to, a happy place, a better place.

That was comforting. Maybe I would see her again, though this weird thought came into my head that she may not be in the same shape and form as I remembered her here on Earth.

I lay awake for the rest of the night till I heard Sean get up for work and start moving around and decided to get up with him. I probably looked like hell after yesterday night and a night of not sleeping.

"Hey, you're up. You didn't have to get up because I'm up, sleep in."

"I think I have to be asleep first to technically sleep in. I thought I would just hang around here today and maybe sleep later."

"That sounds like a plan," replied Sean.

"Tomorrow is your last day, isn't it? I was thinking of going in at lunch to see everyone. If Mr. Gunderson would like a meeting, tell him that's when I will be in."

"Yes, it is my last day. I will tell everyone you're coming tomorrow. I have to get going, help yourself to whatever is here. There's the café downstairs if there is nothing here you like. I put twenty dollars on the kitchen counter. I figured you might need to replace your bank card. Living downtown has its perks; there is every bank you can think of here, so if you decide to go out it shouldn't be far before you find yours."

"I'll keep that in mind. I hadn't really had time to think about what I have to do. I am really tired, but I can't sleep so it might be a rough day. But I will try and do that so I can at least buy things. Solid idea, Sean," I said, smiling a closed lipped smile at him. He gave me a whopper of a kiss; it was a good, heated kiss, but it reminded me that we had to talk at some point.

I think he saw it in my glance at him. The way he looked at me was almost telling, and his posture changed. He knew something was breaking down, and it wasn't just my house.

He left with a goodbye and strolled out the door leaving me to do more contemplation. I must have fallen asleep because I woke at 10:30 a.m. feeling like a new person. Amazing what a couple hours of sleep will do. I could still smell the smoke on my skin so I took another shower, lathering up to try to get the smell out. Sean had sandalwood soap that smelled so good, and that made it easier to get rid of the remnants of smoke and memories. The clothes Sean had bought were perfect for today; the yoga set fit perfectly. I decided I would just forget getting ready because I didn't have anything to get ready with. I used Sean's brush to brush my hair and then went into the kitchen to compile a list of what I had to do to get some semblance of normal. *Call insurance for house, call doctor for new medication that burnt up, find out what caused the fire, find out when I get to go back to the house. Get a bank card, buy necessities, go back to the house and get car.* I thought that list was good enough, considering I didn't actually know what to do when your house burns to the ground. So I did the first two, then called the firehouse that responded and asked to speak to the chief in regards to what started the fire and to see when I could go back and see if anything was salvageable. I was told the chief would give me a call back. So that left breakfast and going out to get a bank card to buy the necessities. I didn't really feel like eating, so I thought I would go to the bank and maybe go for lunch at the café.

I went to the bathroom and looked at myself in the mirror.

I looked a little pale from no sleep and no makeup, and my hair dried into curls that I just put my fingers through to get some control. I didn't even have a clip or hair tie. I grabbed the twenty dollars off the counter, the two hundred dollar gift card off the table and car keys out of habit. I realized then that my coat that I grabbed smelled really bad and so it was left in a heap as close to the door as possible. I had my boots, so that was good. I went to the closet and chose a coat from Sean's outerwear. So purchase number one would be a coat.

It was neat being downtown. I didn't have to go far for anything. Where Sean lived was like a hotel with a doorman, shops, a café and a pub. It was really nice … how did he afford such a place? I went to the café and just got a regular coffee to conserve money in case I needed cash. As it turned out, my bank was two blocks down. I could see the sign once I went onto the street. The bank was notified of what happened and they blocked the old card and gave me and new one. Now for some essentials. I went back to the building to see what I could get there. The gift card came in handy. I spent half of it on a jacket, a really lovely jacket. The other half I spent on the sale rack and got some fitted dress pants and a floral cream-colored top. I found a pleather black jacket for cheap and grabbed it too to go over top. Now I had a work outfit to at least be presentable. I did pretty good, I thought. I didn't see a store to buy the little things I would need, like a grocery store or a pharmacy-type store.

I looked it up and the nearest one was about five blocks. I sure got my exercise being downtown, but having this convenience without a car was awesome. I decided on the walk to call the doctor and tell him to call in my prescription into the pharmacy I was headed to.

That way I could pick it up right away. I felt like I had some momentum built up by getting things done. Maybe I just needed to get as much as possible done, have a couple days off and get back to work.

I felt better on the move. What was I going to do, take time off just to mope around? Movement was what I needed, with the warning bells going off in my head from what the spirit said, but I couldn't be afraid of life. I had to keep going. I made it to the pharmacy and picked up another two hundred dollars' worth of makeup, hair products, a toothbrush and paste and hair appliances. Then I re-purchased my prescription. Now that I had more than a few bags, I felt like an uptown girl.

I kept going in the opposite direction of Sean's, wanting to see what else was down in this area. I had never really looked around here before. I walked passed a restaurant and saw Sean—he was having lunch with a very pretty dark-haired woman. I thought one of the partners at the new job he had was a woman, so maybe that was her? She was very beautiful with wavy dark hair and a red dress with what looked like very expensive shoes, not to mention the place they were eating at looked like money too. His hand then went over hers, and she smiled and picked up her wine glass and took a sip and caressed his hand back. I kept walking, stunned. Did I have it wrong? Maybe we are not exclusively dating. I mean, I was pretty sure that's what he said he wanted, but did he say those words exactly?

Yes, he did say that, or did I? I wanted to slow down this relationship … should I even care? Yes! I think I should! What the hell!

I wasn't seeing anybody else and that was no business lunch I happened to see. The fact that he was ten blocks from his place where I could potentially see him floored me. I was so confused. I kept walking and contemplating and the scenario kept playing out in my head. It had my mind reeling, and I was making it out to be more than what it was with them kissing and cooing at each other. I was making myself angrier. Then I would play devil's advocate and play it as if it were nothing at all, that I was just confusing what I had actually seen. I don't know how far I walked in the wrong direction from Sean's place, but the bags were getting heavy and my mind switched to thinking about what to do next.

"Ms. Stenson?"

Deacon Hall? I thought he was in Victoria now. I was wondering if I had my information wrong. "Deacon, what on earth are you doing here? I heard you had a promotion in Victoria with a new firm?"

"I am, I mean I do. I'm here on business. I just saw you walking by, so I thought you might care to join me for lunch. I already have a table. I was inside by the window when I saw you coming down the sidewalk. Here, I can help you with your purchases."

"I don't think it's a … you know what, it's a perfect idea, Deacon. I would love to have lunch with you." Deacon grabbed my bags and led me to his table. He had a glass of wine sitting there, and it did look kind of lonely. I sat down and Deacon waved a waiter over.

I ordered a glass of a white wine and asked what Deacon was having off the menu. "I haven't ordered yet, but I was going to try the special."

"Today it is salmon, ma'am," the waiter interjected.

"Great I'll have that as well." The waiter left, and I said to Deacon, "Seems you just can't stay away from Vancouver whether you live in Calgary or in Victoria. What brings you here today?" I smiled at him, hoping he knew I was just teasing.

"Yes, it does seem that way. No matter where I live, I end up here. I should have just moved here." Smiling back at me for poking fun at him, he gave me his real answer, "I already have a criminal case they want me to look further into. I don't have many cases at the moment, so I plan to knock their socks off with this one so they know I plan on kicking ass and taking names."

"Well, I hope it goes well for you. It must be a lot different being in a firm than being a lawyer for a manufacturer."

"Yes, but it's not my first rodeo. I was at a firm before, here in Vancouver. I have connections here that helped get me a seat at the firm in Victoria. When I left my position here, I was to be engaged to someone in Calgary. I took the position as lawyer for a company who manufactures. That was out of my wheelhouse by quite a bit. The engagement fell through almost right away, but I had this new job, and didn't quite know what to do at the time.

That was over a year ago, and it wasn't till recently that I got the nerve to pack up, move back to BC and get the job I wanted, not to mention the job I know better."

"Wow, Deacon, I'm sorry to hear about your engagement, that's awful."

"I'm not sorry. It was what it was. I moved on quite a while ago. I stayed in Calgary because in the legal business it doesn't look to good if you're always jumping around, so I stuck it out in Calgary for a bit." He grinned and paused. "What about you? What's new since I saw you?"

I thought about everything, it would be pretty hard to pretend everything was great.

"Are you okay? Your reticence is not unnoticed. If you would rather not say, that's okay."

"Well, I'm kind of a black-and-white kind of woman. I'm either going to tell you everything is wonderful and continue to talk about the meal and the weather, or I'm going to blurt everything out like a whirlwind."

"Which is the truth?"

"Unfortunately, the latter."

"Well, let's go with that one," Deacon said.

"Well, my house burnt down, quite literally. I haven't gone back to see what's left and I don't even know why it burnt down yet . I am guessing electrical; that has always been a problem, I think.

I'm not sure if I'm allowed back. The fire department is supposed to call me back, hopefully today. So I'm staying with Sean, or at least I did last night. I just ran into him having a very cozy lunch with a raven-haired goddess. So that's my day. How's yours going?"

"That's completely terrible. Boy, when life punches you it hits hard, doesn't it? I am so sorry this has happened," he replied.

"Someone recently told me that if life is happening too fast and in the wrong direction, this is the universe's way of trying to slow me down, give me time to figure out who I am. Stopping life, friends, work and such is hard, because I don't want time to think. I just want to go to work and not think about anything."

"Well, if the universe speaks, it has a large voice and it is hard to ignore. I wouldn't try it if I were you. Not that you asked for my unsolicited advice."

"Is that your legal opinion?" I joked

"It is, and my personal one as well. I know I don't know you well, but I seem to care about you and I would like to know you better."

"Well, if there is one thing I know about you, Deacon, it's that you definitely don't give up."

Deacon smiled and cleared his throat. "So what will you do about Sean?"

"Well, you certainly don't beat around the bush," I said.

"I'm a lawyer. I find getting to the point is my best option."

"I think I'll go back and confront him, of course. It has been a little weird. I planned on talking to him tonight anyway so I think he knows it's coming. Then maybe I'll find the girls and go for a much-needed night out. Unfortunately, I can't go far from here without my car and until I figure out what is going on I'm staying just down the road at Sean's. Actually, I think I walked a good ways. I'm not sure how far he lives from here." I laughed.

"I'll drive you to wherever you want to go."

Just then my phone rang. "Hello?" It was a long minute before I said anything to the caller. "I see,… I don't think so no! How could that be? When can I go back home to see what I have left? I appreciate that thank you." I hung up the phone and stared at Deacon, shock evident on my face I'm sure.

"I don't understand," I said to Deacon. "It was arson—how could that be? I don't have any enemies, or not that I know of. I've hardly been here long enough to make friends, never mind enemies. That's what they asked me … if I had somebody that might want to hurt me. I can't think of anybody. Who would do such a thing?"

"I can't imagine what you're feeling right now. If you would like, we can finish up here and I can take you back to Sean's house."

"Yes, thank you, I think that would be best. It seems I have more to figure out."

"Are you fine at Sean's? Will you be okay?"

"I think so. I think I'll be fine."

"Here's my number, Cali, if you need anything." I took the card. Who knows, I probably did need a lawyer … I mean, arson? Deacon paid the bill for both of us and I thanked him as he picked up my bags and led me out the door.

We got to his black Mercedes SUV and he put my things in the back of the vehicle and opened the door for me. As we were driving I asked, "This isn't weird right? You driving me to Sean's?"

"Not at all. If that is where you're staying and that is where you feel safe, I have no problem helping you out."

"Thank you, Deacon, you are very kind."

"When do you get to go back to your home to see it?"

"Tomorrow. The fire department chief will meet me there after his shift with an on-duty officer. He says it's too dangerous to be rooting around in a hazard of a burned-down house, so he will be there to make sure I'm safe and that I'm only going to designated areas. Maybe I can call the girls from the office to come with me and then go for a drink."

We got to the building and I got my bags from the back of his SUV and thanked Deacon again. "I will call and tell you how things went. I mean, if you would like to know?" I said with a blush

"Yes, absolutely, I would like to know."

I went into the building and asked the door man to let me up to Sean's apartment. Just as Sean said, it was no problem, and he came up the elevator with me, took my bags, opened the door to Sean's and put my bags inside and left. That was what I called nice and easy living. Wow. I called the office and Tracy picked up the phone. "Hey Tracy, I was wondering if you had plans tomorrow. I kind of need your help."

"Hey lady, nice of you to call. How are you?"

"As it turns out not so good, I don't know what Sean has told you, but there was a fire last night. My house burned down. Out of shock I called Sean and he picked me up. I stayed at his place last night. They said I could go back to my place tomorrow to salvage anything that might be salvageable."

"Oh my God, Cali, I'm so glad you're okay. Do you want my help tomorrow? Is that why you're calling?"

"Yes, I was hoping you would come with me, and maybe after I think we might need a drink."

"Of course I'll come with you. I'll tell Ashley too, and if she can come she will help. What about Todd and Sean? Should I tell them the plan too?"

"Actually, I was hoping for a girls' night."

"That sounds good to me. When do we go?"

"I have to meet the fire chief at 3:00 p.m. I know you're all working then, but I need the daylight to help me find things. I just thought I might need boxes and help packing anything I do find, and I need a place to put them."

"What about support, Cali? You can't walk into that by yourself!"

"I don't have a choice. The whole office can't take the afternoon off because I need help. I'm already going to be fired, I'm sure, for not showing up."

"Hold off on coming into work tomorrow. I'm calling in sick tomorrow afternoon."

"You are a good friend, Tracy, but that is exactly why I cannot ask you to do anything like that."

"You're not asking, I am telling you I will be there at 3:00 p.m. tomorrow and I won't be late. Ashley can come later. I'll tell her to meet us after work on the down-low so I don't get my cover blown. Apparently I have a gynecology appointment at three tomorrow. They won't question that because they won't want to."

I laughed. "Okay, thank you. I love you for being there for me."

"Of course, who else would be there? Me! That's who!"

"You, my dear, are awesome! Thank you and I will talk to you later."

"Sure thing."

We signed off of our phone call, and I put all my things in the spare room and sat for a bit, wondering if I just had bad luck that someone chose my house to burn down. I didn't know them or deserve to have this happen. Or did I somehow make an enemy? But who? There was some commotion at the door that knocked me from my reverence. I got up and rounded the sofa as Sean came in. "You're back early. It's only five o'clock."

"Yes, well, it seemed earlier like you had something on your mind, like you had something to say, so let's hear it." He seemed very agitated. He was not speaking in a tone that sounded caring or concerned— it was mainly questioning and accusatory.

"Is there something wrong? Sean, you seem upset."

"Isn't there always something wrong when you're around?"

My eyes were set ablaze. How dare he make light of my situation. "If you need to say something, Sean, just say it, the asshole routine can wait till later." He slapped me and the shock and force made me fall against the sofa. I rolled over the top of the sofa to put distance between me and him. Now the sofa was between us.

"You first. Why don't you start with why you and Deacon had lunch together while you're staying here? Why do I keep coming to your rescue when you're obviously so hot for someone else!"

"First of all, you giant asshat, never touch me again! Second, I am no longer staying here. Third, why don't you explain why you had lunch with

143

the raven-haired woman, and why you were holding hands at lunch and leaning into each other. Business meeting, I suppose?"

"Yes, it was a meeting! Where are you going to go, are you going to stay on the streets?" He laughed. He came around to me, and that's when everything came crashing in. Like a speed version of my dream, as he was rounding the sofa, I remembered where I had seen this room before. I had been in this room in my dream; it was almost exact. The shock of not realizing it before was too much. I ran the opposite way around toward the bedrooms. I looked in Sean's room as I walked by to the spare. It was an exact replica of the dream with Sean turning into the demon. This couldn't be happening. "Well, it looks like someone is off in la la land again. Did you just come to a realization?"

"Just leave me alone, Sean. I'm getting the few things I have here and I'm out of your hair for good."

"Oh, I don't think so. I spent too much time getting you here—you're not going anywhere!"

Stunned, I stared at him like a deer caught in the head lights. His six-foot frame was coming at me. What was I going to do? He grabbed my arm, and I still had my hand on the door handle to the spare room, so I used my opposite leg on the door frame and tugged his body enough to have his arm stick through and I slammed the door on his arm, leaving him inside the spare room. Then I ran to the front door and grabbed the entire bowl of keys, which contained his keys and my keys. Thank goodness I had been talking on the phone or I may not have had it with me now. I ran into the hall and pushed the elevator button as I headed for the stairs. Taking the steps two at a time, before he found me. I took the contents of the bowl and put it all in my yoga pants' pocket, which stretched to a huge bulge and left the key bowl there on the steps. Once down the stairs I made it to the front doors and that's when a hand grabbed mine while Charles the doorman held the door open for us. "I believe you have something of mine?" Sean replied politely.

"Yes, of course, your keys," I said, giving his keys back as I walked out the door. I didn't want him out in front of me not knowing where he was, so I left the building and walked few stores down where he grabbed me again by the shoulders. It wasn't anything alarming. I was sure no one even would notice unless they knew the person and could tell something was off.

"You think this is a game, you using me, and then literally having me chase you down? You think that is funny?" Sean was very agitated.

"So, this is wonderful weather we're having, isn't it, Sean? I can see why you picked today to harass or assault Cali. Do you mind taking your hands off her so I don't have to break them in public?" said an equally agitated baritone voice.

Sean let go. "Of course you're here, Deacon. I mean, why wouldn't you be skulking around the bottom of my apartment now that Cali is here?"

"I was having a beer after dropping her off when you put on the window show for everyone in the bar to see. Cali are you fine or would you like me to get you away from the situation?"

"I would like to get the stuff I left in Sean's apartment after he hit me, and then I would like to get the hell out."

"We can get you new stuff; you don't want seedy, shady things in your life anyway."

"I suppose you're right, Deacon," I replied. It looked like Sean wanted to put up a fight, but I think he knew that would not end well for him. Deacon was no slouch, at six foot four and built half as wide, he was not someone I think anyone would want to mess with, especially if he was pissed off like he was now. He shouldered passed Sean and led me to his SUV.

"We will talk later, Cali, I promise," said Sean.

Deacon turned so fast I thought it would be Sean's last breath. Within two strides he reached Sean. "If you call her, contact her, or harm her in any way I will slap a restraining order on you so fast your head will spin.

In fact, I have enough information here that maybe we will make a stop at the police department and press charges for assault and battery. That always looks nice on a resume. What was the new firm you're working at called? Doesn't matter … it's my job to find out. Behave, Sean, or I will make you very miserable."

Deacon turned on his heel and strode back to me. His voice was so low I wish I could have heard what he had said to Sean, who looked like he has just been bested. We got in the vehicle. "What did you say?" I asked.

"Nothing, just told him the threats won't work."

"Well, whatever you said, he seemed to believe you."

"I'm staying at the Fairmont. Let's go see if they have a room there close to mine. With Sean's outburst, you should consider staying away from him."

"I can't stay at the hotel. I don't make the same money you and Sean do, and I have absolutely nothing."

"I can expense it. I had the choice to bring a secretary and chose not to. I haven't chosen a secretary yet, so at this point they won't give it a second look." Deacon continued like that offer was no big deal, "What did you leave over at Sean's? It's still early, so we can pick up some things if you need anything right away."

"Well, as you can see I have no jacket, or footwear and I have no way to get ready in the mornings, which is why I look like hell today."

"We will go to the hotel first and make sure there's a room available and I will grab a small jacket, which will most likely be like a trench coat on you, but we will go find something right away, then we will get the rest of the things you need. You look beautiful, by the way, not like hell. You have natural beauty and you will never look like hell." He smiled at me and of course I blushed back.

"Thanks for your help back there; it was unexpected but definitely not unwelcome. I'm sure I could have handled it, but things have been more unusual as of late, so I wouldn't count on the argument not getting out of hand with Sean."

"I'm glad I was there too, Cali. It was just lucky that I stopped for that drink before continuing on with my day."

We stopped at the Fairmont and he got me a room two doors down across the hall. Since I didn't have anything to put away, we went to the nearby shops to buy the essentials. It was hard to not keep looking over my shoulder since we were still in the same neighborhood as Sean. "How about we go for dinner at the hotel. We can stay in tonight and I'll keep you company," Deacon said.

"That sounds pretty good. I am hungry. That's two meals in one day I've had with you. Sean will be out of his mind if he finds out." Deacons lips pursed into a grimace but he did not remark on what I said. We both knew it was true.

When we got back to the hotel we put my things away in my room and then I changed into a business outfit I'd bought so we could go for dinner downstairs. Once we were seated at the table, Deacon asked, "If you don't mind me asking, how did it come to that with you and Sean today?"

"It seems like a long story, but it really isn't." I explained how Sean used to treat me at work and then how he had changed. I told him about the art exhibit and how I had no idea Sean had been using me as a subject, and then I told him how Sean had been there for me with all the dramatic events. I explained how it ended today with him slapping my face because I had lunch out with someone else. "It has been really weird. I can hardly say we've been dating; we hardly know each other, but I get in a car accident and he's there to help, my house burns down and he's there to help. He always seems to be in the right place to help me or I call him and he's there right away. I have only been on one date with him, and the in the time that I have known him it has been very hot and cold as well as very absurd relationship. I wanted to talk to him about it, but he wanted to talk about why you and I were having lunch and that's what started the fight. I never had a chance to explain, not that I should have needed to, but he felt I owed him for everything he has done."

Deacon stared in silence like he was contemplating something.

I interrupted the silence. "Do you mind if we change the subject? That's the end of that story, anyway."

"Of course, I was just thinking ... well, I don't mean to pry. If you would rather not talk about it we can find plenty to talk about."

"What were you thinking?" I said, now curious as to what had been going through his mind.

"You know, you're right, we should talk about something else. I would rather not pass judgement on him, but I can't help wondering if ... perhaps I could do a background check on him. It really is none of my business, so if you would rather I stay out of it, I will most definitely abide by that. Something just doesn't seem or feel right, and my instincts are throwing red flags like crazy. Maybe he's not who you think he is."

CHAPTER 10
There Is No Place Like Home

I MADE IT BACK TO MY HOTEL ROOM AFTER DINNER WITH DEACON. THE DAY had put more questions in my head than answers. Was Deacon concerned truly with who Sean really was? Or was this a man thing? I was not some princess who needed a constant savior. Yes, my life was hectic and weird, yes, I had absolutely had some unsavory circumstances happen. But this was my life, and while things may have picked up in the weird department, the fact remained that I had been living with weird my whole life. If Deacon was using my issues with Sean because he thought it would further himself with me, he had another thing coming. But what if Deacon was right? What if Sean was not the person I thought he was? I had not been working with him long and I really didn't know him personally. The things I did know about him were because of our outlandish relationship. He had been there when I needed him, but he also had a very hot and cold temper. What about the paintings? Was that a red flag on the play and I missed it? Deacon had also discussed with me if I wanted to press charges against Sean for hitting me.

I had to use extra makeup on my face because where he hit me was red and puffy, but it didn't leave a bruise or mark. I really didn't want to prolong the situation by having to deal with police and go through everything with them. Then I would either have to go to court, which would prolong the situation further, or the police would do absolutely nothing anyway, which in my experience was the case, so why bother going through all of that?

No, I think after today I would just avoid Sean. If Deacon truly wanted to help then I might take him up on it, but I definitely would make it clear that there was no need for a new knight in shining armor. I wondered if Deacon was right about doing the background check. Did he truly believe something was really off with Sean?

Maybe I needed to start over yet again. Maybe it would mean no Sean, no job at Tony's, and no choice in the home aspect of things. I would have to look for a rental property tomorrow. I couldn't stay in an expensive hotel till I found out what was going to happen with my house. My insurance was going to skyrocket with claims on my car insurance and a claim on my house insurance. That was not the best scenario. I needed to start making big adjustments to my life. But how? That was the question. The out-of-control spiraling in my life had to stop; I needed to gain control and perspective. That got me wondering about the pharmaceuticals. I opened the bag and looked inside at the prescription. I decided I was not going to use them. I was going to keep them just in case, I had gained and lost a lot in a very short amount of time. As for the drug to get rid of the hallucinations…maybe I wasn't hallucinating, Todd can see exactly what I can. Maybe I need to come to terms with what is actually happening, the dreams and spirits or whatever they were, that had been part of my life for a long time. It affected people around me, not because I was driving them crazy—because they felt or heard or saw what I did, which meant everyone I knew must need drugs. Or maybe I did not. Maybe it's time to face the fact the unreal, is actually happening.

I was about to go to bed when my phone rang.

"Hey, Mom, what up?"

"Hello, my Cali-Lily, how is everything going out on the west coast?"

"Well, it was going great, but now… not so much. As soon as I make it through this mess all will be well."

"Why, what's happened, Cals?"

"I just had a house fire, Mom. I think everything is gone. I'm not sure. I go tomorrow to see what's salvageable."

"What! Oh, my girl. I'm glad you're okay!"

"Yes, Mom, I'm fine. It's just been a rough few days, that's for sure, and I can't find my Dallas," I said as tears started to well in my eyes. "I haven't called home because I really haven't had time with this mess out here."

"Are you going to come home?"

" I'm not sure, mom. I don't feel quite ready to throw in the towel yet. I feel like I need to get past this and do this on my own. However, if I can't seem to dig myself out of this hole then perhaps I would come home. Just don't expect me quite yet. I have a plan I'm hoping to get into place in the next couple days."

"I'm sorry to be calling with more bad news. Grandma Betty died. She was just old ... nothing really happened as far as we know; she died in her sleep. I wanted you to know. You don't have to come home unless you really want to. Grandma Betty's will says no funeral or prayer service, she didn't want it. So really, you don't have to come home unless you feel like it."

"Oh, Mom. I'm sorry your mom died. I will miss her very much. Are you sure you don't need me home? I can come home for you if you need me. It's is very upsetting news. If you want me there, say the words. I will come home."

"No, I have your dad, your sister has us and her boyfriend, and there is no service of any kind. We knew this was coming. She was old and not a really healthy person, so it was just a matter of time. If you need someone to come home to, I'm here."

"I have friends out here now and I do have a big mess to clean up. If you're all okay I will be okay out here. If there is no service then I will just pray for Grandma's safe return home."

We said our goodbyes. Mom didn't usually call unless I hadn't checked in for a long time or if something there was wrong. It was pretty sad about Grandma and not having a goodbye. But if Grandma would rather not do the ceremonies, that was definitely her prerogative. I felt like I should have been there more when she was alive, but there certainly wasn't anything I could do for her now. More sadness leaked into my heart.

I got into bed and tried hard to shut my eyes and go to sleep. With the news of Grandma and knowing all that I had to do tomorrow, sleep was hard to come by. I waited till the early wee hours of the morning, staring at the ceiling, and finally was able to fall to sleep.

My alarm on my phone went off at 7:00 a.m. I needed an early start. I couldn't live in a posh hotel because I didn't make that kind of money, and if I went through with my plan I may not have any money coming in at all for a while. I gathered my meager belongings, went downstairs to have break- fast and read over the morning paper and also went online on my phone to see what there were for rental properties. I realized by the time they were printed in the paper those rentals were probably already rented, so online was the better choice. Rentals went fast and they were expensive here in British Columbia, especially on the island and Vancouver. I circled a few and stared at one that really had my attention. It was a central location, not too far from the area where my house was, so I would be familiar with my surroundings, and it was a basement suite. I wouldn't be completely alone because there would be someone living upstairs. The rent, in my opinion, was a little high. It was the same rate as my mortgage, but I would only have half the house. That was how it worked here, though. I called that one right away—well, as soon as the clock struck 8:30. I didn't want to call too early, but it was the place I wanted to see first. The woman answered the phone and we discussed the rental. I answered all her questions about myself and we agreed to meet that morning.

The other place I had phoned about was an apartment building. I decided I would go see that one right after breakfast, but I didn't think I could afford it. I didn't know where I stood with my job, and I didn't know if I wanted that job anymore. I definitely didn't want to be where Sean could show up. I also had a new car to pay for. So the odds of me affording this apartment didn't look great; "house poor" would be my best option and best-case scenario.

I wondered if I should be texting Deacon or calling him and letting him know I would be on my way out soon. I guessed I should say thank you again for putting me up for the night and let him know I was leaving. I texted just that and I paid my breakfast bill and left. As it turned out Deacon was already off to work, so he said he would contact me later to see how everything went today.

I was right about the apartment; it was super small and it was in an area that would have me driving forever if I did keep my job a Tony's. Even on my salary there I couldn't afford this place. From there I went to the next and only other place on my list. The house was dated inside and out, but it did feel homey and the woman was really nice. She lived alone so it would be a quiet atmosphere. I didn't hesitate. I told her I would take the basement suite and move in as soon as I could. She informed me that is was available right away, which was great timing for me—no more hotel living. The furniture that was down there was hers, and she said she could move it to storage on the weekend if I wanted to use my own stuff.

I informed her I had no stuff, so coming into a fully furnished place was a full-blown miracle.

I had to go back to the bank and get a money order since my cheque book had not come in yet and I had to cancel the old ones because of the fire. I paid her first and last months' rent on a six-month lease, plus a damage deposit. With my luck, I couldn't say that this was not warranted. If I were her I would have tripled it if I had known my full background.

After all the running around and the excitement of a new place I decided to have a late lunch just down the road from my burnt-up house. I might be a bit early to the house but that was okay. Cabbing around had cost quite a bit today so it would be nice to get my car back.

I was right. When I got to my place, I was the only one there. The cab driver dropped me off, and I went directly to my car, sat down and broke into tears in the neighbor's driveway. I heard a car pull up and it was Tracy. I got out of the car as I heard her say, "Oh my God" as she looked at the mess that was my house. There was caution tape all around the property with a sign that said "keep out" in the lawn. The house was black and charred and the back half was almost completely gone. "Oh Cali, I am so sorry you went through this."

I had gotten out tissue from the car and was drying my eyes. "I didn't know how bad it was until I got here and saw it in the daylight." I had not even walked past the caution tape when I could hear the female whispers saying, "*WHAT IS SHE DOING HERE? LEAVE. LEAVE.*" It sounded like it was coming from around me, but at the moment I didn't see any spying neighbors. I didn't see anyone at all other than the fire department SUV coming down the road.

The vehicle parked and the fire chief got out. After our introductions, he explained where in the house I could go, which was not far. I was allowed in the living room and kitchen area and if there was anything by the stairs in the basement I could get that stuff, but I wasn't allowed past the stairs. The floors beneath the hall and the bedrooms were unstable and could fall at any time. There was not much to salvage. Anything cloth had to stay, as it was wet and smoke-filled. I was able to save electronics in the living room; strangely they were just dirty from the fire.

Same went for the living room table. I looked at the painting I just bought—salvageable but unwanted. It made me sick how things had gone so wrong. I was also able to save my kitchenware. It was all dirty, and some things on the back wall were or had been wet but they could be washed. The kitchen table and chairs were the only other things in the kitchen I could save. Just stuff, my heart sank. "This is just stuff I can replace," I said to Tracy as I walked through what was left. I could see my friend's heart break for me.

"I will haul out the living room TV and stand and I'll get the coffee table," she said. "I'll give you a moment."

That's when I remembered what was in the bottom of the curio unit in the corner near the door. I never really used it, but I rushed to it. Grandma's china. Grandma's tea set and crystal, all still there the curio. It looked like hell, but everything inside was in great shape. Then I opened the doors I was afraid to open. Photo albums and a terabyte storage unit were all intact. The memories of my family get-togethers were all fine. I yelled outside to Tracy, "Get me a couple boxes please!" I think she could hear the excitement in my voice because she was there in a nanosecond.

"What did you find, Cali?"

"Grandma's things. She just passed away, and I have all my photo albums! Can you believe that!"

"That's great. I'm happy for you! Your computer was also on the shelf underneath the coffee table. It might be okay, so if there is anything on there that's pertinent, hopefully it's salvageable."

"That's really good too!" This trip wasn't going to be as miserable as I had thought. Important recoveries were made. Tracy helped pack things up and we took the larger stuff outside together. I decided to open the basement door and go downstairs. The fire chief was right there at the top of the step watching to make sure I didn't go further. Two things I saw right away were the washer and dryer. They were wet and gross, but maybe salvageable, and there were clothes in both. I wondered if smoke and grossness got into the machines? They were locked pretty tight. I would have to hire help to get those, but at least they were right by the stairs.

I put the dry clothes in a garbage bag Tracy gave me, and I put the wet clothes in the hamper on top of the dryer that I had wiped out the best

I could with paper towel from my car. I would salvage whatever clothes I could, considering I had two outfits at the moment.

Over in the far corner I gleaned something from the corner of my eye. Then I really had to stare at it—it looked like someone in robes or a blanket hunched over something lying on the ground. I looked harder, and it was a small black furry body on the ground. That's when whatever it was hunched over Dallas stood tall, and its old-man face reminded me of Freddy Krueger. It whizzed through the basement and right past me so fast it was like a blurry trail going by. I grabbed a sheet from the dirty laundry on the floor and ran.

I picked up Dallas's cold, stiff body with the sheet and wrapped it up and hurried back to the stairs while the fire chief yelled at me to come back as he hurried down the stairs.

"You can't be down here anymore. It's time to go back upstairs. That was very dangerous what you did!" he said.

Tracy looked at my sad face and then the little thing wrapped in a sheet. "Dallas," was the only thing I could say. I would take her to the closest vet and have her cremated. I didn't want to look again, but I wanted to keep Dallas's collar so I opened the little package, removed her collar and wrapped her back up. At least she would get a proper sendoff and not just be buried in the rubble of a burned-out house. As we were leaving the premises and everything was packed into vehicles, the two of them gave me a few moments.

"WHERE ARE YOU GOING?"

The rough sounding man's voice questioned. It came out of thin air and for some reason I replied, "I am leaving for good."

"AAAAAGGH! GET BACK HERE!" he said, I felt like something was rushing toward me. I was so done with this place. Terrified, I bolted out the front entrance and to my vehicle.

It was a terribly exhausting afternoon. Tracy followed me to the vet to dispose of Dallas properly. I would miss her very much, but after I had a final good cry, I knew it was just Dallas's body—the real Dallas had gone to be wherever spirits go. I would miss her very much.

Tracy hopped in her car and I hopped in mine, and we went to the new place I was renting. She helped me put all my things inside. The landlady from upstairs was happy I had a few things of my own after such an ordeal and took her tables out of the basement and let me put my own things in.

There really wasn't much to move, but I was grateful to have a few familiar things around me. I was glad to be out of the house; I was so done with its spookiness and malevolence. I cleaned up my face a bit and added some makeup. Tracy and I were meeting Ashley at the pub for dinner and drinks.

When we arrived, Ashley was already there. "Hey, how did it go today?" she asked.

"It went better than expected, but after being there at the burnt-up place today I am more than ready to move on."

Over in the corner, in a dimly lit area, sat a man who suspiciously looked like Sean. He was sitting by himself gawking at our table. At the same time, as if reading my mind, Ashley said, "Well, today was Sean's last day, and Tracy is officially the boss now. Too bad you missed it. I thought you were going to come in today to see your boyfriend on his last day before dealing with your house."

I looked back over to the corner and the table was empty. "Pretty sure the romance is over. We broke up."

"Did we, though? I don't remember any of those words being said," replied Sean from out of nowhere.

"Words didn't have to be said, asshat, after you slapped me. Girls, I'm sorry but the interruption has me turned off my dinner. I have to leave." I got up and left the ladies with befuddled looks on their faces. I didn't care what Sean said or told them. I was out of there. I got in the car, locked the doors, and got out my phone and started texting. *"Do what you have to do, Deacon. Sean just showed up out of nowhere while I was out with my friends. Run the background check."*

I got a text back that said, *"Okay I will get that done."*

There was a knock at my window. "You are crazier than I thought if you think I'm going to open the door or window for you, Sean," I said and I started up my car.

"I want to talk to you," said Sean. "Open the window."

"Yeah, after the other day, I don't think so." He looked at the locks and the door lock flicked up. I hit reverse and the gas so fast I didn't care if he was in the way. I got the hell out of there. Did he just do that? Did he somehow flip the lock in my car? It sure looked like he did. If not, that was one hell of a coincidence. I sped out of the parking lot and headed home.

When I got to my new place I made myself a bowl of soup. I talked to Tracy on the phone while I ate and filled her in on the Sean and I fiasco and she filled me in on Sean's antics after I left. He said I just blew things out of proportion, and it was just a silly fight and I would be back at his place soon. That was just nuts and so not going to happen. I had a place—he just didn't know it yet.

It was going to take a bit till this basement suite felt like home. It was oddly quiet and unfamiliar. Kind of like staying in a hotel. For the first time in a long time I felt alone in the silence. Lying on the sofa that wasn't mine was strange and not comforting at all, but neither was sleeping in a bedroom that wasn't mine. I figured if I eventually fell asleep with the TV on I would get used to the idea of being here. I also called Mr. Gunderson at work and left a cowardly message. I didn't want to take the chance that for some reason Sean would be there, even though he was supposed to be at his new job. I actually had no idea what Mr. Gunderson knew at all. I had left everything at work in the hands of Sean, which I now realized was really stupid. In my message, I covered the basics even though Sean had said he kept him in the loop as to what was happening and why I had not been at work. But things had not gotten any easier, I said, so I was not coming back in at all. That was my message—flat out and to the point. I had not disclosed my problem with Sean, and that was why I was being cowardly and leaving a message instead of holding a meeting. I just wanted out and I didn't want to look back.

I texted Ashley in the middle of the night as well and told her to go after my job before he posted it. As I was lying in the dark on the sofa with the TV on it seemed to get darker. I felt like the shadows were moving, flying past in a hurry out of the corner of my eye. I didn't know if it was because it was a basement suite or if it was in my nature to just be scared all the time, but the darkness felt like it had a life of its own. The shadows moved like smoke around my space, spreading fear into me like a living, breathing thing. I knew it was irrational, but it I felt terrified.

It was like being afraid as a child, with my heart racing and being frozen in place while I shivered with fear. Not only was the fear in my heart and affecting my body, but it got into my mind too. It was visceral, and anxiety wreaked havoc through my system. The panic I felt was illogical, and the fear palpable.

It didn't dissipate or diffuse either. I lay awake all night afraid of fear itself. I didn't know I'd had a few hours' sleep till the phone rang and startled me awake at 8:00 a.m. I answered tiredly, "Hello?"

"Ms. Stenson, this is Mr. Gunderson."

"Oh, hi, Mr. Gunderson. I'm sorry about the message I left. I didn't mean to be so cryptic, but I really can't explain any further without making more questions instead of answers. Sean said he was keeping you informed, but I really should have been thinking straight and checked in with you myself."

"Sean did no such thing. I thought you jumped ship days ago or went missing or something. I found out some of the truth the other day when Tracy tried to use some trumped-up excuse to take half a day off work. When she told me, it was the first I had heard of anything you had been through. I thought you quit without notice because you just weren't showing up. I'm sorry you're having a string of bad luck and hard times, but I have already written up your employment slip with a quit on it. If you like, you can pick it up."

"I'm sorry I relied on someone I thought I could trust to relay information. I should have done it myself. Can you please mail my employment slips to my new address?" I gave him the address and we disengaged the call with displeasure hanging in the air. What was Sean thinking? If he really liked me he sure had a funny way of showing it. Just then I got a call from Deacon.

"Hi Deacon. What's new?"

"I know you haven't formally given me the go-ahead to look into Sean in writing, but I did have a search done. I don't know how this guy is getting employed. He has two restraining orders and an assault charge. It seems like the restraining orders work, as there are no further charges with those people. I think you should think about keeping far away from him and perhaps get a restraining order on him as well."

"Who was the assault charge on, a woman?"

"No, a man, but I wouldn't put it past him to assault a woman. He did already hit you."

"Okay, thanks, Deacon. Right now I'm safe. He doesn't know where I live and I will change the places I go. That should be enough to slow down any ideas to come looking for me."

"I do have an investigator at my disposal. We could tail him and see what he's been up to."

"If you think that's necessary. I think it's overkill. But I would not mind if you started paperwork on a restraining order."

"I think he could be dangerous, and you share a common tie … your three friends. I don't think they know about him and his past. If they share information about you that puts you in danger."

"Okay, if you think it's a good idea. Maybe spend a couple days seeing what he's been up to and a couple days seeing if he's up to no good now. I can't really afford more than that and this is not something I can ask my family for help with. They will hunt me down to bring me back home. I'm not going to let Sean scare me all the way back to Toronto."

"Okay, I will send out the investigator to see if I can find out anything on a couple of past dates like your house fire and where he has been and what he's been doing."

"Okay, thanks, Deacon. Do you think he had something to do with the fire? I don't know if he would take it that far."

"It's just best to check. I have someone who can, so we might as well use him." I gave Deacon my confirmation to go ahead with the investigation and we said goodbye. Today was not going to be an interesting day, and that was good. I spent the day unpacking the boxes from the house. It was amazing how many there were after a fire. There were only two boxes of mementos and treasures, and I decided to save those for last. I started washing up kitchen dishes and pots and pans and putting them away. I didn't have a washer and dryer yet, so I had to leave my clothes in the area where the washer and dryer went.

I made some calls to a local services website and hired someone to bring up the washer and dryer from the old house. They said they could do it right away and be there after supper.

I dealt with burnt-house problems all morning, like shutting off the gas and electricity and water bill so I wasn't paying for them anymore. Insurance was still dealing with the fire department and the police, so there was little I could do there. I spent the rest of the day just trying to make my new quarters home.

I made an early dinner so I could meet the people with my washer and dryer. They really didn't like the idea of going into the old place. I told them we were not going into the off-limit areas at all. I pointed out what I needed and the gentlemen went downstairs, disconnected everything and then brought up the apartment-sized machines one by one. I gave them the address to the new place and they followed me back home to bring in the machines. After they had left, it gave me pause— it could have been really easy, if Sean was a stalker type, to have just followed me from my old place all the way back here and then he would know where I live now.

I didn't see anyone around, but I had not seen him anywhere before— he would pop up out of the blue to rescue me. Deacon called, and I answered, "Hey, Deacon, I wasn't expecting to hear from you tonight."

"Well, it didn't take long to track down leads. Cali, Sean is not who you think he is. I started looking on the days where you had extraordinary days.

The investigator found the person involved in the accident. He wouldn't talk to the investigator, but the guy involved just reiterated what he said in the police reports. His story changed when I said who I was and applied a little pressure to his story. That and he folded just from the sheer size of me. He was given a lot, and I mean a lot, of money to follow you from your door and dissuade you from your final destination. He chose to run you down before you got to where you were going. He wasn't going to get paid otherwise. He did a great job, too; he basically got you to hit him. He didn't even have to accept fault." Deacon continued when I didn't say anything, "Anyway, I gave him a picture the investigator took of Sean and he positively ID'd Sean. He paid to have you in an accident. Cali, he was probably waiting to be the knight in shining armor. He didn't work late. He knew you would call work, the only number you had at the time, or a cab, and he got lucky because you called work and told him where you were. Hell, he was probably already in the parking lot by the time you called him, and he didn't need the work phone to ring. Would someone from middle management at a furniture store forward the work phone and email to their personal phone and email? I mean he's not a real estate mogul he works at a local store! That's what you stated to me after it happened— that's why I figured something was not right. It's a furniture store, not some major business dealing with crises all the time. It just didn't add up."

"I can't believe he would do that. I think I'm in shock," I replied.

"The investigator also talked to the police, and once the investigator gave his card and mine to them, they forwarded all the information of the night of the fire to me as your lawyer.

The police did canvas the block after they were told it was arson. A couple neighbors said they saw a black car with a man waiting inside for quite a while. They didn't say any more than that so we can't be sure he started the fire."

"But why would he do that? What does that accomplish?"

"Need. You would need him, and he would get to fulfill rescuing you, being the hero, as it were. But in his twisted mind, you would also be indebted to him. At least, that's what I think it is, anyway, just from what you've told me."

"I don't feel safe now with him out there and me here. He probably already knows where I am. I quit my job, which apparently I already got let go from because Sean said he told everyone what was happening and he didn't talk to anyone at work. They thought I just decided not to show up. He sabotaged it so I wouldn't able to work there. Why would he do that?"

"Again, need, or maybe he had a plan for you to rely on him. Maybe he thought he could get you closer to him if you weren't working there or control you. He just left his job. I checked and he does actually have another job to go to, so maybe he had plans to have you work closer with him? I don't know. I haven't gotten that far yet."

"Maybe I should just go back to Toronto. I'm not safe here."

"I already had the investigator corollate all the proof for the accident. I also hauled Mike Johnston to the police station; he is the guy that hit you. He told the police everything he knew, plus I had everything the investigator had sent to the station.

They will be looking for Sean by now." There was silence on the line, but Deacon broke it. "Cali, I know you're going through a lot. If I can be so selfish as to say, I don't want you to go back to the other side of the country. If you don't have anything tying you to Vancouver permanently, maybe we could find you a place to stay in Victoria. You could keep your place in Vancouver, but maybe you would like to come see Victoria for a bit."

"I love the idea, but that feels like jumping from the frying pan into the fire. The last time I trusted someone, look where it got me."

"I understand that, Cali. Just know that I want you to be safe. I want nothing from you in return. Hell, if you want me to keep my distance too, I will. We don't have to have any kind of relationship, friendship or any contact beyond the case. But if you don't feel safe there I don't think he would expect you to stay here in Victoria. He doesn't know any of the new information on you yet, where you live, that you're not at your job, though he's probably expecting that one if he set you up. Take advantage and keep him guessing."

"I don't know ...what you say does make sense."

"Whatever you want as far as contact with me is up to you. I am trying to keep my hours on your case to a minimum so its affordable. So if you only want contact with me when you need help or when you need to talk about the case, that's fine by me. Just don't check out of your life because of some sicko."

"I'll think about it, Deacon, but I had only saved up so much money and I burned through it pretty fast. It will be a while before I see any money for the house insurance. So I should really spend time looking for a job."

"Okay, you think about it. In the meantime, stay safe and just be aware of your surroundings. That doesn't mean you have to be paranoid. Just be aware and take care." With that, we signed off from the call. It was late into the night when I went to bed. I noticed this place felt really lonely. I didn't know if it was the place or just a place without Dallas in it that made it feel lonely. It was hard to sleep with the quiet and nothing else to think about except Sean running around out there. In my mind I made him into a monster. I seemed to be afraid all the time now, like the shadows lived and breathed, spreading fear wherever they went.

It took a long time before I fell asleep. I was having my recurring demon dream, but after being dragged down off my bed for the millionth time, it changed.

The demon stops dragging me, its body shifting from its contorted form. Black smoke fills the air, and the demon's shape changes. Then there he is, standing in the form of Sean, but it's not Sean— he doesn't look right. This Sean had deeper shadows, stronger angles to his face and black onyx eyes. "Sean?" I breathe questioningly. "You're a demon?" "No, you stupid girl, I am the demon who has been after you since you decided to live on this plane. Your soul being up for grabs here means one more for me. Sean is just the skin suit I wear. It gives me more influence in the world. I can reach you here, physically let you hear and see me, and as you seen by my test I can physically get to you and touch you …well, throw you, really. That's what I did. Did you enjoy my throwing you about as much as I did?" It's like the demon is waiting for me to answer. I keep silent. *"Sean is tucked away inside, he made it so easy. I can only body jump into complete assholes; evil lets me in. Leave it to the angel to latch onto a boyfriend who belongs in hell!"* The demon laughs, a grating sound to my ears like metal scratching on metal. *"I can't believe after twenty-four years you still can't figure out what you've done. You don't remember, do you?"* I reply out of curiosity, *"What don't I remember? What did I do that you are so interested in?"*

"The creator that creates all things breathes life into humanity by giving the body a soul, a conscience, and the lifeline that connects life to all living things. You hijacked this body trying to get back to Earth. You are an angel in a human body, stuffed inside like a breakfast sausage. YOU did that! They will never let you back home. That's why your life is such a mess, not to blame this evil sack that I borrowed—it's you, you attract everything evil to the bright light that darkness is attracted to for miles. Essentially you turned this human into a beacon for all things to attract to. The best part is you don't remember why, and as long as you traipse around as a human, you will never remember." His chainsaw laugh hackled through my dream. *"I can help with that. If I kill you now, you'll either end up on my side or you'll end up back up there wondering how you can get back down here and finish your mission. I can let Sean here have his way with you, by the way. I know where you are and so will Sean."* He hacks and cackles a laugh.

Finally it was like I was allowed to wake from my dream. I felt like I was captured; no matter how much I wanted to wake up, it was not something I could do. Was it real? Was it just a dream? What about what the possessed Sean said? Why would an angel come back down to Earth? Everyone was always wanting to leave and go up to heaven or utopia and so forth, so why would one want to fight their way back down? It didn't make sense. Angel, ha ha, funny … I think I would know if I were an angel. I was anything but. I was more concerned with what the dream said about Sean knowing everything about me because he was the borrowed soul. It was just a dream, but he was the stalker, so regardless of the dream or no dream, I needed to keep away and ahead of him.

The thing was, these visions differed from dreams because of the way I had all my senses and faculties— the awareness of what was happening around me. This demon dream *was* different; this vision and the last felt real. Yes, it was always the same dream over and over, but in the last two, I didn't feel like I was in a dream state. I just wasn't able to get back to a wakeful state. I had to endure till it was over. Demons could lie, yes, that was for sure. They could make you believe anything. But what was with all the information this time? Why come and give all that information to me? It was very unreal, and very extraordinary. What if this time it was truthful information? It did fit with what the wakeful vision said—the spirits with the purple aura said they could not tell me everything. Demons didn't play by the same rules; they would say and do whatever they could. The spirits also said I didn't belong here, and that's why my life was disheveled and the darkness kept coming at me.

That was basically what the demon said too—that they were after me and I was a beacon for the darkness. Maybe the new vision had unreal but truthful information. If I went with that theory, I would have to figure out the why. I didn't get the angel part of the vision; maybe that was speaking to my innocence and naiveté, and maybe Sean was the demon because I felt scared of him now. I felt stalked by him. Why would someone come back or want to come back down? Who could I ask? Maybe later I could call Todd.

Right now I needed to worry about what information Sean had. That had the utmost of importance. Maybe he was caught by the police? Maybe I was safe? I could call Deacon or the police and see if they had found him. Deacon would probably have more information because he could contact whoever was on that case. I got up and went to the kitchen to put some coffee on. Deacon wouldn't be at work yet, but I could text him. He was probably on the way in to the office soon. *"Hey Deacon, sorry I am texting you this early, do you think they would have caught Sean? I had a pretty rough night and an early morning. I don't know how to handle this. I am afraid to go out, I am afraid to stay home in case he finds out where I am. Maybe he's busy running or with the police? Then I don't have to worry so much."*

I didn't hear back right away, but ten minutes later the phone rang. "Hey Deacon, sorry for texting before you got to work. I was a little bit on overdrive this morning."

"That's understandable. I didn't call back right away. I waited till I could put you on speaker in the car.

I can check for you mid-morning on status update and ask the officers to keep us in the loop as to what's happening with the case. He may not have been expecting them, so they might have been able to find him easily. Let me call in and I'll get back to you."

That gave me comfort, but I didn't know what to do during the day. I didn't know if I should leave the house or stay in. I settled on the fact that the woman upstairs was home if anything weird happened. I made my space a little more homey and moved things around the way I liked them. It was a little weird for me living in a basement suite. I had never done that before and I never had windows that looked mostly at the ground level. I thought maybe I could go to antique stores or garage sales and look for pictures, since I had none of my own. Then I remembered I had family photos. I could send them in for enlargements and decorate a little with the photos I already had. I went through my memory stick on the computer and picked out a few pictures I would like blown up. A family photo of us goofing off in the park, a picture of Grandma, and a scenic picture with a bear in it from my trip to the mountains recently and Dallas in her box. I could drive over to the drug store and pick up a few things and get my pictures in an hour. A grocery shopping trip was in order—I had next to nothing. That got me thinking on what Deacon said. Hopefully he would call soon with good news, and if there was no good news maybe I would go see what Victoria had to offer for a little while and forgo the grocery trip here. I was tired of living scared, tired of the weirdness. It was time to dig in and really figure things out.

CHAPTER 11
Who Do You Think You Are?

I WAS ON MY WAY INTO THE STORE WHEN I GOT A CALL THAT STOPPED ME IN my tracks in the parking lot. "Cali, I'm sorry, but they have not found Sean. He managed somehow to be one step ahead; maybe the investigator's cover was blown or maybe the police were not careful enough. I don't really know where the mistake was made or if there was a mistake, but he found out. The cops are looking for him and he's in the wind. He didn't show for work, and I don't know where he is." I looked all around me, feeling like if he wasn't where he was supposed to be, he was where he shouldn't be and that was around me. "Cali, are you home? We can send an officer there to make sure things are safe. I put an emergency restraining order in place. Paper doesn't usually do the trick with people like Sean, but it's worth a try."

There was silence. I couldn't speak. I was just looking around. I was not home, but should I be? If I went now and he was following me, was that because he knew where I was like in my vision; did he know where I lived already? If I went now would I lead him there? I finally snapped out of it with Deacon repeating my name. "Sorry, I'm here. I just got a little paranoid for a second. Deacon, I am not home. I went to the drug store and was thinking about getting groceries, but now I'm afraid to move. What if he's here watching me, or what if he knows where I live? There have been opportunities to find information out about the changes in my life before we knew who he was, so he may have that information. What if he's already on my tail?"

"Cali, you have nothing holding you there at the moment. Why don't you get in your car and just drive to the ferry? Come down, you can visit me, see my new place, whatever you want to do. We can keep it strictly professional and just meet up about your case at the office if you want. Like I said, I need nothing from you. We can even just stay in contact by phone. I just think he would think twice with you by me. He's a tall, lean, fit guy, but I know the law and I am in contact with the police. I'm also bigger and he knows it. My sheer size and pissed-off attitude usually keeps people away and you will feel better with some distance between you and Sean till he is caught."

"I don't know if I'm just speaking out of fear or not, but that does sound good. I feel like everything I do can lead me to him or the other way around. I just need to get out. If I don't leave Vancouver and go to Victoria then I will go home to Toronto. That's a hell of a lot farther than Victoria if he ends up getting caught. I would have to travel so far for nothing, except for visiting family."

"I will help you and maybe find a nice bed and breakfast you can stay at for a few days."

"Yeah, that sounds good. I can still look for work with an internet connection and I can have distance. Thank you for your help, Deacon."

"Happy to do it. We'll talk soon. Take care and stay safe."

This felt right; not like any of my other decisions. I didn't know the difference till just this second. But the moment I made the decision to go to Victoria, I felt lighter.

I felt a little braver with a plan in place, and I decided to go into the store and get my pictures. I would forgo going for groceries and just pick up some snacks. As I was coming out of the store I scanned outside quickly for black cars and then men in black cars, and particularly Sean, stalking about. Every person in a suit looked like him. I decided to take my chances and scurry to the car like a mouse. That's when I realized Deacon was right. Whether I was in danger or not, I didn't want to live like I had to watch my back and scurry about like a mouse. That was victimizing over and over again. I couldn't do that. I didn't want to be that.

I was back on the road going home, and it was just a few minutes away. When I got home I could pack a quick duffle bag and I was out. Out of my rearview mirror I saw a black car speeding up, and right away I started to freak out. The hairs raised all over my body as Sean's face came into view—this time it was him. I could see him driving behind me clear as day. I was not dreaming this; it was happening right now. What should I do? Sean was now driving right on my tail. I picked up the phone and dialed Deacon. He would know what to do. 911 was the obvious choice, but then I would have to explain the situation, and by then it could be too late. Deacon had the inside track and knew people handling this. "Hey, what's up, did you forget something?" Deacon asked.

"He's driving right behind me. Sean is here and he knows where I am. He's here!"

"Don't panic, just stay on the road and drive in circles if you have to. Just don't stop anywhere. I will call the person in charge of your case at the station. Where are you?"

"I'm on Oak close to the drug store by my place."

"Stay on the line."

Just then, Sean pulled up beside me, his face cut in hard lines; he was pissed off and obviously blamed me for his current predicament. He sped past me and kept going at an alarming rate. As he rushed through a red light, I came upon the light and stopped. "The cops are on their way. Stay calm, Cali," Deacon said as he returned to the phone.

"He is gone, and he is also visibly pissed right now. I think I'm in danger."

"Where are you now? Hang up and call 911. The emergency dispatch will ping your phone and your location will show up. Just say who you are and say the police are already on the way, but you are calling with an exact location."

I said okay, hung up and did as I was told. "911, what is your emergency, police, fire or ambulance?"

"This is Cali Stenson, police are already on their way. I was told to call so you can ping my phone for an exact location so the police know where to go."

"I am picking you up right now just turning off Oak Street."

"Yes, I am pulling into the 7/11 parking lot right now. I will stop and wait here."

"Are you in immediate danger?"

"Yes, I have a restraining order against the man who is coming after me. He was just here, he sped up and then fled but I don't know if he is coming back around."

"Stay on the line. The officers will be right there, okay?"

The officers came a moment later and I hung up the phone. I had to try and give a description and I was all shaken up and scared. I did the best I could with the description and another cop car was already out looking and searching the area. The officer I was talking to went on his radio to give the description and his partner wrote everything down. "Do you think you know where he might be or where he might go if he is not here with you?"

"I don't really know him that well. I can guess he's not going to work because he was wearing a t-shirt and regular jacket. I've never seen him before without a suit. I'm afraid he's at my place. That isn't far from here and he's probably waiting for me."

"You live nearby?" the officer questioned. I nodded. "Address please." He got on his radio and gave the address to the other officers.

"Is there anything else? I just want to go home and then get the hell out of here."

"Are you going somewhere?" asked the officer

"I am leaving for a few days to Victoria. Hopefully by then you will have Sean in custody, but till then I don't want to be around."

The cop nodded. "If you don't live far, I will follow you home and meet up with the other officers to see if they had any indication of him being around your place."

"Thank you," I said.

When we arrived at the house there didn't seem to be anything amiss. It was very quiet and luckily the lady wasn't upstairs to see her home crawling with officers, though she would probably hear it from the neighbors.

"Ms. Stenson, can I go in with you and check it out on the inside?"

"Sure," I said as I unlocked the door. The officer didn't miss a thing; he was looking to see if the door was even locked when I was trying to unlock it. He kind of nodded in approval or maybe to check the mental box in his head that the door was indeed locked. We went in and I stood in the kitchen while the officer checked out the tiny place. That's when I noticed a folded note on the table in the living room. I thought maybe it was just from the landlady.

"This is all your fault, you did this! You called the cops on me! What a joke you are, all I ever did was want to be close to you, all I did was help your stupid ass with you stupid problems. I took you in, you dumb bitch! I am not going to lie, once I finally got you there to my apartment I didn't want you to leave. I did a lot of careful planning for you to get to know me and

come to be in my apartment. Then you left like I had done
nothing for you. You will pay for putting me through this."

"Well, he's not here," the officer said as I was reading the note. I lifted up my hand with the note. I just stared at the officer with my mouth open, jaw dropped to the floor and eyes wide with shock.

"He got in. He was here while I was talking with you!" The officer got on his radio and talked to the officers outside in the cars and one car took off, probably looking for Sean.

"I have got to get out of here." I grabbed a garbage bag and threw a few days' worth of clothes in the bag, and all my bathroom stuff into a smaller plastic bag.

"I can escort you to the ferry," the officer said. "We will do it as discreetly as possible. If you run into any problems leaving town, let me know. I suggest you get someone to meet you on the other side as well."

I got on my phone. "Deacon, it's me. Can you meet me after work at the ferry? I'm getting an escort there, and they want someone on the other side to meet me."

"Yes, of course, no problem, just let me know when."

Once I got to the port, I bought a ticket. The wait could be long without prior booking. The officers couldn't sit and wait for four hours for the ferry, so the officer made sure I was on the ferry that left in an hour, like a police emergency or something. I was able to load right away and then I just had to wait for it to leave. I stayed out of view as much as possible in case somehow Sean would know this was my next move.

That's when I had the idea and I phoned the officer. "I bet he's at the airport! I bet he thinks he scared me so bad he's going to wait and see if I show up on whatever flight goes to Toronto from here next, Toronto is where I am from."

"I will radio that in to the search area team and have someone at the office look up flights while I watch the ferry and departures area. Thanks for the information."

Next I texted Deacon the departure information and arrival information. He confirmed that he would be there.

I looked forward to finding out if he found a place for me to stay a while and I needed to figure out what I was going to do while I was in Victoria.

What was I going to do about work back in Vancouver? It wasn't that long a ride to Victoria. We had texted a place to meet so I could park my vehicle at the end of the parking lot and we could chat about the next step. I parked and he followed me to where he suggested we meet. "Hi," I said as he got out of his vehicle. "Thanks for meeting me."

"No problem. I thought if you wanted we could go to dinner, since it's that time. There's not much development, but I can fill you in with what I know. We could go just around the corner so it's nice and easy. Nothing too far so you don't get lost."

"Sure, I'm starving. Even soup and sandwiches would be great." We drove for a couple minutes and ended up at a diner with soup, sandwiches and pizza. We ordered and then Deacon interrupted the awkward silence.

"The place you are staying at is a bed and breakfast. Here's the address. It's booked for the week, but if you don't end up staying that long you can let them know."

"Thank you for handling that. I know that goes above and beyond what you do as someone's lawyer."

"It was no problem. So there is some development in your case. Mr. Johnston was arrested for his part in your accident. Also, we found out that Sean may have two cars."

"Oh, shoot, he used to have a Jag. I just assumed he sold it when he got that new fancy car."

"Yes, we think he traded that car for a white sedan so it blends in. They are still trying to locate Sean. I need all your friends' numbers. We are going to call and see if they've had any contact with him."

I opened my phone and gave him the numbers I had for Tracy, Ashley and Todd. He texted them to someone else, the investigator, I presumed. I'd better call them—they would be so mad if they found out what had been happening from someone else. "We won't know if Sean had a hand in the fire till the police are able to bring him in for questioning. They have no leads as to who started the fire, just how it was started."

"I just hope it's soon. I quit my job, I'm running out of money and I'm pretty sure that I'm not going to see house insurance money for a month. It's up to me to put the land up for sale, and that could take time. I'm a little worried on all fronts right now."

"I have an idea. Take it or leave it, that is up to you. I could really use a secretary. I have not been able to find a legal secretary, but at the moment, I'm falling behind and any type of secretary would do. You did data entry and worked in the office. Maybe we could help each other. You help with the inner workings of the office and I will pay you; both our problems solved." He continued with a smile and mischief on his face. "Unfortunately for me, we would have to be strictly professional in terms of how we maintain a relationship, but we get along fairly well and from what I see we could probably work well together as well. What do you think?"

"Wow, that's quite the offer, Deacon." I paused, trying to take in all the information. "What about my place in Vancouver?"

"Well, the way I see it is that you have a brilliant opportunity to try out a new position. You have already paid your rent there for a month. That means you have a month to try things here. If you like it, you stay and find a place to live, and if you don't, you find work in Vancouver and go home to your place."

"I have a lease there for six months, and at some point won't you need someone with a legal background?"

"We can cross those bridges when we come to them. I can probably get you out of the lease if need be, or throw money at the problem and make it go away. Right now that's a month away, so we can figure that out when you decide if you want that place or not.

Right now you do, and its already paid for. I will help with that when it is time. As for you not being qualified, we shall see what you can learn in a months' time. If you can keep learning, and you do enjoy the work, maybe you would want to take some courses at night. If not, you have given me a month to find someone else and for you to find something else." He put up his finger like he needed a moment, got up, got an extra napkin and wrote on it. It was a salary figure he was offering. It was quite a good salary more than I would make at Tony's Furniture.

"Are, you serious? You're sure making this an offer I can't refuse!" I said with a smile and my eyes wide.

"Well, I do really need someone at the office. You would be saving my bacon again."

"And relationship-wise we would be colleagues and friends? Strictly professional?" I asked.

"I promise to you I will stay strictly professional."

"Okay, I mean, this is an opportunity in a new field for me, and I can't pass that up. If you will help me when it comes time to deal with the lease, I will take this opportunity you provided. Wow! This is really exciting!"

"This is great news! I have a secretary. I never thought I would find one. Of course I will help you with the lease and when the time comes we can look at a course for legal secretary if you wish. But let's not get ahead of ourselves. Let's see if you can stand working with me.

You know ... I should have warned you first, but in my profession I am considered a bit of a hard ass," he said with a grin.

"I can deal with a hard ass, not to worry," I said with my chin pulled high, confidence in my posture and a grin on my face.

"I believe you," Deacon quipped back.

After dinner I located the bed and breakfast. I had talked to the owners in great detail about my current situation, and I gave them my credit information. They were quite generous in helping me, as I would not have a place here for a month. They had a discounted rate and said they could let me stay for three weeks. After that they had a bookings for the following two weeks. I thanked them profusely for their kindness and generosity and I texted Deacon right away. I was so excited to tell him I had a place for the next three weeks. I also told him for the next little while I would like to be paid weekly so I could afford to live and pay that rent. He agreed to do so for the first month.

I couldn't believe how things were just working out. I could tell the difference in my decisions too. I could feel I was making the right choices, and they didn't feel heavy and obligatory, they felt light and like I had made the right choice and just knew it. I decided to have a group phone call with Ashley and Tracy. I filled them in on everything and told them that if the police called them that was my doing, as the police were trying to locate Sean.

I let them know to stay away from him as well, but said if he did call or get in contact to find out what they could about his whereabouts, as safely as they could. Then I resigned myself to late-night TV and infomercial shows. This was the fourth bed that wasn't mine that I had slept in within weeks.

It felt odd and lonely, but I couldn't think about that right now. Late at night my mind just wondered, but if I thought about all that had happened I would break. I was turning what I thought was a new leaf, and I was not going to ruin that by bringing myself down in the doldrums.

I dreamed of work and solving problems, a normal work day with my friends at my side doing the same job I was doing. The dream switched and we were in the break room laughing and catching up with coffees in hand, enjoying a normal-looking day. The dream switched again, and I recognized the voice. The lady with the purple aura interrupted me. "Cali, I must tell you now that the truth is out. You must know it to be true, what the demon said—you went down to earth with a purpose, your spirit was angelic the demon did not lie. Right now, Cali, we need you. I cannot enter where you must go, but you are also human. You are both, and you must go." "Go where?" The dream switched and I was acutely aware of the switch from my office to this place which was like Earth but not Earth. Everything changed from color to black and white, like the color had leeched out of the world. There was something raining from the sky, but it was not rain, not snow; it looked like ash. Everything was the color of ash, everything was covered in ash.

The dream switched again and I was thrust in front of Grandma. "Grandma! How did you get here?" She did not speak, and at the same time I knew I had to get her out of there. I took her hand and we ran as fast as she could. I didn't want to leave her behind and I knew instinctively this was why I was sent. Grandma somehow got turned around, lost in the afterlife. She was not where she was supposed to be. This wasn't purgatory, but it wasn't like what people imagined hell to be either. I didn't know where we were, but when I turned around, a very large predatory creature was turning the corner and coming down the street we were on. It seemed to be as tall as the buildings and the same color as everything else. It walked upright and wasn't all that different than TV monsters. It looked as if T-Rex and the creature from Alien had a baby. I needed to get her out of here; how had Grandma lasted so long? We ran and ducked into a store and not surprisingly the store looked the same as everything else; it was destroyed, like a bomb had gone off. Everything was the color of ash, and the store was a mess. The demon or creature or whatever it was crept by, and once it rounded the corner I grabbed Grandma's hand and we crept out of the store and ran. We rounded a corner, because it seemed somehow to be brighter there, just as a demon came around another corner behind us. "Grandma, just a little further." "I can't sweetie, I can't." My instincts were driving me. I knew I had to get her to the end of the road. I ducked in a clothing store that looked demolished, like the drugstore we were just in. "We just need to go to the end of the street, okay?" I didn't wait for an answer. I dragged her towards the end of the street. There was a shining ball of light there that was lighting up and bringing color to the street.

That's why my instincts were humming; it wasn't normal, but it was as close to normal as I was going to get here. I got about fifteen feet from the glowing sphere, and then Grandma just disappeared from my grasp. I knew she was safe now I lead her to the place where she was supposed to be.

I woke up like I had landed in my bed, but I felt like I had accomplished whatever it was I was supposed to accomplish. I knew I wasn't going to be back there, but what the heck was Grandma doing there? Had she gotten so lost in her journey to find peace? Why would I be picked to go? Then I realized I needed to accept the weird in my life. I kept trying to fight it. I had been taught my whole life that those situations were false, that hallucinations or illness were way more common than seeing and hearing what I heard because of spirits. It was all in my head, I had been told, and maybe so, but I knew Todd and I saw the same thing, the same day and at the same time.

I knew I didn't go around breaking my house up or lighting it on fire. I knew Dallas was afraid of everything and everyone. Also, I was not special when it came to this matter. I would bet half the population of this world was like me and either they accepted it, like few did, or they fought it, like many did. Some people may have illness and or medication that caused this, but it was not the same; medication did not cause your back to be lacerated because you were thrown into a mirror in your dream. Did I believe an angel spirit was inside with my soul? Well, honestly, that one was a hard pill to swallow and a new one on me.

Maybe Todd could help or maybe his dad that raised him, the shaman. Would it really help if they told me the exact same thing the demon and spirit did?

I needed human confirmation, as though that would somehow make it acceptable. What if they told me I was out to lunch … then what? I knew what just happened with Grandma to be true. It was unreal, but I knew it to have happened, just as I knew I took the ferry the other day. I got up, got in the shower and as I was thinking things through and lathering up, a very tall, dark shadow wove around me. When it stopped in front of me, images went through my head in seconds flat. Three murders. There was a young boy with his head bashed in from a rock, and another man just lying there face forward in the mud. He was in his thirties and had dark-blond hair and blue eyes. The other was a burly outdoors-type man, older, like maybe fifty, who was shot in the back of the head. Then the shadow disappeared, and I was left stunned, standing in the shower. I rinsed the shampoo out of my hair. When I opened my eyes, something was writing on the shower wall. *DEMON*. I sprang out of the shower so fast I almost took down the shower curtain with me trying to get a way. I ran to my room and I quickly got dressed. I was heading out my bedroom to leave when I decided to go back and check the bathroom.

Sure enough, the writing was on the wall, plain as day. It was just written in the water. I put my finger to it trying to figure out how it got there, how I watched it write while I showered. It looked like my handwriting— that's what got me curious. I was confused …did I do this? Did I make this happen? Did I zone out and write it? I tried to write a word in the water just below and it wouldn't work; I couldn't tell there was anything there.

I tried with conditioner on my hand and then shampoo, to see if it would stay on the wall where I could see it. Nothing, and now the walls were starting to dry up so even the word *Demon* was disappearing. I quickly wiped the wall so it wouldn't be there the next time I showered.

I was going to go upstairs for breakfast, but it wasn't till 8:30. I decided I needed fresh air and I would walk a good distance out of the neighborhood to go to the coffee shop. I put the coffeeshop into my phone and mapped out the route so I wouldn't get lost or take the wrong street. I was glad to be out of the house, but let's face it, it was not the house, it was me. It didn't matter where I went.

I was at the coffee shop a good while and when I returned back to the B&B there was a white car parked out front that was not there that morning. When I walked to the door a man said something to the owner and turned and walked outside. The calmness wiped from my face and I backed down the stairs.

"What, you didn't think I wasn't going to stop and see you while you were here, did you?"

"Sean, what are you doing here? How did you find out I was in Victoria?" The owner disappeared from the doorway quickly and I was left with Sean on the small porch staring up at him from the stairs.

"Well, Todd is a little worse for wear, but Ashley, she is a smart girl, so she told me right away...well, not right away. Todd's nose had to break first, then she told me. You should not have mentioned where you were to Tracy and Ashley if you didn't want me to come say hello."

"I, I didn't. I don't think I told them what place I was staying ... What do you want Sean, what do you want from me?"

"Well, now that you mention it, why don't we go for a ride in this fancy new car?"

"You're crazy if you think I'm going anywhere with you."

Right then Bev, the lady that owned the house, showed back up at the door. "Don't call me crazy, you bitch, you are the one who put me in this mess," Sean said in a low growly voice.

"I did no such thing, Sean, this is not the first time this has happened, has it? You have done this before and failed. You have had restraining orders and charges brought against you before. What else did you do? I mean, you tried to have me injured or killed in a car accident, I don't know which. What else have you done?"

"You mean like the house fire? Are you trying to figure out if I did it? Well, I did! I wasn't myself okay, something ... something happened. It took me over. I don't know, it wasn't me. I don't even remember how I got to your house that night! All I know is I was standing there with a rather large empty gas can in my hand and your house was already engulfed in flames. So the question becomes, what did you do, you witch? I was fine before I met you, and now I am burning down houses with no memory of it!"

"Were you, Sean ... fine, before you met me? You had previous charges against you, you yelled at me, and secretly painted portraits of me and took pictures of me while I was alone having coffee. You hit me, Sean, do you really think that's fine?" Just then a black SUV came screeching around the corner. I noticed it had cop lights on the top and when it stopped the cops turned on the lights without the siren.

"What have you done, witch?" Sean lunged for me and I almost fell from the step I was on as I tried to run for the SUV. The cops got out and Sean tried to break for it instead of chase me down. The cop ran and pointed a gun at Sean and told him to stop. Two prongs shot out and attached to Sean, and he convulsed as he hit the ground from the officer's taser. The other officer jumped on Sean and handcuffed him in seconds. As Sean got up his eyes were as black as onyx and then they went blue again as he stared me down with hate in his eyes and drool on his chin; he looked like a wild man. Another SUV came around the corner and this time Deacon flew out of the driver's side door in a mad sprint after he had parked the car.

"Are you okay?"

"I think so. I'm really shaken … how did they know to come here? How did you know to come here and that I needed help?"

"I left Bev my number, and she called me and I called the cops. I think he'll be put away for a long time. I have quite a case building on him."

"He said he burnt my house down. He did it and doesn't remember."

When Sean was safely confined in the SUV, Bev came out. "I heard that part. I was standing right behind him in the doorway. I can fill out some kind of form saying what I heard and saw."

"Thank you, Bev, that would be great." Chuck, Bev's husband, was apparently right behind Bev and I didn't see him till he came out as well. "Thank you for helping and knowing what to do today. I think you saved my life, so thank you."

"It was no problem, dearie. We knew there was a slim chance he could show up here and we were to just call Deacon and the cops would come."

I turned to Deacon. "Thanks for showing up. I know your workday was probably just starting."

"It's no problem. I need to talk to the arresting officers now anyway."

"What do I do now?" I asked.

"Now you can relax. It's over with Sean."

CHAPTER 12

No More Secrets

I WAS REALLY RAMPED UP AFTER SEAN LEFT. I DIDN'T FEEL LIKE SITTING IN A house full of strangers. They were nice enough people, but this was not home. If it were, I would probably just hibernate under a rock and take down time. "You don't look well," Deacon said. "You are not okay right now. Do you want to go for coffee? I can take you somewhere close, or if you want we can go somewhere close to the office. You can see where you'll be working, and we can draft a work agreement. Maybe keeping you busy is the key. I don't think sitting around here all day will help you."

"Neither do I. You have to go to work, don't you? You don't have time for coffee."

"I can make time. We can chat for a bit, and then I will have to leave for work, but you can either hang out and see what Victoria has to offer or look for a place." or you can come to the office and see what it's like there. Are you still planning to stay in Victoria or are you going back right away? I imagine this might have scared you off. Did it?" "No, I mean I don't think so. How did he know I was here and not Toronto?" "I will find out what the investigators know and fill you in."

"He said something about hurting Todd. I'm afraid to call and find out what that means."

"Lets get out of here and we can at find out," Deacon suggested.

I decided to meet him at the coffee shop near his work so he could get to work faster and do what he needed to do. I didn't want to hold him up all day. Plus, I wanted my own car so I could come and go as I pleased. I felt really unsettled and going home to Toronto with my tail tucked between my legs was sounding awfully tempting. I was going to have to phone Todd and find out if he was okay, but I was just afraid to. I am afraid after all this that they would just hate me, especially if Todd got hurt. I made a mental note to buck up, and make sure to call him after I was done with talking with Deacon.

Deacon had already grabbed a table at the coffee shop. Funny how I was up in arms and my mind was exploding with the odd daily events and tragedies but I could still notice what a handsome man Deacon was. In fact I also noticed I was not the only one noticing. Was he blind to all the attention or did he just not care? Deacon in a tailored suit was something to behold. His tall and muscled frame meant that suit hardly had to work at all; he made the suit, not the other way around. He could probably show up in a sack and look good. Deacon's dark hair was done with precision, and his brown eyes held a bright gleam. That's when I noticed he was looking at me. How long had I been staring? Oh God, I hope not that long. I could feel my cheeks heat and I gave myself a mental pep talk to chill my embarrassment of being caught staring at him before marching over to where he was sitting.

"Did you order a coffee already, Deacon?"

"No, I was waiting for you."

"What will you have? I'll grab coffee today."

"Just a large black coffee, thanks, Cali. That's nice of you." I went to the counter and ordered Deacon's coffee. I decided a vanilla-bean latte was most definitely in order.

***

It was hard not to notice when Cali walked in the door. Even in her everyday clothes and disheveled from a horrible experience, she held herself with confidence. She was gorgeous, too, and that didn't help the attraction I felt towards her. I had promised to cool it and so I had better. That's when she had stopped and noticed him. I didn't think she had noticed that I was looking right back at her, as she was lost in thought. She took a look around the room and a quick smile sprang to her face … that beautiful smile. Did she just give me the once-over? It was quick, but I was sure she looked me up and down. Maybe there was interest there after all. I hadn't been sure till just then when she snapped out of her gaze and headed over. Honestly, I zoned out at her beauty. She was saying something, but all I caught was that she was getting coffee and I told her black coffee. Which was not at all what I drank, but he was in awe of how together she seemed after what had just happened. While she ordered the coffee I went to the side bar and got cream and sugar.

***

I came back to the table and Deacon seemed as zoned out as I was. "You seem a little lost in thought," I said as I sat down.

"I'm just thinking about you, and how together you seem after what you were just put through."

"In my consternation, I feel like it's not over … like, I can't believe what just happened actually happened, but I feel like I expect more to come, you know?"

"Cali, you don't have to worry. He's in cuffs now. I will get the station down in Vancouver to get Todd in for questioning so we can get his and Ashley's statements. That alone will land Sean in hot water, as well as him physically trying to harass you at your residence and then showing up in a different city to find you. Plus, we have arrested the other person involved in the accident and traced down the money transfer so he can't recant his statement. You will be safe from him from now on. You just have trust me. He is out of your hair, and as long as I have something to say about it, it will stay that way." I tried to give Deacon a smile of appreciation, but I just couldn't believe it was over. My relationship started drastically with Sean and ended just the same, so if I thought of it that way it made sense he was gone now. "Why don't you come check out the office? You might as well see if it's something you want to do before you say yes. I mean, now that Sean is gone you could just go back to Vancouver if you wanted. To your place, to your friends."

"That's I good idea. I never thought of that."

"Stupid me to remind you," he said with a smirk. "But it's the truth. I am not going to hold you to anything that is not wholly your decision. As I said, this is not about me. You decide your comings and goings." He paused for effect. "Despite my disappointment if you leave."

I couldn't help but smile back; a 6'4" male facetiously pouting just didn't look right, and it was funny. "I somehow feel safer here even though Sean got to me here. But you're right, let's check out the office. I mean, I heard through the grapevine a real hard ass is the boss." We finished our coffee and Deacon showed me where the parking garage was and then we went up so he could show me the building and front security desk and clearance protocols. It wasn't a big building; we were on the 4th floor, which was the top floor. Deacon worked with three other lawyers, but they seemed to have their own businesses and offices, like they were separate.

Deacon's looked like a classic lawyer's office. It was a corner office with wall full of windows stretching out to a view of Victoria. There was a large dark wooded desk with files all over it, a computer that was turned off and a wall of books behind it. File cabinets took up a wall. To the left of that was another room, and we walked by another door to the right, which went behind the wall of books and into the other office. "This is my office." Every wall had shelved books except one, which had a mini bar and file cabinets. It was decorated with a tall plant and abstract art. "This is very nice, Deacon."

"Let me show you the break room." We walked to the closed door behind the wall of books.

"Best break room I've seen, wow!" It consisted of a fridge, microwave, apartment-size stove and my favorite espresso machine. There was a small table and a couple of five-foot plants.

We left and went back to the overloaded desk out front. "I'm afraid this desk is yours," he said. "And that this is all for filing. But once you find the bottom of the pile, the desk is quite nice. By the time the calls get to this phone, you just have to answer 'Deacon Hall's office.' The main secretary would have directed the call here." There was a pregnant pause as I was lost in thought. "So, what do you think? Will you help me out here?" I looked up at Deacon, which was like looking up at a demigod, but before I could get lost in his handsomeness, I remembered what he said about keeping it professional.

"I do want to help you out. I think working here is a good idea. But I need to go home first to Vancouver. I want to be upfront with the landlady, since I just started renting. Maybe she will cut me some slack instead of waiting till I'm a month into a lease. I also miss my friends and I think they deserve a face-to-face before I just up and leave. I need to check on Todd. I'm worried he will never speak to me again. As long as you really think I'm safe, I would like to do this right away. Too much has happened in the last couple days. I need to reconcile all of it in my head and heart and with my friends that got hurt in the process."

"I think you'll be safe now if you want to go back to tie things up and talk with your friends is important before you take up a new life here." He put his hands on my arms and looked into my eyes. "Are you sure you're okay? If you don't want to do this, I am not forcing you in any way. You can leave at any time. We don't even have to be friends; we can just keep it professional co-workers. I feel like maybe you're worried about being here with me."

"No, Deacon, I'm not worried about you. I am a little worried about the co-workers bit. I think maybe I find you a little distracting, so this is going to be hard." I smiled at him, blushing a little. "I just need to make sure everyone is okay and that is not something I want to do over the phone. I feel like I'm the one who put them in danger. I need to be there."

"Okay, you go, Cali, take care of your friends. I can hold down the fort here a little while longer." I smiled, got up from my desk chair and walked towards the door. "For the record," he said, "it's not going to be easy sitting in the same office as a talented, brilliant, beautiful and caring woman who sits just outside my door. I promised I would be every bit the gentlemen and co-worker, and I will be, and I'll try not to be so distracting."

I grinned, maybe a little flirtatiously, as I left the office. It was going to be hard keeping it on the up and up with Deacon. He was all male, all masculine, gorgeous in every way and obviously brilliant. Even though his frame was bigger than a doorway, I never feel threatened by him. He made me feel safe, and he was straightforward. There was no hidden agenda with Deacon. I either worked for him or I didn't. I either got to know him or I didn't. I found that very interesting and refreshing. There was no pressure. I could just do what I felt was right for me and he would do whatever it was Deacon Hall did.

I walked down the street a bit, and I came across a store that sold purses, bags and suitcases. I went in and bought myself a cheap small suitcase so I didn't have to haul my stuff around in a garbage bag anymore. I got in my car and went to the B&B and packed my things. I told them I was leaving for a day or maybe two.

I was late when I got to the ferry, and I didn't have the police there to get me on the first ferry outbound, so I had to wait. When I got to my place in Vancouver, the landlady's lights were all out. I would have to talk to her in the morning and then go find Tracy, Ashley and Todd. I headed to bed and took a sleeping pill. This place somehow seemed lonelier than the B&B.

I am sleeping, but I feel fully awake lying in bed. At the foot of the bed is something; I focus on what I am looking at, and it is just wrong, the feeling of it / him being there is wrong; it feels dark. It is huge and seven feet tall. The body is well built and the bottom is animalistic and had hooves. I am grabbed by the ankles and dragged out the bottom of my bed, across the floor and down the hall. I see the demon crawling low to the ground on all fours, with my ankles in its hands, its legs moving in unparalleled movements, unnatural-like movements, jerking and twisting about. I then look into the face of a smiling, red-eyed demon, its skin melted and haggard. Its face is contorted and the skin on its body is not clothed. It is a weird shade of brown/grey. It stops, and I try and kick out. "I have been here before, asshole, and I am not afraid. You have no power over me. I am a temple of the Creator and any demon who tries to destroy this temple shall be destroyed by the Creator. It is written, so shall it be done. You have no power here, asshole. Begone!"

One simple sentence and it was so; he was gone. I had done some internet reading and decided after my experiences to have a little faith in the Creator. It was as simple as quoting from the books, any one of the books, really—pick one. The Bible, The Torah, The Koran. There were scriptures and writings from long before those religions even existed.

Even writings from mother earth and so forth said to give no power, because they had no power and that was why they took it. Pretty much every belief system had something that said they had no power unless you gave it, and if that was not the case then the writing said how to get them out of your life for good.

I woke up and I had accomplished something, because I was aware in my sleep state. I knew finally that it was not a dream or vision that would recur.

It was done. I asked for help, I was given help and I just had to keep the faith strong.

Now that I was a little more than motivated, I had to get on with my day. It was the weekend, so I could just call Tracy and hopefully meet for coffee. I texted Tracy first thing to give her time to reply. *"Hey Tracy, how is everything, I am back in town can we meet for coffee?"* I got a response almost right away, so I got ready in monumental time. *"Meet you at Bean Stalk Cafe. 10:30"*

Good, that worked. I ran up to the landlady's door and spoke with her about my predicament. I told her I wanted to work with Deacon, as it was a great opportunity, so I couldn't string either one of these people along. I had made my choice. She was upset that I had taken the place and now decided not to. She kept the first month's rent and damage deposit and refunded me my last month's rent. I figured after screwing her over that was a fair deal, but she also needed me out right away. I told her I would be back this afternoon around lunch to pack up and be gone by morning.

It wasn't like I had a lot, so I would just rent a small U-haul trailer and attach it to the Rav4. Good thing I didn't have a small car anymore. I took off in a flash and secured the U-haul and went to meet Tracy at the coffee shop.

Tracy wasn't there yet so I ordered myself a mocha and waited for her. As I sat at a table, Tracy gracefully swayed in like the goddess she was. "Hi, I am so glad to see you're all right."

I stood to give her a hug and replied, "I'm fine, or will be now. I'm glad to see you're all right. Is everything okay with you?"

"Yes, I'm fine. Did you hear about Todd and Ashley?"

"I unfortunately did from the source himself. I'm so sorry I caused all this. I feel so bad."

"Cali, this wasn't you! You have to realize that. This was Sean and his doing; you were a victim as much as Todd and Ashley. We all knew him, and we all knew him a lot longer than you did and we didn't see this coming. How could you have?"

"I just feel so bad that others were involved."

"What about you? You say he told you what he did? That means he followed you all the way there?"

"He did, and he said he beat it out of Todd." A tear came to my eye and fell a little down my cheek before I could wipe it away and pretend I wasn't crying in public.

I told her everything that had happened at the B&B. "They caught him and he is in custody now, so everyone should be safe. I had hired Deacon as my lawyer so he has built a case to keep him there."

"I'm so glad you're okay. What a situation to go through."

"I plan on seeing Ashley and Todd … do you think that will be okay?"

"Don't be silly. I'm sure that's fine. Give them a call and see what they say."

I texted Ashley, "*Hey Ashley, I am in town do you think you and Todd would like to get together? I heard about what happened, I am so sorry you were involved, I would really like to come and see you.*" It felt like forever before there was a reply.

"*Why don't you meet us, tomorrow morning at John's house, Todds dad's place? We are staying overnight, would you mind coming over here for breakfast? Its John's idea.*"

"*That sounds great, just text me the address and time and I will be there. Tell him thanks for the offer.*"

"You were right, they want me to meet them tomorrow."

"See, I told you it would be fine, and Todd will be fine too. He doesn't blame you. We all feel a little bit like heels because none of us saw this coming."

"Thanks for your support, Tracy. I love you guys for always being there for me, even though it's like all the time." I laughed nervously. "Things are starting to settle down, I feel it happening."

"Well, we have lots of time to catch up on, and what are friends for if not to rely on and help out when you need a helping hand? What kind of person would that make me as a friend if I was never there?" I smiled at her with gratefulness and a little awe that this person who was so kind and caring was my friend.

The smile came off my face with the thought of my other news. "Actually, time is of the essence. I quit slash got fired from Tony's warehouse. I took a job with Deacon, and I have two weeks to find a place to live." I gave a laugh of excitement. Tracy hit me in the shoulder while grinning like a fool.

"I knew it! I knew something was going to happen between you two. I should have taken bets." This time I hit her in the shoulder with a mock look of surprise.

"He told me we will keep it strictly professional. I just hope I can. Listen, I have got to get going. I told the landlady I would be out of her hair before she woke up tomorrow. I have to grab my trailer rental and pack it up."

"Okay, but you better keep in touch. I want to see you regularly and hear from you more than once a week."

"I will, Tracy. I would have never gotten through this without you guys; you all are the best friends a woman could ask for. Maybe you could meet me at John's place? I'm very nervous about seeing Todd. It will be a last hurrah breakfast and I finally get to meet John."

"Sounds like a plan." I hugged Tracy and we said our goodbyes till tomorrow.

I hadn't bothered to buy groceries for more than a couple days and I didn't know what I had at the basement suite, so I stopped to buy some already fried chicken and bread for the morning. Once I got to the house and put my minuscule amount of groceries away I started to pack. It wasn't much, so it took me till dinnertime to pack everything up again and haul it out to the trailer. Twice lucky, I saved the boxes from earlier and had them in the garage, so that made packing easier. I noticed the landlady had a dolly in the garage. I'd never attempted using one before, but I needed to get my washer and dryer back out of the house. I asked the landlady if I could borrow it, and I practiced with my living room table before attempting the big stuff. It wasn't really that they were super heavy, but they were super awkward to move and that's what dollies were for. I made the first trip no problem with the dryer, and the second trip was a little heavy but I managed to get it all the way to the trailer. *Look at me being all self-sufficient,* I told myself as I patted myself on the back.

It occurred to me that I had always had someone to rely on. I needed to rely on myself more. I was strong. I had been on my own for almost two years, and I just needed to give myself the chance to be more confident in myself and in my life. Once I was finished the last heavy load

I sat down to cold fried chicken, which was a favorite of mine, with a glass of soda and put the TV on. I zoned out watching some show where the bride was trying to plan her wedding.

The next thing I knew I was back in the beautiful forest where I saw the two spirits with the purple aura, the lady and the young girl. *I wasn't sleeping, was I?* How did I get outside? How do I get back inside? It was not exactly warm out. Where was I and was there anybody else there?

"When help comes from the Creator you don't get to ask how or when. You asked me to stop the demon attacks and I gave you a way to do it yourself. You asked if it was possible to be an angel. I'll give you an answer. You are wrong; there isn't a hijacking of your body by an angel. There is no angel squashed inside beside your soul. Angels do not hijack bodies, that is what demons do. However, there was an angel that wanted to go back down to Earth." I could not see where the voice was coming from. I looked around and found no place the voice could come from. It was coming from all around me and also from within my head like a thought. For some reason I know who it was, like the way you know a cow is called a cow and a tree is called a tree. I had known this voice since I was small.

This was who had watched over me even with all the bad things and good things that happened. This was the same voice when Dallas died when I got my warning. *"This spirit was done its course of life and I had appointed them a new angel. They were not happy with the guilt they still felt because the angel was not happy with who they were when they lived on Earth. She was not a good person, in her mind, and could not forgive herself or forget.*

Dangerous business, eternally speaking, not being able to forgive others or yourself. She has been forgiven and shown her deliverance by transforming her into an angel, thus, forgiveness by the Creator. The angel could not forgive herself for past life mistakes and came back to re-live life and try and live life fuller and with more grace. To be a better person than she was in her other lives, a second chance to do it right. The creator of all things chose to let the angel go back, but this spirit always belonged to you, before and after it was deemed angelic. The spirit and soul belonged to you when you were in a life as a nurse in a nursing home and stole from the elderly to get by while you were almost living on the streets from a bad divorce . You did ask for forgiveness, but never gave it to yourself; you were filled with guilt. The spirit belonged to you when you were sent to live as a farmer's wife and shot your husband for beating you badly. It also belonged to you when you were burned in Salem as a witch and lost your seventeen-year-old son to the mob as he watched you burn and he was stoned to death. You also died by tidal wave as a leader to your people. These were the cycles that you needed to learn here on Earth.

None of the actions are justifiable on Earth; these are bad things. The Creator can forgive many things if you can forgive yourself truly. Humans do all kinds of sin and evil all the time, and forgiveness is needed between themselves and others, between them and what they believe spiritually and forgiving themselves. Evildoing is the easy part, reconciling it is the hard part. Repenting is the hard part. These lives lived are the way they are for a reason. They are a path that you are put on and you must live to the best of your ability.

"The demon showed me three men and has written in the shower to tell me who showed me these things. Are they the three from past lives?" I asked

Yes, they were, but demons like to twist the information, and do not tell the whole truth. You were done your lifecycle. You had done in those lives what was needed to be done, what was needed to be learned, and you were to come home. But you were still not happy with yourself, with your progress, and you could not forgive you own transgressions. The deaths were people you knew in you past lives. I allowed you back to free yourself from your own mind, your own guilt, when you figured you could do it better this time. Now that you understand forgiveness, you know I forgive you and you have learned to forgive others and yourself. If you wish to remain on Earth you can. I will bind you to the human body and you will live out your days wholly human and your angelic nature will be stripped away. You can come home now, but the body of Cali Stenson will be no more. You cannot live without a spirit and soul." Then I asked, "But as Cali I was carving out a good, decent life. I have love and friends and a life, and I am trying hard to be a good person. I want the chance to live as I am in this life, human."

The next thing I knew I was thrust back in to the basement suite living room. The TV was still on and the plates from dinner were still out. I looked at the clock and it was close to midnight. I lost a whole evening. It seemed that about four or five hours of my time were missing. What did that mean?

Do I get to live out my life as I was? Did I dream it all? Or was I going to be ripped from space and time to go home to be in my true form?

"Why can't I just dream of a shitty day at work like normal people, or a love affair? What the hell was that?" I was supposed to meet everyone in the morning, so I hauled myself off the sofa and shook off the vision. I went to the bedroom, got ready for bed and curled up and tucked in for the night.

Four spirits at my bed— the Creator who created all sent them. I wake to find four dark entities, human in form but not human, and very ethereal, not solid. Bright auras of light surround each and blur what they look like. "We were sent to strip the spirit and soul of the angelic title and essence so you will live out your days as a human." They disappear and I become aware of dark black symbols in my dream, one after another, in curving and striking features. Light brighter than any imaginable source lifted from my body and ethereally went up in a shot and was gone. It left me with a warm spiritual feeling— the feeling of being full of life and love.

The alarm went off at about 8:00 a.m. I quickly got out of bed and showered and realized I'd had a very refreshing sleep. I didn't remember dreaming anything after the suppertime vision. I was going to have to drive and ferry back to Victoria today so I just dressed in jeans and a t-shirt, grabbed my new jacket and gave the place a once over to make sure I had everything that was mine. I went upstairs and got the landlady and told her I was on my way. She looked over the suite and then I was on my way to the address Ashley texted me.

It was about a half-hour drive to John's house. I seemed to be the last to arrive, as Tracy's car was already there.

I walked up to the door and Ashley opened it before I even reached the steps. "Hey, Cali how are you? You look well for everything you have been put through these past days. I can't even believe it."

I hugged Ashley hello and walked in the door to see Todd standing right there with his eyes black and his nose set with some weird bandage. I burst into tears on the spot at the sight of him and went to hug him. "Aw, come on now," Todd said gently. "I can't look that horrid." He tried to lighten the mood with a smile.

"Todd, I am so sorry you were involved. I don't even remember telling Ashley where I was, never mind getting you hurt for it."

"Thank the lord you told me. I don't know if he would have stopped hitting Todd had I not given in. I'm the one who's sorry. I totally cracked and gave the information up on you, Cali." Now Ashley was upset.

"I don't blame you, Ashley, at all. I would have wanted to save Todd too," I said.

"I didn't even call you to tell you what happened. I should have called you even if it was in the wee hours of the morning and told you I gave up your information, and I didn't even call you," said Ashley.

"It's over now. I have news, so why don't I fill you all in," I told the group.

"Yes, let the lady in," said a voice I didn't recognize. "I am John"

"Very nice to meet you, John" I've heard a lot of good things about you," I said.

The group gathered in the kitchen and set the table and got ready for breakfast. We ate a delicious pancake breakfast thanks to John, and I filled everyone in on what had happened once getting to Victoria. "Deacon said he would be in touch with Todd and you too, Ashley, for statements. He said he has a pretty strong case against Sean and needs to speak with you," I said by way of ending the conversation on Sean. "I am moving there to Victoria," I said to the group.

"That explains the little trailer," said Todd.

"I'm going to be a secretary for Deacon. If I'm any good at it I might take college courses on becoming a legal secretary, but we will see how this goes first."

"Oh, I know how it goes," teased Tracy.

"It's not like that. We're going to be colleagues, not on a porn special. We will be very professional all the time; in fact, he promised," I said with a smile. "It's getting late, and I still need to get over to Victoria and find storage and a house to live in. I have a lot of work to do in the next couple weeks. I should get going, but I will keep in contact and call you all very soon." With that, everyone got up from the table to say goodbyes. I hugged them and thanked John for the lovely invite and delicious breakfast.

He pulled me closer but did not bother to whisper. He said, "You will be fine, Cali, you will go on living your life normally. Don't be afraid of what comes in the night. You shine bright. It's time you live and enjoy life just as Cali Stenson and nothing more."

I pursed my lips and tried to smile. I wasn't sure exactly what he meant, but I had a pretty good idea. Todd was right, this guy really could see everything—he was good. Whatever he saw for my future and who I was to be sounded like it was going to turn out all right.

I drove to the ferry and told Deacon I was on my way back. I was hoping we could meet up tomorrow. I got a text saying that actually he would like to meet me off the ferry, if that was okay. We set up the same meeting plans as last time and hours later I was on the Island. I parked my car and Deacon was already out of his car. He turned around as I was walking up to him and there was a little orange fur ball in his arms. "I couldn't resist the charms of this kitten. I hope you don't mind. He's for you," he said with a bit of worry on his face. "He was named Rai at the SPCA here in Victoria. I felt it was fate, because guess where he came from?"

"Where?" I asked.

"Texas… Dallas, Texas."

Screw being professional, I kissed him with the kitten pressed in between us.

"I think Victoria is going to be good for me. I think you're good for me. Rai is a lovely little kitten, and it does sound like fate that he came from Dallas," I said with a tear welling in my eye. The kitten mewed and stretched to come to me like he knew we belonged together. "I think this new life of mine here in Victoria is going to be wonderful." No more nightmares, no more existential crisis, just a new start to a new life.

THE END

ABOUT THE AUTHOR

AN AVID READER OF YOUNG ADULT, ADULT fiction and erotic novels, Terah Marie's love of reading is what inspired her to write. She wrote this book because she wanted people to know that supernatural phenomena is widely experienced by others and she doesn't feel the topic should be avoided. She has worked as a hair stylist, medical transcriptionist and customer service representative, but her biggest joy was raising her daughter, who is now a young lady. Terah enjoys painting and making jewelry, and she also plays several instruments, including piano, trombone and violin. She lives with her husband, Jeff, her eleven-year-old daughter, Railyn, and her two dogs, Riley and Beemer, in Edmonton, Alberta.

CPSIA information can be obtained
at www.ICGtesting.com
Printed in the USA
LVHW091554180219
607899LV00002B/468/P